Tracy swallowed audibly.
She wasn't going to lie to him.

Especially since she'd so obviously enjoyed his kiss. And because she desperately wanted his trust.

"I didn't want my purpose for being here, my wish to know Seth, to get tangled up in what I was feeling toward you."

"And I didn't want my desire for you to cloud my judgment of your purpose. But you showed me today—" he whispered as he trailed kisses along the line of her jaw and throat "—that you have an incredible core of strength. No matter how fragile… your appearance, you proved…you are no pushover."

Though his compliment warmed her heart, her gut tightened. She squeezed her eyes closed, feeling like a fraud. "I didn't feel strong," she admitted. "I felt horribly vulnerable." She tightened her grip around his shoulders as the chilling horror of those moments washed through her again. She buried her head under his chin, her ear pressed to his breastbone and shivered. "I did what I had to to protect Seth, but…I was scared to death."

**

Be sure to check out the next books in
The Coltons of Oklahoma series.

The Coltons of Oklahoma:

COLTON COWBOY PROTECTOR

BY
BETH CORNELISON

MILLS & BOON

Published in Great Britain 2015
by Mills & Boon, an imprint of Harlequin (UK) Limited,
Eton House, 18-24 Paradise Road, Richmond, Surrey, TW9 1SR

© 2015 Harlequin Books S.A.

Special thanks and acknowledgement are given to Beth Cornelison for her contribution to the The Coltons of Oklahoma series.

ISBN: 978-0-263-91543-3

18-0615

Harlequin (UK) Limited's policy is to use papers that are natural, renewable and recyclable products and made from wood grown in sustainable forests. The logging and manufacturing processes conform to the legal environmental regulations of the country of origin.

Printed and bound in Spain
by CPI, Barcelona

Beth Cornelison started writing stories as a child when she penned a tale about the adventures of her cat, Ajax. A Georgia native, she received her bachelor's degree in public relations from the University of Georgia. After working in public relations for a little more than a year, she moved with her husband to Louisiana, where she decided to pursue her love of writing fiction.

Since that first time, Beth has written many more stories of adventure and romantic suspense and has won numerous honors for her work, including a coveted Golden Heart Award in romantic suspense from Romance Writers of America. She is active on the board of directors for the North Louisiana Storytellers and Authors of Romance (NOLA STARS) and loves reading, traveling, *Peanuts'* Snoopy and spending downtime with her family.

She writes from her home in Louisiana, where she lives with her husband, one son and two cats who think they are people. Beth loves to hear from her readers. You can write to her at PO Box 5418, Bossier City, LA 71171, USA, or visit her website, bethcornelison.com.

To my family, the whole loving, supportive,
often goofy bunch of you!

Thank you to Deborah Boyd,
who won the chance to have her kitty Oh La La
Sleek (Sleekie) memorialized in this book
through the Brenda Novak Auction for the Cure.

Prologue

The man reminded her of a wolf. His pale eyes held a feral quality, his heavily graying black hair was shaggy and thick, and his thin, sloped nose brought to mind a canine muzzle. She shivered as he slid into the front seat next to her, but his wild appearance boded well. She needed him to be the deadly predator he resembled. The two-faced mouse that had ruined her life and stolen her child from her needed to pay.

They'd parked in the farthest corner of the parking lot outside the range of the security cameras. She knew the spot was safe, because she'd checked the surveillance tapes herself. As it was after hours, few cars were left in the lot, and darkness added another layer of cover.

She slid the wolf man a file and gave him a hard stare. "I hired you because I was told you're the best. Naturally, discretion is of utmost importance. This can't be traced back to me or my husband."

"Naturally," he deadpanned. He reached into his front shirt pocket and pulled out a pack of cigarettes. Tapping one out, he flicked a silver lighter and lit his smoke. The tip glowed red like an evil eye in the dark.

She balled her hands in her lap, watching him uneasily as he flipped through the file. "I'll want proof when the job is complete."

Blowing smoke after her, he sent her a snide look, as if her request was beneath him. "I'll finish the job."

"Be sure you do. You don't get the last of your fee until I know that she's paid for what she did to my son."

He slapped the file shut and curled his lip in a sneer that revealed a lupine-like incisor. "Oh, she'll pay. Your son was my friend, my partner in a deal that went south when he died. I lost a small fortune. This job is personal. I won't rest until his death is avenged and that backstabbing bitch is dead."

Chapter 1

"In one hundred feet, turn right onto access road," the stilted voice of the rental car's GPS intoned.

With a deep breath for courage, Tracy McCain signaled the turn. She noted with interest that the car ahead of her on the isolated stretch of rural Oklahoma highway also made a right onto the side road leading to the sprawling ranch of cattleman John "Big J" Colton.

More interesting were the three cars that followed her onto the long driveway, including a television news van complete with a satellite dish on top. What the heck was going on at the Lucky C ranch today?

The iron gates, normally requiring someone at the main house to buzz you in, stood agape, allowing the parade of cars to continue up to the house unimpeded. As Tracy passed through the stone-walled entry, she noticed the Lucky C logo, an upright, good-luck horseshoe with a C inside, atop the posts on either side of the iron gate.

She hoped the logo boded well for her. She could use a bit of good luck today for her mission. From what her cousin had told her, the Coltons were a stubborn bunch, hard-nosed and highly protective of their family and their business.

Tracy wiped her sweaty palms on the legs of her slacks as the string of vehicles rolled closer to the ranch buildings, past acre upon acre of prime grazing fields. She looked for a place to pull off and park as they approached the main house, but, trapped between the SUV in front of her and the news van behind her, she had no real choice but to pull right up the drive to the front door of the Colton mansion. Laura had told her the Coltons were wealthy, but the glorious estate before her sent a fresh roll of trepidation through her. Holy cow—or maybe she should say holy *cowboy*—the place was big…and beautiful.

She knew how David must have felt going up against Goliath. What were the odds that she, an unemployed widow, a down-on-her-luck nobody with only a tenuous right to the claim she wanted to stake, could hold sway with the mighty Coltons?

She glanced at the snapshot of a small boy that she'd laid on the passenger seat, and her spirits lifted. Seth was worth the effort. And she owed Laura. Big time.

When the line of cars stopped on the cobbled drive in front of the stone-facade mansion, a man in a white button-down shirt and black pants yanked open her driver-side door.

Tracy gasped and shrank away as he stuck a hand toward her. "Wh-what are you doing?"

He flashed a lopsided grin. "Offering you a hand out. We cowboys are raised to be helpful to ladies."

"Oh…thanks, but no." She glanced around at the manicured lawn. "Where should I park?"

"You don't."

She jerked a startled look back to the dark-haired man, who either had a head start on his summer tan or an enviable heritage lending him his copper-toned skin. "Pardon?"

Had she been recognized as an interloper? Was she being dismissed even without getting to state her case?

The cowboy chuckled and wiggled his fingers, indicating she should get out of the car. "Parking is my job today. But don't worry. I drive cars as well as I drive cattle. I won't scratch it."

A car horn blasted behind her, and another man in a white shirt leaned out of a vehicle behind her and shouted, "Come on, Daniel. Schmooze the ladies on your own time, man. You're holding up the line!"

The cowboy-valet at her door smiled at his cohort and deliberately scratched his temple with his middle finger. Offering his hand to her again, he said, "Ma'am."

With a nervous grin, she grabbed her purse off the floor and took his callused hand to slip out of the rental car. As the valet—Daniel, the other man had called him—climbed behind the wheel, she remembered her messenger bag. "Wait! I need that."

She pointed past him to the passenger seat. But instead of the bag, he zeroed in on her snapshot. He picked up the photo with a curious frown. "Hey, isn't this—?"

She snatched the picture, drawing a deeper scowl from him. "My bag. Please."

Daniel retrieved the satchel and handed it to her, along with a small piece of paper. "Write your tag number on this and give it to whoever's manning the front door when you're ready to leave. Someone will bring your car around."

With that, he closed the door and sped away.

"But I don't know—" She quickly shifted her attention to the rental car's license plate and caught the first few digits before her valet-cowboy turned out of the circular drive and headed toward the back of the property. As she crossed the driveway, headed for the front door, she stuck the photo in her purse, then fumbled for a pen to write the plate numbers down.

Tracy joined the stylishly dressed reporter and bored-looking cameraman from the news station, climbing the decorative concrete steps to the front door. The reporter knocked on the dark wood door inset with an ornate glass window. While they waited for an answer, Tracy practiced in her head what she would say when she confronted her cousin's ex. Honesty was a good policy, but how open would the Coltons be to her proposal, if they knew her past? She didn't have long to mull over the question, as the door was answered quickly by an effusive older woman with a dark bob.

"Veronica Hamm, KRQY News," the reporter said, offering her hand.

"Of course! I'd know that pretty face anywhere!" the woman at the door gushed, ignoring the proffered hand and swooping in for a girlie hug and air kisses on each cheek. "Come in, come in! I'm Abra Colton. Thank you for coming."

Tracy's stomach flip-flopped. *Abra Colton. Seth's grandmother.* As matriarch of the Colton clan, Abra could be key to whether Tracy was accepted by the family or not.

Their hostess waved the cameraman and Tracy through the door without so much as a "hello." Abra clearly had use only for the newswoman, and she continued buzzing over her like a bee to the sweetest rose. "The media room is to the right at the back. We'll have our big announcement in just a little while." She hooked arms with Veronica, ignoring Tracy and the cameraman as she walked the reporter into the house. "In the meantime, help yourself to the buffet out by the pool, and a glass of champagne. Big J and I ordered cases of the best bubbly from France for the occasion!"

As the cameraman trailed after Abra and Veronica like an obedient puppy, Tracy lingered awkwardly in the entry hall. She glanced around at the high ceilings, marble floors and triple arches leading into the formal living room, and her pulse picked up speed.

How had Laura walked away from all this grandeur and wealth? Seth clearly had a better life here than what she could have offered, but leaving her son behind had been harder on Laura than she pretended to the Coltons. She'd done what she had because she'd wanted the security and opportunity that a life with his father could afford Seth.

"A little less ogling and a little more giddy-up if you don't want to get separated from the rest of your crew."

Tracy gasped and spun to face the man who'd spoken. She found herself staring up into the bright green eyes of a cowboy with broad shoulders, shaggy chestnut hair and a somewhat surly expression.

Her mouth dried as she held his level stare. He had the rugged good looks Laura had said the Colton men all shared, and a commanding presence that made Tracy's toes curl in feminine appreciation, despite his less than welcoming greeting.

"I'm, um…not with the news crew."

Tall, Dark and Sullen grunted. "In that case, the food

is out by the pool. Eat up, 'cause your hostess spent as much on that buffet as two pure-blood, registered breeding bulls would cost at auction." With that, he strode away, his gait brisk and confident, and disappeared into the crowd of guests.

When the doorbell sounded a few seconds later, Tracy was still standing in the foyer, gaping at the spot in the mingling crowd where the devilishly handsome but curt cowboy had joined the soirée. A woman wearing a housekeeper's uniform and her silver hair twisted up in a bun scurried out from a side door and balked when she saw Tracy.

"For Pete's sake, don't just stand there, girl!" The older woman flapped her thin hands as if to shoo her out of the entry hall. "There are guests to serve and drinks to be poured. Get busy! Don't make me report you to the catering company."

Tracy gave a self-conscious chuckle. "I'm not with the caterers. I'm looking for—"

The woman jostled her out of the way to open the front door. Tracy's opportunity to ask for directions was lost as the housekeeper greeted the arriving guests with enthusiastic smiles and hospitality.

Rather than continue to stand at the door like a bump on a log, Tracy sidled into the living room. She clutched her messenger bag close to her body to avoid jostling anyone or knocking over one of the numerous champagne flutes resting on trays in the exquisitely furnished room. Dressed in basic khakis and a simple print blouse the same caramel color as her hair, she noted that she was underdressed for whatever event the Coltons were celebrating. Feeling all the more out of place, and hoping to camouflage herself against the French-vanilla walls, she began inching her way through the clusters of guests.

Maybe she should just leave. Clearly, now was not the time to approach Jack. She was an uninvited interloper at a high-society event. She didn't belong. Story of her life.

Sighing with resignation, she'd started weaving her way back toward the front door when a large, boisterous man with a thick shock of silver hair caught her arm. "Hey, little darlin'. Whatcha doin'?"

Busted.

"I—I'm sorry. I was just leaving..."

"Leaving? Hell, darlin', the party's just getting started good."

She recognized the green eyes that flashed at her with mirth. Tall, Dark and Surly's eyes had mesmerized her with the same bright emerald shade, and the gruff cowboy could be this flirtatious gentleman in thirty years... if he added this man's playful smile.

"Why is your hand empty? You should have a glass of bubbly. This is a celebration, darlin'!" He snagged a glass of champagne off a passing tray and shoved it at her. "Bottoms up!"

"Oh, I'm not—" She stopped short as she realized who this animated man was. She'd seen his picture when she'd researched the Lucky C on Google before coming to Oklahoma. "You're Big J! I mean...J-John Colton."

Though John laughed and nodded amiably, she felt her cheeks heat with embarrassment. Great. She'd just called one of the wealthiest and most powerful men in the ranching industry—heck, in all of the United States' agribusiness—by his nickname. *Way to make a good first impression...*

"Yes, I am, darlin'. Yes, I am." He took a step back and gave her a slow once-over that brought the stinging flush back to her cheeks. "And who might you be? I believe I'd remember meeting you, if I'd ever had the pleasure."

"Tracy McCain. I'm actually here to speak to Jack. Can you point me toward him?"

"I could, but…I'm still enjoying your company." The older man winked. "Besides, Jack is probably hiding somewhere until time for the announcement."

"Announcement?"

Big J gave her a you've-got-to-be-kidding look. "Greta's engagement. That's why we're all here lifting a glass."

"Oh." Tracy fumbled for anything Laura might have told her about Greta.

But Big J seemed oblivious to her mental catch-up and helped her out by adding, "It's not every day a daddy gets to toast his only daughter getting hitched, so we went all out for my Greta."

Only daughter…of course. Greta was Jack's sister. The youngest of the Colton children. Tracy smiled and raised the glass John had foisted on her. "Well, here's to Greta."

"To Greta!" Big J clinked his glass with hers, so hard the contents of both drinks sloshed out.

Without warning, he gave a shrill whistle, startling Tracy so much that a shot of adrenaline raced through her, tripping her pulse.

"Brett! C'mere, son." Big J waved someone over, and a tall, athletic-looking man with short brown hair separated himself from a circle of cloying women and strutted across the room.

Tracy goggled as he approached. Dear God, did the Coltons have an account at hunkycowboys.com? She had yet to meet one who didn't look as if he'd walked off the pages of a hot-ranch-hands catalog.

Big J put his hand on Brett's shoulder when he reached them, and jerked his glass toward Tracy. "Brett, my boy. This lovely filly is Tracy McCann."

"Um…McCain."

"I am going to leave her in your good hands," Big J continued, as if he hadn't heard her correction. "She's looking for Jack. But before she talks to your brother, I think she needs something to eat."

"No, really, I'm not here to eat. I just need to speak to Jack." Tracy's stomach chose that inopportune moment to growl. Thankfully, the din of the party conversation and background country music muffled the sound.

Brett took her hand and, rather than shaking it, merely left his fingers wrapped warmly around hers as he gave her a smile that twinkled in his trademark Colton-green eyes. "My dad's right. You don't want to meet my brother on an empty stomach. Besides, the brisket is so tender it will melt in your mouth. Follow me."

He tugged her hand as he led the way out to the pool, where a small acoustic band was playing the country tunes she'd heard inside. Brett steered her to a buffet table piled high with beef brisket, rolls, fresh fruit, veggies and dips, cheeses of all types, and an array of the most sumptuous-looking desserts Tracy had ever seen. Her mouth watered, and she decided it would be a good idea to have at least a *little* something to eat. She and Brett both picked up plates and started down the buffet. "Wow!"

He chuckled. "I know, right? Abra knows how to put out a spread, huh?" He used the tongs from a tray of cheeses to pile sliced beef and bite-size meat pastries onto Tracy's plate. When melodic laughter drifted to them from a small group by the desserts, he called, "Hey, Ryan, save some of those brownies for the rest of us."

"You snooze, you lose," a muscular man with tell-tale green eyes marking him as another Colton quipped. "Greta said I could have hers."

The brunette woman beside Ryan elbowed him. "I said you could have mine, not the rest of the tray!"

Brett hitched his head toward the group. "Tracy, have you met this crew? My brother, Detective Ryan Colton of the Tulsa PD, and of course, the honorees, my baby sister, Greta, and her fiancé, Mark You-Better-Be-Good-to-Her-or-I'll-Kick-Your-Ass Stanton."

The russet-haired man next to Greta laughed as he offered his hand to Tracy. Brett's face sobered, and he gave Mark a squinty-eyed glare. "I'm not joking, man."

Greta shoved her brother's shoulder. "Brett, stop trying to intimidate my fiancé, you big goof."

Brett grinned broadly. "Yeah, okay." But when Mark smiled in relief, Brett blanked his face again in an instant and raised an eyebrow. "But I mean it."

"I already warned Mark that I know a hundred ways to kill a man and hide the body without being caught," Ryan deadpanned.

Tracy gave Mark a sympathetic look. "Tough gig, marrying into a family with this much testosterone."

"Yeah," Mark said with a sappy grin as he kissed his fiancée's temple, "but Greta's worth it."

Brett made a gagging noise, then flinched as a cold jet of water spritzed them all.

Tracy heard a youthful giggle as Brett spun around with a playful growl. She leaned to her left to see who was behind him and spotted a familiar-looking little boy with a water gun.

Her heart seized. *Seth.*

She gaped at the boy who so obviously resembled his paternal family, and a knot of emotion clogged her throat. Seeing her cousin's son, her only living family, in the flesh for the first time was no less poignant in this setting than if she'd been greeting him five years ago when he was a newborn in the hospital nursery.

"All right, pal. You asked for it!" Brett said, sweeping him up and over his shoulder.

Seth's laughter rang over the party sounds as Brett took three long steps to the deep end of the swimming pool and tossed his nephew in, clothes and all.

Tracy gasped and took a step toward the pool, prepared to dive in after Seth if needed. But the little boy broke the surface of the water, still grinning from ear to ear and clutching his water gun. He swam skillfully to the ladder to climb out, calling, "Okay, Uncle Brett, this is war!"

Brett grinned as his nephew shook his wet hair. "Bring it on, Seth. I'm ready for you, buddy."

Seth aimed his gun and blasted Brett and several other guests with a jet of cold water. Tracy bit her bottom lip to cover a smile.

Abra strode briskly through the French doors, clearly not amused. She clattered out onto the patio, her high heels clicking on the concrete, and gave Brett a stern frown. "The two of you cut that out at once! I'll not have you ruining Greta's party," she said, barely keeping her tone above a hiss. She quickly schooled her face and smiled at her guests. "I'm so sorry for my grandson's behavior. He can be rather a handful sometimes."

Tracy bristled, ready to fly to Seth's defense, just as Greta touched her arm and spoke to her. "So, Tracy, are you a friend of Mark's?" She divided a curious look between Tracy and her fiancé.

Mark shook his head, at the same time that Tracy said, "Um…actually, I'm not here for the party. I came to see Jack. On a personal matter."

Greta's eyes widened, and she sent Ryan a knowing look that said, *Well, well...interesting.*

Tracy's cheeks flamed again, and she cleared her throat. "Could you point me toward him, please?"

Greta blinked. "You don't know what he looks like?"

"Well, no. I mean, based on the Coltons I've met so far today, I'm assuming he's green-eyed, dark-haired and gorgeous, but beyond that…"

An amused grin tugged the corner of Ryan's mouth, and he sent a glance around the area, using his advantageous height to see over the heads of the assembled guests. With the glass in his hand, he motioned to the far side of the pool. "That's him over there, wrapping Seth up in the towel."

Tracy turned to look, and her breath caught. The man draping Seth in a beach towel was none other than the cowboy she'd encountered in the foyer. Mr. Tall, Dark and Surly himself.

Chapter 2

With his gaze, Jack Colton followed the sounds of splashing water and his son's playful laugh to the swimming pool and cracked a small grin. Seth's carefree, sometimes mischievous nature reminded him of himself when he was younger, before life, fatherhood and the demands of a large cattle ranch replaced his wild ways with a more responsible attitude. The mirthful sounds were silenced by a rebuke from Jack's mother, and he tensed.

Wasn't it bad enough that Abra was putting on this dog-and-pony show, flaunting Greta's engagement to the world in order to boost her own social standing? The media was here, for cripes' sake! Not that Jack wasn't happy for his sister. Greta's engagement deserved to be toasted and celebrated. Just not so publicly. This spectacle was an embarrassment.

Jack strode quickly to the pool to retrieve his son, noting that Brett had been the one egging the boy on. Jack appreciated the rapport his brother had with five-year-old Seth, but not when it led his son down the wrong path... namely one that crossed Abra's.

"Seth," Jack said calmly, but with a tone and volume that brooked no resistance. His son glanced up, and Jack gave a subtle head jerk. As Seth obediently scurried out of the water, Jack turned his gaze to Brett and sent him a false smile. "Thanks."

His brother held up both hands, laughing, "He started it."

"Yeah, but you're an adult. Act like one."

Brett gave him a who-whizzed-in-your-Wheaties look and turned to join the conversation behind him. No doubt ragging on his grumpy big brother. When had Jack become such a grandpa?

Jack dragged a hand over his mouth and sighed. He was feeling edgy today, and it wasn't Brett's fault. This lavish party—$20,000 for champagne?—chafed his practical business sense. Anything frivolous that ate away the bottom line was a burr under his saddle. This party was the whole prickly bush. Grunting in frustration, he swiped a beach towel off a lounge chair and held it out for Seth.

"Sorry, Daddy," Seth said mournfully, his eyes downcast as he slopped over in his wet clothes and shoes.

"Didn't I ask you this morning to be on your best behavior?" Squatting, Jack wrapped the towel around him and rubbed an end over his shaggy brown hair.

"Yes, sir." Seth lifted a rebellious look. "But this party is so *boring*! There are no kids to play with and no bouncy castle or games."

Jack was bored, too, and eager to get out in the north pasture to check on the most recently born calves. "Tell you what. Go change into dry clothes, behave like the good boy I know you can be for the rest of the party and we'll get ice cream in town tonight. Deal?"

Seth's face brightened. "Two scoops?"

Jack raised an eyebrow. "A wheeler-dealer like your grandpa, I see."

Seth grinned at the comparison. "Pa Pa says, 'never take the first offer. Always ask for a more better deal.'"

"Just 'better.' Not 'more better.'"

Seth wrinkled his nose. "Huh?"

Inside the house, Seth's Pa Pa, Big J, gave a bellowing laugh that reached all the way to the pool. Jack shook his head. Seth could do worse than to emulate Big J. Poor grammar aside.

"Sure. Two scoops. If you eat a good dinner." Great, now Jack sounded like someone's mother. Not *his* mother, though. Abra had never cared whether he ate his vegetables or brushed his teeth. She still barely bothered herself with her children, unless it served her purposes. Case in point, Greta's engagement party.

"Excuse me."

Jack angled his head to meet the gaze of the woman beside him who'd spoken. He squinted against the bright Oklahoma sun, which backlit her.

"Are you Jack Colton?" she asked.

"I am."

"May I have a word with you?" Her voice was noticeably thin and unsteady. She cleared her throat and added, "Privately?"

In his head, Jack groaned. What now?

He swatted Seth on the bottom. "Go get changed, Spud."

With a curious glance at the woman, Seth nodded and squished across the lawn toward the old ranch house.

Jack pushed to his feet, his knee cracking thanks to

an old rodeo injury, and faced the woman at eye level. Well, almost eye level. Though tall for a woman, she was still a good five or six inches shorter than his six foot one. He recognized her as the woman he'd seen earlier lurking in the foyer, practically casing the main house. "And you are…?"

He suspected she was a reporter, based on the messenger bag hanging from her shoulder, though why a reporter would need to speak privately with him was beyond him. He had nothing to say to any reporter, privately or otherwise.

She took a deep breath and nervously wet her lips. "Tracy McCain."

The name didn't ring any bells, but when she extended her hand in greeting, he shook it.

She added a shy smile, her porcelain cheeks flushing, and a stir of attraction tickled Jack deep inside. Hell, more than a stir. He gave her a leisurely scrutiny, sizing her up. She might be tall and thin, but she still had womanly curves to go with her delicate china-doll face. "Am I supposed to know you?"

Her smile dropped. "Laura never mentioned me?"

His ex-wife's name instantly raised his hackles and his defenses. His eyes narrowed. "Not that I recall. How do you know Laura?"

"I'm her cousin. Her maternal aunt's daughter. From Colorado Springs."

Jack gritted his back teeth. Laura had been dead only a few months and already relations she'd never mentioned were crawling out of the woodwork like roaches after the light's turned off. The allure of the Colton wealth had attracted more than one gold-digging pest over the years. "You should know, Laura signed an agreement when we divorced. She got a tidy settlement in place of any alimony. The agreement meant she gave up any further financial claim on Colton money or the Lucky C."

Tracy lifted her chin. "I'm aware."

"So you're barking up the wrong tree, if you're looking for cash."

Tracy blinked her pale blue eyes, and her expression shifted, hardened. "I'm not after money," she said, with frost in her tone.

Jack scratched his chin and tipped his head, giving her a skeptical glare. "Then what?"

She waved a hand toward the house, then, as if realizing they'd have no more privacy inside than here by the pool, she frowned. "Is there someplace quiet we can talk?"

Ten minutes ago, Jack had been dying for an excuse to ditch Abra's party. Now he had the excuse he'd been looking for, but his gut told him he'd be no better off hearing Miss Blue Eyes out.

"Fine." He huffed an exasperated sigh and headed across the lawn, leaving her to follow or not. Her choice.

The main house was a good distance from the stable, barn, bunkhouse and other outbuildings— two miles by the dirt road, a little less if you cut across fields and grassy lawns. He had driven one of the ranch's utility vehicles over to the party, but some peevish rebellion in him decided to walk now. If Tracy wanted to talk to him, she could hoof it to the stable. Ninety-five degree Oklahoma heat and gravel road be damned.

He walked too quickly for her to match his long-legged stride, but to her credit, she didn't fall too far behind. As they neared the stable, cutting across a corner of one of the holding pens, he aimed a finger at one of the many cow patties, warning, "Watch your step."

She drew a quick breath and took a last-minute side

step to avoid a pile. For what it was worth. Her modest brown dress pumps were caked in mud, the heels likely ruined by the gravel. Jack experienced a moment of compunction for her destroyed shoes, but he pushed it aside. She should have known better than to wear shoes like that to a ranch.

He wiped sweat from his brow as he entered the shade of the stable, where large fans circulated the scents of manure, straw and leather in the stuffy alley between horse stalls. In a shady corner of an empty stall, their black barn cat, Sleek, napped between hunting expeditions. The family wanted Sleek to catch mice, which she did, but the feline seemed more interested in birds…and sneaking into the old ranch house to sleep on Seth's bed when Jack wasn't looking.

Jack gave a pat to one of the mares, which stuck her nose out as he passed, then made his way to Buck's stall. His buckskin gelding tossed his black mane when Jack opened the stall door and led him out.

When Tracy caught up to him, she was breathing heavily and perspiration rolled down her face and neck. The fine, sweat-dampened hair around her temples and ears curled in sweet golden ringlets, and over the musty smell of the stable, a floral scent wafted to him with the fan's breeze. The sweet aroma was completely out of place here, much like the woman wearing the perfume, and the heady scent made lust curl in his belly. Her stylish khaki slacks and simple print blouse were more suited to a boardroom than a tack room, and Tracy's knitted brow as she scanned the horse stalls spoke for her uneasiness on his turf.

He took a currycomb from a shelf and started grooming Buck. "You wanted privacy, you got it. So talk."

She let the messenger bag slide off her arm and thud

onto a nearby bench. "There wasn't anyplace…closer?" she panted.

He shrugged. "Sure there was. But I figured if I could groom ole Buck while we talked, I could get a jump on my to-do list for the day."

And if he kept himself busy combing Buck, maybe he wouldn't be as easily distracted by her lush lips and doe-like blue eyes. Her fragile, china-doll appearance made her seem vulnerable, and until he knew what she was after, Jack didn't want to feel any weakness or sympathy toward her.

She dabbed ineffectually at her damp cheeks and brow, then flapped the front of her blouse, trying to cool down. "Okay, so…I wanted to talk about Seth."

Jack tensed, his gut filling with acid. He squeezed the currycomb with a death grip and grated, "No."

"I… What do you mean, no? You haven't even heard what I want to—"

"I don't need to hear. My son is off-limits. Nonnegotiable." With an effort, Jack loosened his grip on the currycomb and continued stroking Buck's beige hide.

Tracy was silent for a moment, shifting her weight and swatting at a horsefly that was as drawn to her perfume as Jack was.

"All I want is the opportunity to get to know my cousin's son. I want Seth to know things about Laura that he might not know."

Jack shook his head and aimed the currycomb at Tracy. "He knows all he needs to know, and I won't have you filling his head with information that will lead to questions best left alone, or truths about his mother that will only hurt him."

Tracy straightened her spine, her expression affronted.

"I have no intention of hurting him. I… What would I say about his mother that would hurt Seth?"

"The truth. She abandoned him when he was a baby."

"Abandoned?" Tracy chuffed a humorless laugh. "She did no such thing!"

Jack paused from the grooming to face her, cocking his head. "Really? What would you call it?"

"Laura loved Seth!" Tracy clapped a hand to her chest, pleading her case with wide, earnest eyes. "She did what she thought was best for him. She saw that he'd have a better life here on the Lucky C with you and your family than she could give him as an unemployed single mother. She never forgot a birthday, always sent Christmas presents—"

He scoffed. "You can't buy a kid's affection. Presents are no substitute for being there."

"I know that. And…so did she." Tracy looked at the ground as she said the last, not sounding at all sure of her claim.

"Doesn't matter. I didn't give him her gifts or cards."

Tracy's chin jerked up. "What? Why not?"

"It would have only confused him."

Now she tilted her head to the side, her eyes suspicious. "Confused him why?"

"I told Seth his mother died when he was a baby."

Tracy gasped in outrage.

Jack turned back to Buck and patted the gelding's neck. "I thought that would be easier for him to handle than knowing she chose to walk away."

"She didn't— You shouldn't—" Tracy sputtered. "You had as much to do with her leaving as she did! You knew she wasn't suited to ranch life. You encouraged her to go her own way when you saw how unhappy she was."

Jack gritted his back teeth, feeling a knot in his stomach. The failure of his marriage was the last thing he wanted to rehash today…or ever. Seth was the only good thing that came out of his years with Laura. He took a slow breath and swallowed the bitter taste at the back of his throat. "Water under the bridge," he said in a low, even tone.

He raised the currycomb to continue his work, but Tracy strode over and caught his wrist. "Would you stop that long enough to hear me out? My cousin was not the monster you're making her out to be!"

He heaved a put-upon sigh and tossed the currycomb aside. "No one said she was a monster," he said under his breath. Then, only a little louder, he added, "I wouldn't have married her if she were a monster. She had her good points, and at one time, I thought I loved her."

He angled a look over his shoulder at Tracy. She was swiping at the sweat on her face with her wrist, her pale skin flushed from the heat. He stepped over to the shelf where he kept his personal tack equipment and fished a bandanna out of his saddlebag. He held it out to her, and she eyed it suspiciously. "It's clean. I promise."

With a murmured thank-you, she dried her face and neck, and ambled closer to a fan so the current of air blew in her face. "As I was saying…I want the chance to spend time with Seth, to get to know him. After Laura died, I promised her…" Tracy paused and swallowed hard. To his dismay, Jack thought he saw tears fill her eyes. God, no tears! Please! He hated seeing a woman cry. Tears were worse than splinters under his fingernails, and he'd do anything to avoid them.

After a slow breath, Tracy seemed more composed—thank the Lord—and continued. "I promised Laura that I would make sure her son knew how much she loved him, the kind of woman she was and everything she did for me. She deserves that."

Jack folded his arms over his chest and leaned against a wall. "What she did for you?"

Tracy nodded. "The day of the car accident that killed her…"

"Yeah?"

"…she was helping me. I was in the car with her when she died. She'd saved me from a really bad situation, helped me escape…" Tracy wet her lips and glanced away for a moment before continuing. "The man who ran us off the road was my husband."

Clenching his jaw, Jack recalled what he'd been told about the accident. "He was arrested for vehicular manslaughter. Right?"

She nodded.

"So he's in jail now?"

"He was. But…he was shanked the second night he was in jail and died on the way to the hospital."

Jack arched one eyebrow. He hadn't known that tidbit. "I'm sorry."

A sad smile tugged the corner of her mouth. "I'm not."

Jack stared at her. Read between the lines. "He abused you." It was a statement, not a question. Abuse would explain a lot of the vulnerability he sensed with her.

She said nothing for a minute. Finally, her shoulders slumped, and she nodded. "Verbally. Mentally. He was spiteful and mean. Loved making me cry for sport."

Jack felt a hot ball of rage well in his gut toward the man.

"He only hit me once, though."

Jack barked a laugh of disbelief. "Just once?"

Her eyes rounded, and she took a step back. "Y-yeah."

"As if that makes it all right or wins him points?" He drilled a finger at her. "Once is one time too many."

Her hand fluttered to her throat, where she dabbed again at the sweat collecting there. "I agree. But my point is…I owe Laura. I know how much Seth meant to her and how much it would mean to her—how much it would mean to *me*—if I could spend some time with her son."

Jack rubbed the bridge of his nose. "For what purpose? So he can have another woman walk out of his life in a few days?"

"Who said I wanted to walk out? I don't have a child of my own. Maybe I'm looking for something long-term, something permanent."

Ice slid through Jack's blood, and he lurched away from the wall. "Excuse me?"

Tracy blinked, confused. "I said I wouldn't walk out on him. I want—"

"If you're looking to sue for custody or visitation rights, you should know that the divorce agreement Laura signed denies her *or her family* the right to come back here and try to take Seth from me."

Jack stalked toward Tracy until she'd backed against the far alley wall, and he loomed over her. "Seth is mine. All mine. I have sole custody, and that's how it's gonna stay."

She hunched her shoulders, trying to make herself smaller, and he realized how his power play must have appeared to her. Intimidating, threatening, hostile… Okay, he had meant to intimidate her and drive home his point. But he'd forgotten for a moment how that tactic would play with an abused woman. Damn it!

He eased back a step, giving her breathing room, while still making his point that he was unyielding on the question of custody. He would fight her to his last dollar to keep his son. When he drew a calming lungful of air, he inhaled the sweet scent of her. Heat unrelated to the summer temperatures skittered through him. His pulse kicked harder as he imagined what it might be like to pin her against the wall and kiss her full, frowning lips. Standing this close to her, he could see her chin quiver and hear the agitated rasp of her breathing. Damn the man who'd scarred her psyche this way! And damn himself for finding Tracy so alluring, so sweetly sexy and begging for protection.

He was far more likely to need protection from her and her plans for Seth than she needed protecting.

"I don't want to take him from you." Her voice trembled, and when she raised her gaze, he saw moisture in her eyes. But also defiance. "I don't want to be at odds with you on this matter but…if I have to go to court to win the right to see Seth—" her throat convulsed as she swallowed "—I will."

Chapter 3

After Tracy threw down the gauntlet regarding visitation with Seth, Jack hustled her back to the party, driving one of the MULE side x sides this time, and ordered her off the ranch. He'd not have any relative of his ex-wife blackmailing him into visitations with Seth. Especially not if those visits included the possibility of Seth hearing upsetting truths about his mother. Or if said visits could lead to an attempt for shared custody. Or…*cripes*, the possibilities chilled Jack.

He let Tracy out at the pool area and directed her to leave immediately, before he moved the MULE to the edge of the lawn. When he returned to the party to look for Seth, he spotted Brett near the buffet line, yukking it up with some slick-looking customers in Stetsons too clean and crease-free to be real cowboys. Brett caught his eye and waved him over.

Seeing no graceful way out, Jack crossed the lawn

and gave the men with his brother a half smile as he approached. He could smell big-city investors and rancher wannabes from a mile away. These guys reeked of money and little practical ranching knowledge.

"Jack, I'd like you to meet some gentlemen. Bill and George here are from Dallas and are interested in helping us get started in horse breeding."

Nailed it. Jack gloated silently as he shook the men's hands.

"I've been telling them how I found that stud in OKC with papers and a great bloodline."

Jack lifted one eyebrow. "What stud?"

"I told you about him when I talked to you last week about my idea for breeding cutting horses."

Drawing a slow breath, Jack pinned his brother with a level stare. "As I recall, I told you we weren't making any changes to the business plan for the ranch. I have no interest in breeding cutting horses."

Brett gave the businessmen an awkward grin. "Well, yeah, but *I'm* interested, and so is Daniel. I've been looking into it, and George here says he has connections that can—"

Jack took his brother's arm and pulled him aside. "Excuse us for a minute, gentlemen."

Brett muttered a curse under his breath and glared at Jack. "Don't blow this for us, man. You know Daniel is looking to set up his own breeding program, and if the Lucky C doesn't provide him with the resources, he'll take his talents, and his profits, elsewhere."

"If he wants to leave the ranch, he should."

Brett scowled and angled his head. "You don't mean that. He's family! He belongs at the Lucky C. That means giving him reason to stay here, and Geronimo is a fantastic reason."

Jack exhaled slowly and shoved his hands in his back pockets. "He only belongs here if he wants to stay. I won't be party to strong-arm tactics or guilting him into staying."

Brett squared his shoulders. "He'll want to stay if we own Geronimo. He has the best bloodline in Oklahoma *and* Texas. I've been trying to get these guys to invest in our horse-breeding program for months, and I've got them on the hook."

"The Lucky C doesn't need outside investors. We've done quite well on our own and don't need city boys poking their noses in our business."

Brett met Jack's gaze with a stubborn frown. "We do if you're unwilling to front the cash from the ranch funds to buy Geronimo."

"We're not buying Geronimo or any other studs." Jack leaned close to his brother and kept his volume low but his voice unflinching. "And we're not shifting any resources to raising cutting horses, saddle broncs, race horses or any other wild scheme you've got up your sleeve. Period. I'm the manager of this ranch, and I decide how and where to spend money. Cattle have gotten us where we are today, and they'll continue to be our business as long as I'm in charge. I see no good reason to change direction and risk everything Big J built."

Brett shook his head, clearly frustrated. "Damn it, Jack. I know what I'm doing! Daniel knows his business, and he'll take his business somewhere else if we don't make some changes around here."

Jack scoffed. "What did Daniel say when you proposed all this to him?"

Brett flinched. "I…haven't yet. I wanted to secure the deal before—"

Jack cut him off with a grunt and a head shake. "You

wanted more ammunition to lure Daniel to stay here. But he needs the freedom to decide his life without manipulation or bribes or guilt."

"I have his best interests—the *ranch's* best interests— in mind."

Jack rubbed his eyes with the pads of his fingers before speaking again. "And you're sure the two are one and the same?"

Brett looked confused. "Why wouldn't they be?"

Why, indeed. Except that Jack had often wondered what he'd missed by passing up the chance to strike out on his own when he'd been younger. He'd let the pull of the family business, his role as the eldest son, lock him into a life running his father's empire. He didn't regret his choice, exactly, but sometimes he just felt…constrained.

"Look, Brett, leave the business decisions to me. Okay? Tell your city slickers thanks, but no thanks, and drop this horse-breeding nonsense. Got it? If Daniel wants to stay at the Lucky C, he will…for his own reasons." Jack clapped his brother on the shoulder as he stepped back.

"Jack…" Brett's hands fisted, and his face hardened with displeasure and frustration.

But Jack felt it was better he settle the issue now, no holds barred, than have Brett continue to bug him about it and string the city slickers along. With a nod to the men from Dallas, he stepped away to look for his son. Seth had had plenty of time to change clothes and return to the party.

"Jack Colton!" His sister's voice pulled him up short as he passed the patio doors to the living room. "How dare you!"

He groaned internally as he turned. Now what?

Beside Greta stood a certain caramel-haired china doll, her eyes red from crying. Before he could repeat his order for Laura's cousin to get off the ranch, his sister seized his arm and dragged him through the crowd in the living room to an isolated corner of the foyer. Tracy followed.

"I am ashamed of you, Jack Colton!" Greta said, releasing his arm and scowling darkly. "I just found Tracy at our front door, crying. She says that you ordered her off the property. I hope I heard her wrong, because I can't believe any brother of mine would be so rude and inhospitable. This is *my* engagement party, and you have no right to say who attends and who doesn't."

Jack dragged a hand over his mouth, tamping down the irritation building in his blood. "She's not here because of your party, Greta. Or did she forget to tell you that part?"

"Did you kick her out?" Greta asked pointedly. "Did you not understand that she is *family*?"

He braced his hands on his hips and dug deep for patience. First Brett wrangling to tie Daniel to the ranch, now Greta shoving this woman's connection to Laura down his throat. He loved his family, but sometimes…

"She's Laura's family. Not ours. And yes, I asked her to leave. We'd said all that needed to be said."

"As Laura's family, that makes her Seth's family. And that, then, makes her *our* family."

Jack groaned long and loud. He could see where this was going. "Greta, don't interfere—"

"I've invited her to stay." His sister lifted her chin in a way that said the matter was settled. Being the youngest sibling and the only girl, Greta had gotten her way more often than not growing up. He wouldn't call her spoiled—not exactly—but Big J doted on her, and she was clearly and unequivocally Abra's favorite.

Jack glanced at Tracy, who was studying her shoes

and gnawing her bottom lip. "She didn't come here because of your party. She came to cause trouble with Seth."

Now Tracy's head jerked up. "I did not! I told you the last thing I wanted was to hurt Seth. I just want to meet him, get to know him, spend some quality time with h—"

"And I said *no*." He straightened his spine and clenched his hands at his sides. "Hell, no. No way. Not in a million years."

"Jack!" Greta scolded.

"I'm not stupid," he continued, undeterred by his sister, feeling his blood pressure rise and pulse at his temples. "I know this is a ploy to weasel your way into his life and establish some thin case you can take to a judge, trying to get visitation or shared custody or money or—"

Tracy was shaking her head, her face pale. "You don't listen so well, do you, cowboy? I've told you I don't want custody or your money!"

"But you *do* want to fill my son's head with stories about his mother." Jack aimed an accusing finger at her. "Things that will only raise more questions and—"

"He has a right to the truth!"

Greta gave a shrill referee-like whistle. "Both of you, to your corners!"

Abra appeared in the foyer, her eyes shooting daggers at the trio. "What is going on out here? I have guests! Greta, *you* have guests! And it is almost time for the official announcement. Shouldn't you be freshening up and finding your fiancé and a glass of champagne about now?"

Their mother added a look that said the question was actually a command, and she wouldn't be disobeyed.

"I'll be right there, Mother." Greta faced Jack again. "I have to go now, but Tracy is not going anywhere. I've invited her to stay as my guest. Not just for the party, but for an extended visit. She can have one of the spare rooms here in the main house."

Jack stiffened, feeling as if he'd been kicked in the chest by a bull. "You did what? Greta!"

"I hope for your sake and your son's that you will change your tune about letting her spend time with Seth. He has a right to know the truth, a right to know his maternal family."

Jack turned to glower at the blonde, whose expression had brightened. A pink blush tinted her cheeks, and her dewy blue eyes watched him with a light of expectation and hope. The odd tangle of lust and protectiveness he'd felt toward her in the stable reemerged, sending a shot of heat to his core. Tracy was the first woman in years to turn his head and stir this carnal reaction in him. And she'd be staying at the main house, just a short ride from the old ranch house where he lived with Seth. A cool drink in the midst of a ranch full of hot, thirsty brothers and hired hands. He didn't like the idea of that one bit, nor the flair of possessive jealousy that tickled his gut.

Tightening his jaw, he tore his gaze away, pushing aside the niggling desire.

She might look like an innocent china doll, but he feared she'd prove to be the Bride of Chucky.

He searched for an out and offered, "What is she supposed to do for clothes? I don't see a suitcase."

"She can borrow some of mine," Greta returned.

"Actually…I have a suitcase in my car. I'd planned to stay at a motel in town during my stay in Oklahoma. But if the parking valet could bring my car around from—"

"You planned to stay?" he asked, cutting her off.

She swallowed, then straightened her shoulders. "I hoped to have a few days to spend with Seth."

"See there? All settled." Greta nodded in satisfaction.

"You can…supervise her visits or…lay out parameters or something, if it makes you feel better." Greta waved a hand, clearly making up her suggestions off the cuff. "But since she'll be my guest, you *cannot* kick her off the ranch."

His sister smoothed the skirt of her sundress and stepped back. "Now, I have to go announce my engagement." She added a smile that reflected a touch of nerves. "Make nice, you two."

As she sauntered away, Greta gave him a little gloating grin, as if she'd bested him.

Jack knew better. Greta could allow Laura's cousin to stay in the main house, but he'd see to it Tracy got nowhere near Seth. His son was his whole world, and he'd protect him at all costs.

Tracy stood by herself in the cool marble foyer for long seconds after Jack gave her a warning glare and stomped off to join the party. She'd expected to have to sway Seth's father to her idea, but she'd never imagined he'd be quite so hostile and suspicious of her.

Laura had said there was no love lost between them after the divorce. Jack took his wife's leaving personally, she'd said. Understandable. Broken relationships had a way of being personal. But the wall Jack had erected to keep any hint of Laura or her memory out of his son's life was overkill in Tracy's estimation. She had her work cut out for her, breaking down his defenses and earning his trust.

Her head was telling her to run. Far and fast. She didn't need any part of another overbearing alpha male just months after freeing herself from Cliff. But her heart was telling her Jack Colton's bark wasn't a reflection of the soul inside. Laura had said Jack was a loving man, a softhearted father and a protective husband before things had gone south for them. Protective, Tracy could certainly believe, and she chose to believe that the rest lay beneath the hard surface she'd seen today.

The lean and sexy surface. She fanned herself, despite having long ago cooled off in the frigid AC after their hike to the stable. The heat that swamped her now came from deep inside. A purely female reaction to shaggy dark brown hair, broad shoulders and green eyes that glittered with passion when their owner got riled.

A rustling noise in the hallway to her right drew Tracy's attention, and she craned her neck to see what had caused the disturbance. She saw nothing at first, but when a side table with a large vase moved, rocking the vessel of flowers, she caught a glimpse of the boy who was the spitting image of Jack. "Seth?"

She stepped in that direction, sending the boy scurrying from his hiding place, jostling the side table again. The vase tipped forward, and Tracy rushed to catch it a split second before the crystal urn would have crashed to the floor. "Whoa! That was close."

She smiled at the boy as she righted the vase on the table. "I can't imagine your grandma would be too happy if that broke."

He shook his head, wide-eyed. "I'd have got a whuppin' for sure."

"Your father spanks you?" Tracy frowned, bothered by the notion.

He shook his head again. "Not Daddy. But Pa Pa might've, since it's Grandmother's flower thing. Daddy says he used to get whuppin's when he was bad."

She was relieved to hear Jack didn't spank his son, but tucked away the notion that Big J Colton had used corporal punishment on his. Discipline was one thing, but being all too familiar with domestic violence, Tracy worried where Big J might have drawn the line when spanking his grandson.

She made a mental note to investigate this further. If Seth was in any danger of harm, she'd do what it took to get him away from the Lucky C. For now she focused on the boy, her nephew, and gave him a friendly smile. "So you're Seth, huh?"

He nodded. "Yeah." Scrunching his nose, he corrected, "I mean, yes, ma'am."

Tracy chuckled. "A polite young man. That's nice."

"Daddy says 'specting elders is important." Seth rubbed his hand on his nose.

Tracy winced internally at being classified as an "elder." With a wry half grin, she said, "Manners are a good habit. He's right."

Seth narrowed a wary look on her. "Greta said you knew my mom. That you're…my family?"

Tracy caught her breath. Crouching to his level, she offered him another gentle smile. "You heard, huh?"

His eyes got big. "I wasn't spyin'! Honest! I just… well, I…"

She dismissed his concern with a head shake. "It's okay, hon. Yes, I knew your mom. She was my cousin. That makes you my cousin, too."

His dark eyebrows rose. "Really?"

"I'm your cousin Tracy." She held out a hand to him in greeting, but instead of a handshake, he slanted her a lopsided grin, stepped shyly closer and gave her a bear hug. Tracy's heart somersaulted, then flooded with joy. She blinked back the sting of tears the boy's warm greeting brought to her eyes, and embraced him back. His small body was slim but strong, and he smelled faintly of sweat and the last traces of a fresh soapy scent from his morning bath. Like his father, Seth wore his hair fairly shaggy, and it curled a bit from moisture at his neck.

"Cousin Tracy?" Seth backed out of their hug and wrinkled his nose.

Her chest filled to bursting as she heard him address her with the familial tag. "Yes, sweetie?"

"Why was my daddy mad at you?"

Her gut twisted. Just like that she was walking on eggshells, not wanting to cause problems, and handling delicate questions with the boy. "Well, I don't know that he was so much mad as he was—"

"Yep, he was," Seth said, nodding in certainty. "That was his mad voice, and he was all stiff, with his hands tight like this." He demonstrated the way Jack had fisted his hands. "And his face was bumping like it does when he's mad."

She blinked. "Bumping?"

He pointed to his temple. "Right here. When Daddy gets mad, his head goes bump bump bump."

She twisted her mouth as she deciphered the kid speak and decided Jack must have a blood vessel at his temple pulse point that throbbed when he was angry. "I see. Well...we had disagreed about something earlier, but it's nothing you need to worry about. Okay?"

Seth skewed his lips in thought, then lifted a lean shoulder. "Okay."

From the next room, Tracy her the clink of a utensil on glass and Big J's booming voice calling for the attention of his guests.

"Sounds like it's time for Greta's big announcement. Want to go with me to watch?" She offered her hand to Seth, and he took it with a nod.

"It's just about her and Mr. Mark gettin' married. I already know that stuff, but I'll take you in there."

"Why, thank y—" Before she could finish, he was towing her toward the living room entrance. She stumbled a step or two as she rose too quickly from her crouch. Seth moved with a hurried, boy-like trot that had her hustling to keep up. When they reached the amassed guests in the living room, he wove his way among them, dragging Tracy by the hand and causing her to jostle through the crowd as he led her to the front of the assembly gathered around Greta, Mark and the senior Coltons. Embarrassed to have been so boldly brought to the front, Tracy tried to sidle to the right, away from Abra and Big J's line of sight, but Seth tugged her arm, drawing her back to the center.

"Abra and I were thrilled to welcome our darling Greta to the family twenty-six years ago," Big J said to the room, his glass raised.

Tracy hunched her shoulders, trying to duck lower and make herself less obvious. Could she squat next to Seth? When she tried to stoop, she bumped the lady behind her, who scowled.

"Sorry," she whispered.

"After having four rowdy boys, we treasured our first and only baby girl," Big J continued, beaming at Greta.

Tracy cast a glance around the circle of onlookers, hunting for Jack's rugged face. Her attention snagged on the cowboy who'd parked her car when she arrived. He stood in a corner, his arms crossed over his chest, with a crooked grin on his face as he watched the proceedings. But his amused expression faltered at Big J's last statement. He ducked his chin, casting his gaze to the ground. For just a moment his brow wrinkled, so quickly Tracy almost missed it. But she was sure she'd seen a look that could only be described as hurt or crestfallen flicker across the cowboy's handsome face. A moment later he gave his head a small shake and returned his attention to Big J. Tracy couldn't help but feel a tug of sympathy for the man, without even knowing who he was or what had upset him.

"She's our pride and joy, and we are pleased to announce…"

Tracy's attention left the boisterous glee of the Colton patriarch, sensing rather than seeing Jack's hot stare from across the room. Her gaze darted to his, drawn like a magnet to his bright green eyes. A tingle like an electric shock skittered through her, speeding up her pulse. Her mouth dried, and she wished for one of the drinks the guests had hoisted in salute to the bride-and-groom-to-be. Not just because she stood out all the more for her lack of a glass for toasting, but because she could use something to wet her throat. Preferably something alcoholic, to help calm the flutter of nerves jangling in her core.

She was so entranced by Jack's level stare that when the crowd around her cheered and clapped, she gave a startled jolt. Pulling her hand free of Seth's, she joined the applause. Her appearance at the party with the boy had no doubt added to Jack's consternation. If making peace with Jack in order to gain access to Seth was her goal, she wasn't off to a good start. That needed to change. One way or another, she had to get past Jack's defensiveness, break down his walls and prove to him he could trust her with his son.

As the party ended and the last guests and media crew were sent away with hospitable smiles, Greta found Tracy out by the pool. Tracy had been watching Seth goof around on the grassy lawn with the cowboy who'd been her parking valet.

"Ready to go up and see your room?" Greta asked.

"Sure. Thanks." Tracy stood and smoothed the seat of her slacks, giving Seth and the handsome cowboy a last look. Remembering the expression of sharp disappointment that had crossed the man's face at the engagement announcement, she aimed her thumb over her shoulder as she followed Greta inside. "Who is that roughhousing with Seth?"

Greta glanced to the lawn. "Oh, that's Daniel. Another uncle."

Tracy frowned. "I thought you only had four brothers."

"He's a half brother." She sighed and lowered her voice to a wry, conspiratorial whisper. "The product of an 'indiscretion' on my father's part early in my parents' marriage." As she led Tracy through the living room Greta straightened an iron sculpture that had been knocked askew during the party. "When his mother died, Daniel came to live on the ranch." She raised her eyebrows and angled her head. "Much to my mother's chagrin. But my brothers and I count him as a full sibling and love having him here." She sighed and shook her head. "Mother still won't accept him, though."

"That explains the look, I guess," Tracy muttered to herself.

Greta's clattering footsteps on the marble foyer slowed. "I'm sorry? What look?"

Heat flushed Tracy's cheeks. She didn't need to be poking her nose in private family issues and stirring up problems while at the Lucky C. Her goal was to win favor and get to know her nephew, not be the conscience of the Colton clan.

"Oh, nothing." She forced a smile.

But Greta stopped walking and faced her, arching a well-manicured eyebrow. "Fess up. What do you know?"

Heaving a defeated sigh, Tracy wet her lips. "It's just

that…during your father's speech…when he was announcing your engagement…"

Her hostess's forehead dented with apprehension. "Go on."

"Well…" Tracy shifted her weight from one foot to another, feeling like a grade school tattletale. "I saw a look cross his face when your father was talking about having four sons before you were born. Daniel looked…hurt."

Greta closed her eyes slowly and grimaced.

"It was fleeting, and I could have imagined it, but…"

"Big J did say *four* sons, didn't he? I didn't even catch it at the time, or I'd have said something." Greta huffed in frustration. "No doubt he left Daniel out to appease Abra, but…poor Daniel. He denies to our faces that it still bothers him, but this kind of thing is bound to make him feel like an outsider. *Damn it*." She grumbled the last under her breath as she resumed walking toward the wide stairs to the upper floors. "Thanks for telling me. I'll apologize to Daniel later for—"

"Oh, I…I can't imagine he'd want his discomfiture pointed out. Or the fact that I noticed. I don't want to be a source of trouble or strife in the family."

Greta flicked a dismissive hand. "I'll leave your name out of it."

That was something, but Tracy thought about the icy look Jack had given her earlier at the announcement. "I have enough to deal with earning Jack's trust. He really hated Laura a lot, didn't he?"

"Hated her? Heck, no. He loved her. More than he'll ever admit to any of us. You know how men bury that kind of thing. I think what he puts out there as ill will toward Laura is the manifestation of his deep wounds. Her unhappiness at the ranch disappointed him. Her leaving him and their baby crushed him. Her distance and disinterest in their son after she left angered him. Laura hurt him on many levels, and he's put up walls. But don't be fooled. He never hated her. I think he wishes he could hate her. It'd make it easier to get over her abandonment."

"So his hostility toward me is—"

"Fear, most likely." Greta led her into a large, plushly appointed bedroom with a massive king-size sleigh bed, dark walnut furnishings and a recessed ceiling, framed with elegant crown molding.

Tracy caught her breath, taking in the beautiful decor.

"He's fiercely protective of Seth," Greta continued, apparently unaware of Tracy's momentary rapture. "That boy is everything to him. The idea that you could want to take Seth or disillusion—"

"But I don't!" Tracy countered quickly, snapping from her dazed admiration of the guest room.

Greta raised a hand. "I hear you. But Jack will be harder to convince."

Tracy's shoulders slumped. "Any advice where to start?"

Greta twisted her mouth in thought. "Action. You can talk until you are blue in the face and not convince him of anything. Jack is a doer. A man of action. If he sees you treating Seth with kindness and can witness evidence of your respect for his wishes regarding Seth, that will go further than any promises you make him. Laura made promises she didn't keep. You'll have to prove yourself to him before he'll listen to anything you say."

Chapter 4

That evening, Jack and Seth walked up to the main house to join Jack's parents, sister, Ryan and Brett for a family dinner. When she'd called him about coming to dinner, Greta had informed him that Eric, a trauma surgeon in Tulsa, had planned to be there, but had been called to the hospital. Mark had returned to town on business, and Daniel had begged off, claiming he had other mysterious plans.

Jack had had his fill of socializing for the day, even with his own family, and had been looking forward to a quiet evening with Seth. But his son had overheard the phone call and had bounced on his toes, begging to go. What could he say? Seth loved dinner at the main house, stuffing himself on the home-style foods Maria Sanchez, Abra and Big J's cook, prepared, and teasing with his uncles and aunt. The family connections were good for Seth, and the balanced meal was a far cry from the Tater Tots and hot dogs Jack had planned to make.

So here he was, heading back up to his parents' house with his son chattering animatedly beside him about the snake he'd seen out in the pasture that afternoon.

"Daniel said it wasn't the bad kind." Seth tugged the heavy back door open, his little-boy muscles straining. Jack no longer helped Seth with doors or his shoelaces or buckling his saddle straps—though he did double-check those before he let Seth ride. His boy was old enough to do things for himself and was determined to be self-sufficient. Jack encouraged him to learn ranch chores and be independent but caught himself wondering now and then where his baby boy had gone. Seth was growing up so fast.

"Some snakes are good, 'cause they eat the mice that get in the barn," he continued as they strolled through the mudroom and into the family room. "He says Sleekie can't catch all the critters, so we need some snakes around."

"Snakes?" Abra said as they joined the family. Jack's mother shuddered visibly and turned to speak to the woman next to her. "Vile creatures. Another reason I prefer to stay at the house and avoid the pens."

"I'm no fan of snakes myself," the woman agreed affably.

Jack recognized the voice and whipped his head toward the female guest. Tracy McCain. His gut rolled. He'd forgotten she was still here. Hadn't considered that she'd be at the family dinner. He slanted an irritated glance at his sister, and Greta's returned gaze was triumphant. "Jack, you remember Tracy, right?"

He clenched his back teeth, tightening his jaw and shoving down the growl of frustration that rose in his throat. "Yeah. I remember her." He cast a dark look at their guest that let her know exactly how he felt about her interloping.

"Hi, Tracy!" Seth chirped, peeling away from his father's side and skipping over to greet Laura's cousin.

Laura's cousin, therefore Seth's cousin. Hadn't Jack just thought that family connections were good for Seth? But Tracy's presence filled him with a sense of foreboding and unease that burrowed deep into his bones. Something about her left him off balance, made his skin feel hot and prickly, as if he'd been out in the sun too long. And the way her pale blue eyes watched him with that fragile, wistful expression fired unwelcome feelings of protectiveness in him. Protectiveness and—he gritted his teeth harder—lust. Yes, damn it. The woman's ethereal beauty and delicate femininity drew him in and riled his libido like crazy, a complication he didn't need if he was going to protect his son from her hidden agenda.

He'd opened his mouth to call Seth back to his side when his son opened his arms and fell against Tracy to give her a hug.

"Hi, sweetie," she answered with a warm smile as she returned the embrace. "Good to see you again."

Jack's heartbeat stumbled at Seth's trusting and loving gesture. Not for the first time, Jack wondered what his son was missing, not having a mother in his life. Abra loved her grandson, but had never been the warm, fuzzy type, even with her own children. Greta spoiled Seth when she was around, but she was such a tomboy, Jack didn't count her as a mother figure.

Seth, ever the gregarious soul, beamed up at Tracy and asked, "Do you want to see my pony after supper? His name is Pooh Bear, and he's all mine!"

"Pooh Bear? What a wonderful name. It reminds me of the Winnie the Pooh I had when I was little."

Seth brightened. "Me, too! That's why I named him Pooh!"

"Well, what do you know?" Tracy flashed a grin and combed her fingers through Seth's wild mane of hair. Seth leaned contentedly into the caress, and Jack could almost imagine him purring like a kitten.

His son always got his hair cut when Jack did, but in recent weeks, Jack had been too busy with the herd and calving to bother with a haircut. He dragged a hand through his own shaggy mop and tried not to imagine how it would feel to have Tracy's fingers tangling in his hair or stroking his skin. But his scalp tingled, anyway, with ghost sensations.

"My grandson is well on his way to being a fine horseman and cowboy, Miss McCain," Big J said, and flashed a smile that lacked the spark and full-wattage flirtation that was usually part of the old man's arsenal. Jack gave his father a considering glance and saw other evidence of fatigue. His shoulders were a bit more stooped, his face more lined and his cowboy's tan seemed a tad washed out. The engagement party had been a massive undertaking, but Jack was surprised by Big J's apparent post-party fatigue. His father was widely known to be an unstoppable force of nature. Bigger than life and always the last man standing.

Jack's puzzling over Big J's demeanor was sidetracked when Brett strode into the family room rubbing his belly. "Hey, y'all, when do we eat? I'm famished."

"After all you ate at the party? Where do you put it, you hog?" Greta gave her brother a playful jab.

"I can't help it. I'm a growing boy. Right, Seth?" Brett winked at his nephew, and Seth rolled his eyes.

"Well, now that we're all here, shall we go in?" Abra asked with a prim lift to her chin.

"Go in?" Jack muttered to Brett under his breath.

"Someone's been watching too much *Downton Abbey*," his brother returned quietly.

Jack arched an eyebrow. "And how would you know?"

Brett pulled a face. "I may have watched an episode or two with Greta. She monopolizes the TV in the family room on Sunday nights. The accents the women on that show have are kinda hot."

Jack gave his brother a slap on the back and a snort of laughter as he followed his mother, Greta and Tracy into the dining room.

Speaking of hot… The wispy sundress Tracy had changed into for dinner stopped above her knees and gave a tantalizing view of her slender legs and porcelain shoulders. Jack had the stray thought that Tracy would have to show extreme care with her skin if she went out on the ranch in the scorching June sun. She'd burn quickly and—

He shook his head. Tracy's skin and the relative risks of sun exposure for her were not his concern. If he had his way, she'd be long gone from the ranch before the question of sunburn could be an issue for her.

"Cousin Tracy, you can sit by me!" Seth said, patting the seat of the chair where Jack usually sat. His son blinked up at him. "Is that okay, Daddy?"

Jack paused, his hand on the back of the chair. "Oh… uh, sure." He pulled the seat out for her and helped her push up to the table before taking the only spot left, across the table from his son.

After Maria brought out their dinner, the family bowed their heads to say grace. When the prayer ended, Jack glanced across the table, and his gaze met Tracy's and held for a few lingering seconds. A pink flush filled her cheeks, and he felt his own body temperature rise.

Clearly, his libido recognized that Tracy McCain was an attractive woman. But his head wasn't ready to trust her.

"Tell us about yourself, Miss McCain," Big J said.

His father's voice broke the spell that had kept her staring back at Jack for long seconds. She jerked her attention to the end of the table as Big J passed a tray of roasted chicken and vegetables to her. Jack noticed that his father's hand shook a bit, adding to his earlier impression that Big J seemed uncharacteristically worn out this evening.

"I don't know that there's much to tell. I live in Denver, but I grew up outside of Colorado Springs and graduated from Colorado State with a degree in communications."

"Communications, huh?" Big J grunted. "And what are you doing with that degree?"

"Well, nothing at the moment. My husband didn't want me to work, and since his death, I haven't had much luck finding a job."

Jack paused with the serving spoon of wild rice hovering over his plate as his eyes lifted to Tracy again. She was unemployed? That lent credence to his theory that she was after money.

"You're a widow?" Greta asked, her tone soft and sympathetic. "I'm so sorry."

"What's a widow?" Seth asked, his mouth full of chicken.

"It means her husband passed away," Abra said quietly, when no one else spoke.

"Oh." Seth tucked into his dinner again, but Jack wasn't sure his son understood his grandmother's euphemism.

When Seth picked his chicken leg up with his hands

and took a big bite, Abra scowled. "You have a fork, Seth. Please use it."

"Oh, sorry." He gave her a chagrined look and earned another frown when he wiped his greasy hands on the cloth napkin.

"Can I help you cut your meat?" Tracy offered, reaching for his knife.

Jack opened his mouth to tell Tracy that Seth could cut his own meat, but Seth beamed up at her and nodded. "Sure. Thanks."

Where was his I-can-do-it-myself son? Seth had insisted on cutting his own meat since he was three years old. Jack watched, fascinated, as Tracy doted on him— helping serve him rice and peas, cut his meat and tuck his napkin in his lap—and Seth soaked up the coddling.

"How did your husband die?" Greta asked.

"Greta!" Abra scolded in a hushed tone.

"If you don't mind my asking…" Jack's sister added.

Jack had impertinent questions of his own. He needed to know more about Tracy and her history, her family connections, if he was to be prepared to protect his son.

Tracy flashed Greta an awkward smile, obviously uneasy with the question. She stared at her plate a moment, idly rearranging her English peas before answering.

He recalled their conversation in the stable earlier today. *He was shanked the second night he was in jail…*

"Car accident," she said quietly.

Jack's pulse kicked at the lie. Or was what she'd told him in the stable the lie? Either way, he'd caught her in a deception and intended to confront her about it. Later. He didn't want Seth to be a witness to any story she might invent to weasel out of the snare she'd caught herself in.

"How awful. I'm so sorry." Greta, seated on their

guest's left side, placed a comforting hand on Tracy's wrist.

"Wait," Brett said, screwing his face in a frown of confusion. "Didn't Laura die in a car accident? And she was your cousin, right?"

Tracy turned her face toward Brett, and the color leaked from her cheeks. "Yes."

Jack kicked his brother under the table, and Brett cut a side glare back at him. Jack had told Seth his mother had died right after he was born, and Brett's thoughtless comment threatened to expose the white lie. Clearing his throat and sending his brother a meaningful look, Jack said, "But that was a long time ago. Let's not talk about that now, huh?"

Tracy sent him a curious frown. "Not that long ago. Six months. Wh—"

"So, Greta, have you had any luck breaking that new colt we bought at the auction last month?" Jack asked, eager to change the subject before Seth caught on. The fact that he'd nearly been caught in a lie of his own didn't escape Jack, even if he could justify the disinformation he'd told Seth as being in his son's best interests.

"Jack," Greta said through clenched teeth, her manicured eyebrows dipping low in disapproval. "You interrupted Tracy."

He waved a fork toward their guest. "Oh, sorry," he said, though his tone contradicted him. "You were saying?"

Tracy gave her head a shake. "Forget it." She seemed glad to have the topic diverted from her, and faced Greta. "You train horses?"

Greta arched one scolding eyebrow at Jack, but nodded to Tracy. "I do. I work with the more difficult animals on the ranch and recently started taking clients who want a kinder method of training. I use operant conditioning and positive reinforcement instead of punishment and have had great success with even the most spirited animals." A grin tugged her cheek. "That's how I met Mark. He was a client."

Tracy smiled politely. "How wonderful."

"Did you ever see the movie *The Horse Whisperer*, Miss McCain?" Abra asked.

Tracy nodded. "Beautiful cinematography."

"I agree. Well, our Greta does much the same thing Robert Redford did in the movie." Abra gave her daughter a formal smile. "The term *horse whisperer* is more of a colloquialism than an official term, but you get the idea. Yes?"

"Sure."

"Can you ride a horse, Miss Tracy?" Seth asked, tugging at her arm.

"Well, I rode a pony at a fair when I was a kid, and I went on a trail ride once in Rocky Mountain National Park with my family as a teenager, but I'm not sure that counts."

"It's something," Greta said.

At the same time, Brett chuckled. "Hardly."

Tracy divided a grin between the two for their differing opinions. "Anyway, I haven't been on a horse in probably ten years or more, so I guess my answer is no."

"Oh." Seth's face fell in disappointment.

A thoughtful look crossed Greta's face as she stabbed a bite of chicken. "Ya know…I could take you riding tomorrow before I go back to OKC. Teach you a bit about horsemanship. It'll be fun. I'll show you the lay of the land."

Seth perked up. "Can I go?"

"Sure!" Greta said, just as Jack shook his head.

"Seth, I don't…" He let his sentence trail off as all eyes turned to him with mixed degrees of curiosity, disagreement and disapproval.

"You don't—" Greta prompted him, then immediately finished for him "—have any good reason not to let him join us. I'll keep a close eye on him."

"I know you will. I just…" He scowled at his sister and cast a disgruntled glance toward Tracy. When he hesitated, looking for a way to effectively deny Tracy access to his son, Greta swooped in.

"All right, then. Meet me at the stables tomorrow morning at seven. We'll go out before it gets too hot. Then come back up to the house for a big ranch-style breakfast." She shot Seth a querying look. "Think you can be up that early and meet us?"

Seth glanced to his father, wide-eyed. "Daddy, what time do we get up?"

The truth was Jack typically had Seth up before dawn to help with ranching chores, but he had a perverse notion to let his son sleep in tomorrow. "Pretty early, usually."

"Tell you what," Brett said, then took a bite of biscuit and continued with his mouth full, "I'll pick you up on my way to the pens and help you get Pooh saddled up."

"Thanks, Uncle Brett!"

Jack shot his younger brother a frown that said *Die!* Brett answered with an innocent and bemused look. Clearly, Jack was alone in his mission to keep his ex-wife's scheming family away from Seth.

Fine. If his family was going to pave the way for Tracy to spend time with Seth, then he'd make himself available to monitor her interactions with his son. He wasn't about to let a pretty face and sweet smile fool him. His son was his first priority, and he'd protect his boy from anyone who tried to threaten his happiness or the life Jack had with Seth.

After dinner ended and the family moved to the family room to enjoy a glass of wine or a cold beer, Jack pulled Tracy aside for a private word. Even in the shadows of the small alcove where they stood, her pale blue eyes held a bright gleam of innocence that contradicted the motives he suspected were behind her visit to the ranch. Jack found that incongruity almost as annoying as his body's reaction to her bright, penetrating gaze.

He allowed his hand to linger on her soft skin, telling himself his grasp on her arm was to keep her as his captive audience until he'd said his piece. But a small voice in his head argued that he enjoyed touching her, standing close to her and seeing her eyes widen with anticipation when he hovered over her a bit too much.

"Is something the matter?" she asked.

"We just need to establish some boundaries, get some facts straight if you want to spend any time around my son." He drilled her with a hard look, hoping to assert an air of authority, but holding her gaze sent a shaft of desire to his belly. Damn but she was delicate and beautiful. Captivating in a way that spoke to everything male in him.

"What sort of boundaries?"

"For starters…" He clenched his back teeth, desperately shoving the distracting thoughts down so he could deal with the threat she posed. Like the Trojan horse, she might seem desirable on the outside, but what lurked inside held the real danger. "You're not to spend any time alone with Seth. I have to supervise any activity you do with him."

She rolled her eyes, expressing her opinion of his dictate.

"I'm serious. If I get word of you going behind my back and seeing Seth on the sly, I'll personally escort you off this ranch and have a restraining order filed within the day."

Her brow puckered indignantly. "A restraining order? Don't you think that's a bit excessive? I've told you I have no intention of harming Seth in any way."

"And I've said the truth of that remains to be seen. There are more than a few ways you could hurt him."

She huffed in exasperation and tried to leave. Jack blocked her, hating the tingle that shot through him when his chest and hips collided with hers. She took a step back and trembled visibly, her gaze now downcast. "Do you mind? I'd like to pass."

"We're not done."

Her shoulders drooped, and she seemed to struggle for the fortitude to meet his eyes again.

"I told Seth his mother died shortly after he was born."

Her shoulders snapped back and fire leaped to her eyes. "So you said earlier today. But that's—"

"That's the story you need to stick to. Telling him anything else will only hurt him. It will lead to questions about where she's been, why she left, why—"

"Why you lied to him?" Tracy interjected, her expression self-righteous.

Jack stiffened, his hands fisting at his sides. "I was trying to protect him. I thought it would be easier on him to think his mother died than to know she'd abandoned him. That she willfully walked away from her husband and child and didn't look back."

"What are you talking about? Laura *tried* to have a relationship with her son!" Tracy pressed her mouth into a taut line of disgust. "She tried to reach out to him, but you prevented her attempts to come back for visits. You wouldn't let him come see her, either."

"She made her choice. When she left, she was dead to us."

"Dead to you, maybe, but you had no right to keep Seth from her!"

Anger pulsed through Jack's blood and pounded at his temples. "I had every right! I'm his father!"

"And she was his mother!"

"Not after she threw him away. She signed full custody over to me when she left, in exchange for a tidy settlement. Maybe you can't buy love, but she certainly got paid well when she abandoned Seth."

Tracy looked away, her expression wounded.

"She didn't tell you that, did she? How she accepted a payout in exchange for her promise not to interfere with Seth or try to make any claim to him later in his life. She *sold* her right to my son, his inheritance and this ranch." He paused, then nudged Tracy's collarbone with his index finger. "And by extension, any right *you* or the rest of your family might have."

"I'm not after money. I just want to have a relationship with Seth. Why can't you believe that?"

The quiver of emotion in her voice chipped at the wall he'd erected. He could almost believe she meant what she said. Except...

"I make a habit of not believing known liars."

She stiffened in umbrage and grated, "I'm not a liar."

"Oh? What really happened to your husband? Is he even dead? Because you did, in fact, lie earlier. Either at dinner or in the stable." She blanched, and Jack gave her a smug grin. "Yeah. I caught it. You told me this afternoon your husband was killed in prison, stabbed by another inmate."

Tracy's doll-like features crumpled, and she looked as if she might be ill. "He was. But I couldn't very well say that at dinner with Seth listening."

Jack folded his arms over his chest. "I see. So you plan to base this relationship you want with my son on lies? Can you see why I don't trust you?"

Her shoulders drew back defiantly, causing her small breasts to jut toward him. "I was trying to protect him from the ugliness of the truth! He's too young to hear about such things as prison murders and shanks made from a sharpened toothbrush."

"And when he first asked about his mother, he was too young to know about a mother who could walk away from her family for purely selfish reasons."

Tracy opened her mouth, clearly planning to defend her cousin.

"Don't even start," Jack said, stopping her by pressing a finger to her lips.

Tracy jolted as if his touch had caused a static shock, drawing a sharp breath and flinching.

Too late, he realized the mistake of his move. He, too, felt a crackle of something electric that briefly side-tracked his thoughts and caused a tremble deep in his marrow.

Their gazes clashed for a moment, and he withdrew his hand, rubbing his thumb over the spot in his finger that still tingled.

From the next room he heard Seth's youthful laugh as Brett roughhoused with his nephew, and Jack recalled the point he'd been making. "I was there, not you. I was the one she divorced, the one she argued her case to, the one left cleaning up in her wake. I was the one who paid her settlement and stayed up nights with a colicky baby after she walked out. I have every right to determine what my son knows about Laura and what remains unspoken. You *will not* tell him anything that contradicts what he now knows about his mother. Or you will be removed from the ranch and Seth's life if I have to carry you to the highway myself."

Tracy's gaze flitted to his arms and chest, as if imagining him making good on his threat. She swallowed hard, and her feet shuffled slightly as she shifted her weight. He could see the pulse point at the base of her throat fluttering, and he was swamped by a primitive urge to taste the skin there. To suckle her neck, nip the skin and feel that rhythmic pulsing with his lips.

Hellfire! What was he doing? He didn't need to be indulging in lustful fantasies about this woman if he was going to do his job as a father and protect Seth from her meddling.

Tracy took a step back from him and bumped the wall behind her. Flexing her hands and wiping her palms on the skirt of her dress, she wet her lips and raised her chin. "I won't tell Seth anything that contradicts you." The nervous glint in her liquid eyes belied the set of her shoulders. "But neither will I lie to him if he asks me directly."

Jack gritted his teeth. "Ms. McCain, I'm warning you…"

"You don't need to make threats, Jack. I told you I have Seth's best interests at heart, same as you." She placed a trembling hand on his arm and pushed at him. "Now let me pass."

He didn't move right away, stubbornly keeping her trapped to let her know he would have the final say, not only with Seth but in this discussion. Finally, he stepped aside and swept a hand toward the living room, granting her passage. She stalked away, leaving a hint of her sweet floral scent behind. He experienced an unwanted, but not unpleasant, visceral reaction to the heady honeysuckle aroma she trailed in her wake. Maybe, he thought wryly, the vixen had gotten the last word, after all.

Chapter 5

Early the next morning, Tracy hitched a ride with Brett in a utility vehicle across the wide ranch yard to the outbuildings. First stop, Jack's house to pick up Seth.

As Brett parked in front of the age-worn wood-and-hand-carved-stone house, Tracy admired the ranch-style home where Jack and Seth lived. Where Laura had once lived. How could this gorgeous abode and beautiful setting not have been enough for Laura?

"This used to be the main house, before Abra had the new house built," Brett said, tooting the tinny-sounding horn of the utility vehicle. "It's over a hundred years old, but has been kept in good repair through the years."

Seth came scampering through the front door with Jack close behind. He raced up to her like an eager puppy, grinning ear to ear. "Hi, Miss Tracy!"

"Good morning. Aren't you full of energy so early in the day?" She ruffled the boy's still-sleep-rumpled hair. "What's your secret?"

He gave her an I-don't-know shrug.

"Sugar," Brett said under his breath. "Jack lets the kid eat all the chocolate cereal he wants for breakfast."

"Wrong," Jack said as he drew close to them. "He only gets that crap when he stays at the main house."

Tracy shifted her attention to the older Colton brother, and her pulse did a little morning jig. Jack was obviously fresh from his shower, his hair still damp and curling near his collar. His work clothes were crisp and carried the clean scent of laundry detergent, and he had recently shaved his square jaw and angled cheekbones. Beneath the rim of a black cowboy hat, his eyes held an especially magnetic emerald gleam in the early-morning sun. His blue jeans hugged his lean hips and his muscled thighs in a way that left no secret that Jack was every bit as fit and toned as she imagined a career rancher and horseman would be.

Her mouth dried, and her palms sweated. Good-looking though he was, Brett hadn't had this gut-tightening effect on her when he'd appeared on the back porch, ready to escort her to the stable. Jack had a certain...*something* about him that spoke to her. An elusive additional quality that made her nerves spark and heightened her senses.

"Hop in, buddy. I have things to do," Brett told Seth, aiming a thumb at the back of the MULE.

When Seth started for the backseat of the utility vehicle, Jack caught the back of his shirt and pulled him up short. "Not needed. He can walk over with me. If Seth's going out for a ride on the property, I'm going, too."

Tracy sat taller, a tickle of apprehension in her gut. "You don't have to go. He'll be well cared for. Greta and I will keep a close eye on—"

"Ms. McCain, do you remember our conversation last night in the alcove?"

How could she forget? Cornered by his muscular body and lectured to as if she were a schoolgirl, she should have been frightened. His body language and demeanor had been similar to the intimidation techniques Cliff had used. But she'd sensed two things in Jack that had calmed her fears.

First, a well-controlled restraint. The passion behind Jack's intensity last night had been a love for his son, whereas Cliff's violent and malevolent rages had been rooted in a savage cruelty and lack of self-control.

And second, she'd felt a strong undercurrent of attraction. While she was unnerved by that sensual spark between them, she couldn't call it fear. She felt safe with Jack Colton, yet vulnerable to him because of her body's carnal response to his presence.

"I meant what I said about supervising your time with Seth," he continued. "We'll meet you there in five." His clipped tone left no room for argument.

Oo-kaay. So Jack would be joining them on the horseback excursion around the property. Her stomach fluttered a little with nervous energy. Novice that she was, she prayed she didn't embarrass herself in the saddle in front of Jack.

Greta had arrived at the stable ahead of them and greeted Tracy with a cheery hello. Brett waved goodbye and made a gesture with his hand to indicate she should phone him when she was ready to be driven back up to the main house, since the walk was two miles. Her feet ached from having made the trek yesterday in her "sensible" pumps, which had proved highly unsensible for a ranch. This morning she'd worn tennis shoes and jeans, the only jeans she'd brought with her. Tracy could see that a shopping trip for more practical ranch clothes would be on the agenda for that afternoon or tomorrow.

Her hostess had a dark brown horse with a black mane and tail already saddled and was leading a lighter brown horse out of the stable. "Hey there, Tracy! I've got Mabel all saddled and ready for you."

Tracy eyed the dark brown horse with a bit of trepidation. She'd never spent much time around horses, and she was unsure what to do with the mare. She wanted to exude more confidence than she felt, nonetheless, so she strode forward and reached for Mabel's nose.

"Wait!" Greta called. "Don't approach her from straight on. That's her blind spot. Come at her at an angle so she can see you. Then give her the back of your hand to smell, like when you greet a dog for the first time."

Tracy sucked in a deep breath and edged sideways, adjusting her approach. "Hi, Mabel," she said sweetly and held out her hand as she neared.

The mare snuffled and sniffed her, and when Mabel lowered her nose, Tracy patted her neck.

"That's the way," Greta said with a grin as she slung her saddle over her horse. "Mabel is a sweetheart. She's the horse we always give visitors, since she's so easygoing. Just be firm with her, or she'll want to dally in the fields to nibble all day."

The thud of footsteps drew Tracy's attention as Seth ran up and climbed on the rungs of the corral fence. "Are you gonna ride Mabel, Miss Tracy?"

"Seems so." She gave the mare another pat and glanced past Seth to his father. Once again a bolt of electric attraction streaked through her, stealing her breath. Jack was so ruggedly handsome, his stride so confident and relaxed…

"Let's go, buddy." Jack ruffled his son's hair as he passed. "Bring Pooh out of his stall, and let's get him saddled."

Seth hopped down from the fence and grabbed her hand. "Come on, Miss Tracy. You can help me."

"Oh…uh, Seth, I don't—" The rest of her protest was lost in a gasp as a black animal streaked from the shadows and ran right in front of her, nearly tripping her.

Seth laughed. "You're not scared of Sleekie, are you, Miss Tracy?"

She pressed a hand over her runaway heart and looked for the animal in question. A black cat sat on a hay bale in the corner of the stable, tail swishing. "Is that Sleekie? The cat?"

"Yep," Seth said, tugging her forward again. "Don't worry. Black cats aren't really bad luck. You don't have to be scared."

She smiled sheepishly. "I know. She just startled me is all."

"Her real name is Oh La La Sleek. But we just call her Sleek or Ohla, 'cause Daddy says her real name is a mouthful."

"I see." An amused grin twitched Tracy's lips as she listened to the little boy chatter. Pausing, she cast a backward glance to the end of the stable, where Jack paused to give Sleek a leisurely head scratch before taking a coiled rope off a hook on the wall. His gentle attention to the cat was evidence of what Laura had said about his tender side. *Tough as leather on the outside, but soft as whipped butter toward anyone he loves.* Tracy felt her heart melt like that same butter on a hot waffle.

"I can lead Pooh myself—" Seth called, interrupting her food analogy.

Maria Sanchez had been preparing breakfast as Tracy had left. The aromas of pork and warm maple syrup had made her stomach growl, and she could hardly wait to dig into the bacon and waffles waiting when they returned from their ride.

"—but Daddy has to check my saddle. He says that's just in case. He wants to be sure I'm safe." Seth opened the gate to a stall and walked in to greet his pony. "Morning, Pooh! Wanna go for a ride?"

Tracy approached Pooh from an angle, as Greta had instructed with Mabel, and held her hand out to the pony.

Seth clipped a lead onto the pony's bridle and tugged him forward. "Move it, Pooh!"

Tracy followed as the pony plodded out into the alley, and Jack helped his son ready the small horse for their ride. As Jack worked, Seth kept up his excited dialogue about being the ring bearer in Greta's wedding, the herd of cattle and his first loose tooth, one topic flowing into the next as if they were related. He opened his mouth to point out his wiggling incisor.

"Thee?" Seth lisped around the dirty finger, and Tracy tried not to think about the germs the boy would swallow as a result. Boys and dirt went together, she figured, craning her neck to admire the loose tooth.

"Wow! That's almost ready to come out!" she enthused, then glanced up as Greta strolled into the stable to check on them.

Seth bobbed his head. "I can't wait! Uncle Brett says if I put it under my pillow, the tooth fairy will bring me twenty dollars!"

Jack choked and coughed. He sent his son a wide-eyed look of dismay before pulling a face and returning to the buckles and straps he was adjusting.

Greta laughed and leaned close to her older brother. "Even the tooth fairy is subject to inflation."

"I think Brett's about to owe me money," he muttered

in return. Soon Jack had his saddle buckled and Seth's double-checked, and the group was ready to ride.

When it was her turn to mount up, Jack moved behind Tracy and wrapped his big hands around her waist, giving her a boost into the saddle.

"How much do you remember about riding?" he asked as she settled on Mabel's back.

"Not much. It's been ten years since that trail ride in the Rockies."

He grunted in acknowledgment and let his hand linger on her hip as he handed her the reins. "Leave a little slack in the reins, but not too much. Keep your head up and watch where you are going, not the horse," he said, but she was distracted by the heat of his palm on her hip. His handprint felt seared into her with a tantalizing tingle.

"Keep the ball of your foot in the stirrup. If you need help, don't panic or shout, you'll scare the horse. I'll be right behind you."

She gave a nod of understanding as he pulled Mabel's harness, and the mare followed Greta's horse and Seth's pony as they set out.

Tracy squeezed the leather straps in her hand as they headed across the nearest field. Seth whistled to the cows as if they were dogs and laughed as calves romped and ran to their mothers.

"As long as we're out here," Jack called, loud enough for his sister to hear, "we should use the time to check the fences up in the north pasture."

Greta signaled a thumbs-up and steered her horse toward a gate in the main field. Jack swung down from his saddle to open the gate and let them through before securing the fence and mounting Buck again in one smooth, practiced motion. His athleticism and natural agility prodded Tracy's pulse to a dizzy cadence. Jack personified every romantic cowboy she'd ever seen in movies or read about in novels. Lean, tough, handsome and so sexy.

"Tracy!" he shouted, yanking her guiltily out of her daydreaming. She'd been staring at Jack's snug jeans and the skillful way he managed his horse with subtle body movements and tongue clicks. He motioned for her to join the group, which was leaving her behind. "You have to pull up on her reins and make her obey your direction. Mabel will lollygag all day if you let her."

"Oh…right." Tracy drew and released a cleansing breath, then pulled hard on the reins and goaded her mare. "Time to go, Mabel. Come on, sweetie. Yah!" She tried giving the mare a light kick with her heels. Mabel only chewed another mouthful of prairie grass.

"Let her know you're boss," Greta called. "Pull harder on the reins. Bring her head up."

Tracy tried again, afraid to hurt the horse by tugging too hard. She certainly didn't want to anger the thousand-plus-pound beast she was sitting on.

Jack rode back to her and reached for her reins. "Come on, Mabel." He brought the horse's head up and gave the mare a slap on the rump to get her moving.

Mabel trotted forward, bouncing Tracy in the saddle. After a few minutes, they reached the northern pasture and rode along the fence line so Greta and Jack could survey the condition of the barrier.

"So, uh, what's the goal here?" Tracy asked.

"Maintenance," Jack said, pulling alongside her.

"If ya see a post that's broke, holler," Seth said matter-of-factly, as if he were ranch manager instead of his father.

"Fences are always getting knocked down or damaged

by weather or by…" Greta glanced to Seth and cleared her throat before finishing. "Umm…amorous bulls."

Tracy chuckled. "Pardon?"

"If there is a cow in heat in a neighboring field," Jack explained, "a bull might knock down a fence trying to get to her."

He gave Tracy a level look, and she felt the rising tingle in her cheeks as she flushed. "Oh."

"Generally, we manage the breeding program, which includes keeping the cows and bulls in separate pastures. But every now and then, a bull gets out of containment. The instinct to breed is a powerful thing, and pasture fence won't hold a one-ton bull answering that most primitive impulse."

Jack's gaze lingered, a sensual heat filling his piecing stare. Tracy shifted restlessly on her saddle, her skin suddenly feeling both too tight and prickly, as if sunburned.

"There's one, Daddy!" Seth called, heading off with his pony at a canter.

Tracy jerked her attention away from Jack's weighty gaze to see what Seth had found. By squinting against the morning sun, she spotted a leaning fence post some distance off. "How did he see that?" she muttered.

"The boy's got eagle eyes. Better than his ole dad's," Jack said, before riding ahead to join his son.

Before Tracy could reach them, Seth was already off Pooh and messing with the broken post. While Jack opened a flap on his saddlebag and brought out a few tools, his son pushed on the wooden post and flapped the loose barbed wire. Greta reined her horse next to Tracy and swung down with an easy finesse to help. Tracy gripped the saddle horn and eyed the distance to the ground with trepidation.

Here goes nothing… She stood in her stirrups and

swung her foot over Mabel's back, only to have her already tired muscles wobble as she tried to hop smoothly to the ground. Instead she stumbled awkwardly, nearly landing on her butt. When she regained her balance, she shot a rueful glance toward Jack and found him watching her with an amused grin twitching one cheek.

"Just call me Grace," she said with a good-natured eye roll, earning a wider smile from Jack. The rare smile transformed his face from ruggedly handsome to breathtaking, and Tracy did, in fact, struggle to draw air into her suddenly tight lungs.

A cry from Seth shattered the moment, and both Jack and Tracy whirled toward the boy, who held out his bleeding hand with tears filling his eyes.

She rushed forward, concerned about him, as Jack knelt to examine the injury.

"What happened?" Greta asked, peering over her brother's shoulder.

"I hurt my hand on a poker on the wire. It's bleeding lots!" Seth gaped at his injury with childlike horror.

Jack used his shirttail to wipe the blood from Seth's hand and judge the extent of the wound. "Aw, it's not so bad. Barely a scratch. We'll slap a Band-Aid on there, and you'll be good to go."

When his father rose to retrieve some first-aid supplies from his saddlebag, Seth turned to Tracy with puppy-dog eyes set to full power and his chin quivering. "It really hurts."

Sympathy arrowed through her and, crouching, she held out her arms. Seth fell immediately into her embrace, and she examined his hand herself. "You poor thing. I bet that's sore. Don't worry, we'll make it all better."

Seth snuggled close. "Will you kiss it? Dillon says his mommy kisses his boo-boos."

"Of course I will, sweetie." And she did, giving the palm of his hand a big smacking kiss, plus another on his forehead.

Seth smiled through his sniffles and leaned his head on her shoulder. "Thanks, Miss Tracy."

Jack glanced back at his son and frowned. "Seth, it's not that bad. You've had worse and didn't cry this much over it. Don't be a baby."

Tracy glared at Jack. "He's not a baby, but even big boys need a little TLC from time to time."

Jack pulled a disgruntled face as he brought disinfectant spray, a sterile wipe and a Band-Aid over and knelt in front of them. "Okay, Spud. Let me see it."

"Can Tracy do it?" he asked in a timid voice.

Jack blinked, looking a tad hurt. "Well, I guess."

She sent him a silent apology with her eyes as she accepted the wound-cleansing spray and wipe from him. Holding Seth's hand gently in position, she poised the antibiotic spray. "Okay, close your eyes and think about your favorite video game."

Jack scoffed.

Ignoring Jack, she asked, "Ready?"

Seth bobbed his head and wrinkled his nose in dread.

Tracy spritzed the puncture wound with disinfectant, and Seth whimpered.

"Are you thinking about your favorite game?" Tracy asked and blew gently on the wound.

"Yeah, but it stings."

"I know, sweetie, but you're being very brave."

Jack grunted again, and Tracy elbowed him, shooting him a quelling look.

With a shake of his head and a frown of discontent,

Jack rose and walked away, turning his attention to the fence post that needed to be pounded back in place.

She continued doting on the little boy, savoring the opportunity to mother him, while Jack and Greta replaced the post and tightened the barbed wire.

For her efforts, Seth gave Tracy a kiss on the cheek. The sweet gesture burrowed deep in her heart and stirred an ache for children of her own to cuddle and nurture. As she rose from the ground, her muscles protesting with a stiff throb, she sensed Jack's gaze on her.

A side glance confirmed as much, and rather than avoid him and his reproach, she marched over to him and raised her chin. "I'm sorry if I overstepped, but little boys need motherly coddling every now and then."

Jack raised an eyebrow, clearly skeptical. "He was playing you. He knew you'd fuss over him, so he pulled out the crocodile tears and theatrics for your benefit."

"It may have been an act, but have you considered that maybe he did it because he misses having a mother to dote on him?"

Jack narrowed his eyes and braced a hand on his hip as he faced her. "Are you implying I don't give my son enough attention?"

"Not at all. By all indications, you've been a great father." Her assessment seemed to appease him a bit. "But there's a reason children have a mother and a father. Mothers provide something fathers can't."

Turning back to his saddlebag, where he stowed his tools, he shook his head. "Bull. I'm doing just fine caring for my son alone."

"I'm not criticizing. Single parents raise healthy, well-adjusted children all the time. I don't mean to imply otherwise. I'm just saying a little boy needs what a mother can—"

"Daddy!" Seth called from the back of his pony, interrupting her. "Can I ride ahead with Aunt Greta?"

Jack jerked a nod. "Sure, go on."

The little boy spurred his pony and set off.

When Tracy opened her mouth to continue making her case, Jack cut her off, waving a finger toward Mabel. "Need a hand up?"

Taking her cue that the subject of Seth's need for mothering was closed, she eyed the large horse and grimaced. "I, um…"

He strode over to Mabel and held the stirrup steady. "Come on."

When Tracy fixed her foot in it and pushed off the ground, he planted his hand on her bottom and gave her a needed boost to propel her into the saddle. She gasped at the intimacy of his touch, and desire like Fourth of July sparklers crackled in her veins. Even after he'd sauntered back to Buck and climbed into his own saddle, Tracy could feel the heat of his hand on her buttock, as if he'd branded her. Jack hung back, waiting for her to ride ahead, and she tugged hard on Mabel's reins, bringing her head up from her continued snacking.

"You should consider getting Seth a tetanus shot." Her voice croaked, giving away her lingering jitters as Mabel strolled past Buck and they moved on down the fence line. Tracy sat taller in her saddle, pretending confidence she didn't feel around Jack. Her attraction to him rattled her and undermined her mission to build a relationship with Seth. "Despite your dismissal, that was a pretty deep puncture wound."

"He's had one." Jack paused, then added, "But… thanks." A moment later, he cleared his throat and added, "I appreciate your concern. And your tending to him."

The wind blew a wisp of her hair in her face, and she

tucked it behind her ear as she gave Jack a nod. "My pleasure. He's a wonderful little boy."

A grin ghosted across Jack's lips in acknowledgment, and he fell silent for a moment. His expression grew pensive, then a pained look crossed his face. "He's my life. I'd be lost without him." Jack sighed and cast a side glance her way. "I guess that's why I get so…protective of him. Overprotective, if I feel a threat to him."

"And you see me as a threat?"

He didn't answer right away. Finally, he muttered, "I did."

His use of the past tense startled her. "And now?"

"I believe you don't want to hurt him." Jack's concession on that point was a major victory in her eyes. But then he added, "However…threats come in many forms. What if he grows attached to you and then you go home and…"

He let his sentence trail off, and she recognized a wounded look in his eyes she knew he would never vocalize. One of disappointment and inner pain.

Greta claimed Jack had loved Laura. Had her cousin broken his heart when she'd left? Was the source of his anger and resentment a lingering ache from lost love? Maybe part of Jack's protectiveness for his son was rooted in his own defensive walls. Was he afraid to let a woman back in his life—and therefore his son's— because he had never recovered from the wounds of his broken marriage?

"Miss Tracy!"

She shifted her attention to Seth, who was riding back to them with a fistful of wildflowers. "Whatcha got there, sweetie?"

"Flowers. They're for you." He rode up beside her and handed the scraggly bouquet to her.

Holding the horn of her saddle so she wouldn't fall, she reached down to take the yellow and purple blossoms. "Why, Seth! These are lovely. Thank you."

She took a big sniff for show, though they didn't seem to have any discernible fragrance.

Seth beamed. "Aunt Greta says girls love getting flowers."

"She's right. The best part for me is knowing these are from you."

Clearly pleased with himself, Seth tugged Pooh's reins, turned the pony and rode off again.

When Tracy glanced at Jack, she saw the wrinkle of concern in his brow, and she lifted her chin. "Jack, this doesn't have to end badly. If you'll let me, I could have an ongoing relationship with Seth. I don't want to disappear from his life. I want to know him. Watch him grow up. Be a part of his life in a way Laura never could."

Jack's square jaw tightened, making his countenance appear all the more rough-hewed and severe. "We'll see. One step at a time."

His bright green eyes mirrored the intensity of his voice, and she felt an answering tremor deep in her core. Not of fear, but of yearning. A delicious, tantalizing stirring that made her heart beat faster, her nerves tingle and her breath quake. Jack Colton spoke to the very root of her. Her soul. Her marrow. Her heart.

When planning her mission here to meet Seth, she'd never considered the possibility of falling for Seth's father. But now she needed to examine how that might change things. Because she could feel herself succumbing to Jack Colton's spell.

Tracy had certainly cast her spell over Seth. Jack brought up the rear of their little parade and kept a close eye on the interaction between his son and Laura's cousin. Their conversation was superficial and lighthearted, eliciting frequent laughter from both. His son's giggles never failed to lift his own spirits, the sound so full of youthful glee. And Tracy's laugh had its own mesmerizing effect on him. At first, her chuckling sounded rusty, as if she had to dust it off from infrequent use. That fit the image he'd built of her, his suspicion that she'd come from an unhappy, abusive marriage. As the ride progressed and she relaxed with Seth, her laughter loosened up, the musical notes tickling Jack's gut like bubbles in champagne.

He noticed, too, the comfortable way she sat her horse. For someone who'd been in a saddle only once or twice before, she had a natural grace and skill. And if he found himself staring at the curve of her bottom and the way her slim legs hugged Mabel's flanks, it was because he was admiring her horsemanship and not the way her jeans fit her trim build. *Yeah, right, Colton. Who do you think you're kidding?*

He blew out a sigh, tamping down the kick of lust that coiled like a rattlesnake in his core. After ten years of a reckless, wild lifestyle, followed by a short marriage, he'd been virtually celibate for the past five years. His choice. He'd wanted to focus all his energy and attention on Seth, and making the ranch prosper during tough economic times. But the sexual drought had left him all the more primed and tuned to chemistry he sensed with Tracy—or that's what he told himself. Admitting he had a natural rapport and physical connection to Laura's cousin left him edgy and off balance.

"Jack, do you see this?" Greta called from the front of their group. The uneasy tone of her voice as much as her question brought him out of his reverie.

He followed her pointing finger to the old family cemetery, situated under the branches of a large, sprawling oak tree, where Big J's ancestors had been buried. Jack didn't see what had disturbed Greta right away, but when he looked closer, squinting against the bright sun, he saw the small pile of dirt and the shovel that lay next to a hole in the ground. Was there a grave robber loose on the Lucky C?

"What is it, Daddy?" Seth asked, standing in his stirrups to see across the meadow.

"I don't know." Jack tugged Buck's reins and headed toward the cemetery. "Seth, wait here with Tracy while I take a closer look."

"Why can't I come?" Seth whined, but Jack didn't linger to debate his order. Greta fell in behind him, and they dismounted together at the edge of the low fence that surrounded the small family graveyard.

Jack walked first to the pile of dirt and lifted the shovel that had been left there. He recognized it as one used in the stable for mucking out stalls.

Greta rounded the small pile of dirt and peered into the hole that had been dug. "It's not one of the marked graves, but—" She stopped abruptly, gasping and stumbling back from the freshly dug pit.

"Greta?" Jack hurried to his sister. "Are you all right?"

She aimed a shaky finger toward the hole. "I'm better than whoever that is." When he frowned in question, she pointed again. "Look."

Even before he peered down into the earth, apprehension tightened his gut. At the bottom of the freshly dug hole lay the pale bones of a tiny human skeleton.

"It's a baby, isn't it?" Greta asked, her voice choked with tears.

Jack clenched his back teeth so hard his jaw ached. "Seems to be, judging from the size."

"Who is it?" she asked, her voice trembling. "Or maybe I should ask *whose* is it, considering there's no headstone."

"Good question." He swiped a hand over his face and stepped back from the grave. He had no way of guessing how old the bones might be or how long they'd been buried.

Greta edged closer to him and rested a hand on his forearm. "What do you think happened to it? Did Big J ever mention to you about a baby being buried here?"

Jack shook his head. "Not that I remember. If it was a relative of Big J's, why isn't there a headstone?"

"I don't like this, Jack." Greta's voice cracked, and her breathing was shallow. "It doesn't feel right. And I don't just mean because a baby died. Why would someone dig up the bones? Why would they leave the grave open like this? Just…abandoned and exposed?"

"It's not right." He turned slowly, surveying the area for further clues about what had happened and who'd been there. "It's not right at all."

"What is it, Dad?" Seth's voice called from the bottom of the hill.

"Stay put!" Jack shouted back. He didn't need his son having nightmares about dead babies and open graves. Bad enough the sight was burned into his own brain and Greta's.

"What do we do?" his sister asked, her fingers tightening on his arm.

"We do nothing. Treat it like a crime scene, and don't touch anything." He pulled out his cell phone and checked for signal strength. As with many of the more remote spots on the ranch, he had no reception here. He put his arm around his sister's shoulders and guided her toward the horses. "When I get back to the house, I'll call

Ryan. If there's no official record of the baby's burial, I'm guessing the coroner will have to exhume the remains."

Greta cast another worried glance over her shoulder to the cemetery before mounting her horse. "What good will that do?"

"They may be able to tell us how long ago the baby died, and if it died from foul play. A DNA profile could tell us more about who the baby is."

Greta gave a visible shudder before snapping her reins and heading back down the hill. "It's so creepy…and sad. That poor baby!"

"There could be a simple explanation," Jack said, trying to reassure his sister, though the image of the tiny skeleton still haunted him, as well. "Remember, infant mortality was much higher even as recently as fifty years ago."

"What was it?" Seth asked again as they approached.

"Nothing for you to worry about. Let's head back to the house. We all have work to do."

Tracy rode up close to Jack as Greta turned for the stable with Seth leading the way.

"Well?" she asked in a quiet tone.

He hesitated, casting a grim glance at her. "Someone dug up an unmarked grave, exposing the skeleton of a baby."

Tracy's hand flew to her mouth. "Oh, dear Lord! Who—what—?"

"Yeah. My sentiments exactly."

"Oh, Jack…" Beneath the hint of sunburn that colored her cheeks, Tracy's face was as white as a ghost. Her blue eyes grew wide and looked haunted. A knot of regret twisted inside him for the lost joviality she and Seth had shared earlier. Jack already missed the bubbly sound of her laughter and the light of her teasing smile.

He put away the reasons for his powerful reaction to her, to examine later. Right now they had the upsetting find at the cemetery to deal with and a ranch to run. His unexplained attraction to Tracy would wait for another day.

Chapter 6

Half an hour later, they returned to the stable, and though stiff and a bit sore, Tracy had to admit she'd found the horseback ride exhilarating—save for the gruesome discovery at the cemetery.

When she said as much, Greta offered to give her an official riding lesson. It would help reduce her aches by training her to stand in the stirrups instead of bouncing in the saddle.

"I'd love that. Thanks." Tracy watched from the corner of her eye as Jack led his horse and hers into the stable and started removing the saddles and blankets.

"I have wedding-related appointments this week in Oklahoma City, but…" Greta pinched the bridge of her nose and shook her head, clearly still rattled by her sad find. "Um…I'll be back Thursday afternoon. So maybe that evening?"

Tracy followed Greta into the shade of the stable and

blinked as her eyes adjusted to the dimmer light. "Sure. It's a date."

Seth was already sponging Pooh off, cooling the pony down. Tracy watched him for a moment, amazed at what he could do at age five. If Seth could tend Pooh, she needed to learn to care for Mabel. Stepping over to Jack, she held her hand out for the sponge he was using to clean the gentle mare.

"Shouldn't I be doing that?"

He considered her proffered hand and raised an eyebrow. "It's the mark of a good horseman to properly care for your horse."

"I'll take that as a yes." She took the wet sponge from him and faced Mabel's flank. "Show me what to do."

He stepped close behind Tracy, covering her hand with his, his chest nestled against her back. "Like this. You want to clean the sweat and dirt left under the saddle," he said, but she could barely hear his instructions over the heady buzzing in her ears. "Do a visual check for sores or other wounds that may need attention."

Cool water rippled down Mabel's sides as Jack guided Tracy's hand in long strokes. When Mabel snuffled and tossed her mane, Jack chuckled. "You like that, girl?"

She couldn't speak for Mabel, but Tracy was enjoying the grooming lesson quite a bit. The press of Jack's body against hers was heavenly. Despite the odors of horse sweat and straw, she caught a hint of the crisp masculine scent that clung to him, a heady blend of soap and spice. He stepped back from her, taking the sponge with him to refresh in the water bucket, and she shook herself from her trance. This time when he handed her the sponge, he stayed where he was, letting her wipe Mabel down without his help.

"That's the way. When you're done with that, you'll

dry her off with the same long strokes." He pointed out a towel waiting on a hook by Mabel's stall. "And when you've finished that, call me, and I'll help you check her hooves for stones or other problems."

He stepped aside, unclipping his cell phone from his belt and thumbing in a number from memory. "Hey, Ryan. It's Jack…yeah, we have a situation out here. At the old Colton cemetery on the north property…" His voice faded as he stalked toward the other end of the stable.

Shuddering at the thought of the skeleton Jack had found, Tracy wiped the perspiration from her temple with her arm, careful to avoid wetting herself with the sponge. Strands of hair fell in her face, and she carefully plucked at them with her damp fingers. She'd need a shower after this for sure.

Greta strolled past and nudged her with an elbow. "Here." She held a ponytail holder on her palm, which Tracy accepted gratefully. "You'll find it's most practical to wear your hair back on the ranch. I have a bunch of these bands up at the house if you want a few."

"Thanks." Tracy contemplated the sponge in one hand and the elastic hair holder in the other for a second before Greta chuckled.

"Let me." Jack's sister took the elastic band back from her and finger-combed Tracy's hair into a respectably neat ponytail. "There." Greta stepped in front of her to inspect her handiwork, and an odd expression crossed her face.

Tracy frowned. "What's wrong? You still thinking about the baby?"

Her new friend shook her head and smiled. "Yes and no. It's just…nice to have another woman around. Being the only female on a ranch full of testosterone-reeking cowboys can get old."

Tracy pulled a face. "Aw, poor Greta. Surrounded by too many good-looking men?"

She snorted. "Most of whom are my brothers, remember."

Tracy shrugged, conceding the point. "Ah, well…"

"But you should enjoy yourself while you're here." Greta waggled her eyebrows at her and flashed a smug grin. "Maybe a little vacation fling?"

"M-me?" The idea flustered Tracy so much, she choked and ended up coughing and gasping for a breath.

Greta laughed and pounded her on the back. "Yes, you. Why not?"

Tracy cast a side glance at Jack, who'd finished his phone call, and found him watching them with a frown.

"Maybe Brett? He's quite the catch, if a bit of a playboy," Greta suggested.

"Um…" Tracy watched Jack's scowl deepen. Was it the idea of her having a fling that upset him, or just the notion she might have one with Brett?

"Or Daniel? Eric… No, he doesn't seem interested in dating. Let's see, I could introduce you to H—"

"Leave her alone, Greta, and stop pimping out your brothers."

"Aw," Greta said with a teasing pout, "is Jackie jealous I didn't suggest him?"

In answer, Jack swatted his sister's butt with the towel he'd used to dry off Buck and shot her an unamused grin. "You're funny."

Greta sauntered away, grinning smugly. "Think about it, Tracy. And I'll see you Thursday for your riding lesson."

Tracy waved to her new friend and turned back to Mabel, all too aware of Jack's gaze on her. Oh, she'd think about a fling, all right. She'd already entertained the notion. Too bad the object of that fantasy seemed too tightly wound, too dead set on challenging her at every turn.

The next morning, after eating a large country-style breakfast with Abra, Big J and Brett, Tracy hitched a ride with Big J down to Jack's house, hoping to beg a favor. He seemed startled to see her and his father on his porch, but he stepped back and waved them inside with a courteous nod.

"Jack," Big J started, "I've been on the phone with Ralph Menger down at First National. We've discussed reallocating some funds for the ranch, and I need you to run into town this afternoon and sign the paperwork."

Jack squared his shoulders. "What sort of reallocations?"

"Don't get your undies in a twist. Just the changes you and I discussed last week. Ralph made some other suggestions, which he'll show you when you go in. I'd go myself, but I didn't sleep well last night, and, well, I'm just feeling a bit off today."

Jack eyed his father with obvious concern. "Maybe Eric should stop by and check your—"

Big J cut him off with a scoff and flapped a hand in dismissal. "Don't bother your brother. He's busy at the hospital, and I don't have a thing wrong with me that a nap and a nip of Maker's Mark won't cure."

Tracy cleared her throat, dragging Jack's worried frown to her. "And I was hoping I could tag along into town. I seem to have brought entirely inappropriate clothes for the ranch, and I'd like to shop for jeans and boots. Maybe some more casual shirts, as well."

Jack scratched his stubble-dusted chin. "Why doesn't Greta take you shopping? Or Abra?"

"Abra is busy, and Greta is in Oklahoma City until

Thursday." Tracy paused, shifting her weight uneasily. "If it's an imposition, maybe I can—"

"No. It's fine." His tone contradicted him, but she didn't argue.

Big J clapped his son on the shoulder. "All right, then. Ralph's expecting you in an hour. Ms. McCain." He tugged the brim of his cowboy hat as he nodded a goodbye to her and opened the door. "Thank you, son."

An awkward silence filled the foyer after Big J left. Jack studied her, his lips twisted in thought.

She glanced into the living room. "Where's Seth? Will he come with us?"

"Is that what this is about? An excuse to see Seth?"

"No," she said with a sigh, getting a bit tired of Jack's paranoia regarding his son. "It's about needing ranch clothes. I was just wondering where Seth is."

"He's getting a riding lesson with Daniel."

"A riding lesson? I thought he did quite well on Pooh yesterday."

"There's more to riding a horse than staying in the saddle. Daniel's likely got him on one of the cutting horses, teaching him some basics about roping."

"A cutting horse? But he's only five years old!"

Jack gave a dismissive shrug. "I learned to ride a cutting horse when I was five. So did Brett. I rode a bull in my first rodeo when I was thirteen."

She shook her head in dismay. "Good gravy!"

He flipped a hand, as if his early start in the dangerous sport was nothing. "Thing is, Daniel won't push Seth past what he's capable of." Jack stepped past her, snagging his black Stetson from a peg on the wall. "Come on, I'll show you."

Tracy followed him out into the ranch yard. Even before they reached the practice pen, she could hear Daniel's whoops and Seth's laughter. Jack stopped at the fence and leaned against a post to watch his son race around the pen on the back of a dark brown horse twice the size of Pooh. Tracy held her breath as Seth wove between barrels and galloped past them. While she hadn't yet been formally introduced to Daniel, she immediately recognized the tall copper-skinned cowboy who'd parked her car the day she'd arrived, the half brother who'd been excluded from Big J's toast to Greta. His teeth flashed white against his dark complexion as he grinned and shouted to Seth. "That's the way, buddy! One more time, and then bring him in."

Tracy nodded her head toward Seth's riding coach. "So Daniel is your half brother?"

"Yep." Jack cut a side look at her. "Who told you that?"

"Greta. She said that Abra is none too happy to have him living on the ranch, but the rest of you consider him family."

"He *is* family. And a damn fine rancher and horseman, too. He's an asset to the ranch, even if my mother can't see it."

Tracy eyed Daniel and his tall, muscular frame. The term "tall, dark and handsome" had surely been coined with Daniel in mind. "Was his mother Hispanic?"

"No. Cherokee."

Jack didn't elaborate on his relationship with Daniel, so Tracy let the subject drop. The tone of his voice as he defended Daniel's status in the Colton clan indicated the affection Jack felt for Big J's illegitimate son.

Once Seth had made another circuit in the ring, he reined the horse and trotted up to Daniel. His uncle lifted him down from the saddle and ruffled his hair. "Well done, partner. You need to work on keeping a firm grip on the reins and controlling your horse, but we'll work on that another day."

"Can I help you cool him down and feed him?" Seth asked eagerly.

"You better," Daniel said, picking Seth up like a sack of potatoes and tucking him under his arm. "I'm not doing all of your dirty work, kid."

Seth squealed in delight as Daniel toted him into one of the horse stalls.

Jack pushed away from the fence, and as they passed the door to the stable, he called, "Daniel, can you keep an eye on Seth for a while? I'm running an errand in town and won't be back for a few hours."

Daniel glanced in their direction and arched a speculative dark eyebrow when he spotted Tracy. He set Seth's feet on the ground before nodding to Jack. "Sure thing. Take your time. All I had planned this afternoon was going over some paperwork with Megan. When I finish that, I'll challenge Shorty here to 'Mario Kart.' It's been a while since I kicked his butt at video games."

"No way!" Seth said with a laugh. "I'll kick *your* butt!"

Jack's lips twitched in a grin, and he tugged the brim of his Stetson. "Thanks, Daniel, I owe you one."

Daniel barked a laugh. "You owe me about twenty, but who's counting?"

Jack took Tracy's elbow and steered her toward the ranch yard. "We should go if I'm expected at the bank in an hour."

"He's good with Seth. Does Daniel have any kids of his own?"

"Naw. Seth is Big J's only grandchild to date. But you're right. Daniel has a good rapport with Seth. He's patient and soft-spoken but firm, which is why he's so good with his horses, too."

Tracy sputtered a chuckle. "Did you just compare your son to a horse?"

"You laugh, but the same traits that make Daniel a good horse trainer will serve him well raising his own kids one day."

"Touché," Tracy conceded, with a last glance over her shoulder to the gentle giant ruffling Seth's hair in the stable.

If Seth was surrounded by the strong, caring role models his uncles and aunt clearly provided, had a father who guarded him and loved him beyond all else, and had the security and joys of his ranch home, what did she really think she had to offer the boy? Maybe she was wrong to try to insert herself into his life. Laura had believed Seth was better off at the Lucky C, even as much as she'd loved her only child. A quiver started low in Tracy's belly. Was her own purpose in being at the ranch misguided? Selfish?

She bit her bottom lip, and as she mulled the question over, she remembered how Seth had gobbled up the attention she'd lavished on him when he'd hurt his hand. His green eyes had been bright with a needy plea, a clear longing for a mother's touch.

Jack might think his young son was capable beyond his years, encouraging Seth to be independent, responsible, and to attempt tasks beyond what Tracy felt a five-year-old should be asked to perform. But she saw the still very little boy. She saw how Seth longed to please his father, saw his need for comfort, care and cuddling. Those things she could provide. Her heart was full of a tender longing to nurture Seth as she would her own child.

She followed Jack to his truck, a mud-splattered F-250 with an extended cab, and eyed the giant step up into the passenger seat with dismay. Not that she couldn't hoist herself up, but her muscles were still stiff and achy from the ride yesterday morning.

Seeing her hesitation, Jack twitched a grin and kicked the running board with his boot. "Use this to step up."

She tipped her head, giving him a how-dumb-do-I-look glance. "I know *how* to climb up. I'm just dreading it. My legs are rather sore from yesterday."

"Understandable." He put a hand under her elbow, and a crackling awareness shimmied through her. "I'll give ya a boost."

His grip was warm and firm, and his spare hand rested at her back, steadying her. Sparks raced through her blood, and her breath caught. She flashed back to the last boost he'd given her, when he'd palmed her behind. Many more helping hands from Jack, and she'd be a puddle of goo. After he'd closed the door, she released the breath she held in a tremulous gush. Who was this giddy schoolgirl she became in Jack's company?

The ride into Tulsa took about twenty-five minutes. Tracy tried to engage Jack in conversation, curious to learn more about the man her cousin had married. Though he answered all her questions willingly enough, his responses were terse, often no more than a yes or no. She'd hoped that if she and Jack got to know each other better, he'd loosen up a bit about her spending time with Seth.

"Will Seth start kindergarten in the fall?" she asked, clutching the passenger armrest as he took the tight turn of an interstate exit ramp.

His expression hardened. "No."

"Why not? He's five, isn't he?"

"Yeah, but I'm holding him out until next year."

She frowned. "Why would you do that?"

Jack gave her a peevish look. "Because I'm his father, and don't think he's ready."

Tracy blinked, surprised at this. By all indications, Seth was unusually bright, inquisitive and extremely verbal. "Is it Seth that's not ready for kindergarten…or you?"

Jack's face grew darker as he glanced at her while negotiating traffic. "What does that mean?"

"He certainly seems ready for school to me. How can you think he's old enough to ride a cutting horse but not go to kindergarten?"

Jack squeezed the steering wheel tighter and cut her an irritated glare. "They're totally different."

She gnawed her lip as she studied him. "I can't help but wonder… Does your decision mean you're not ready for him to grow up? Maybe you want to keep him under your wing another year before letting him leave the ranch all day?"

A muscle in Jack's jaw flexed as he gritted his teeth. "And maybe you're overstepping your boundaries. I know what's best for Seth."

She raised a conceding hand. "My apologies. I only mean to say he seems intellectually advanced for his age to me. Probably because he spends so much time around adults."

Jack's mouth pressed in a grim line. "Is that another criticism?"

"No! Not at all. I think it is wonderful Seth has so many uncles and Greta to dote on him. I think it's contributed to his verbal skills and curiosity."

Jack stopped at a red light and bumped the steering wheel with his fist. "Edith thinks I should send him to school in September. She thinks he needs to be around kids his own age."

"I have to agree." Tracy paused, racking her memory. "Who is Edith, again?"

"The housekeeper at the main house. She was more mother to us growing up than Abra was. Abra traveled a lot when we were kids, and Edith helped our nannies. Now she helps me out with Seth."

"Oh. So she would know what she's talking about." When he turned to her with an impatient scowl, Tracy added quickly, "I know you don't care what I think, but… have you asked Seth what he wants?"

Jack's expression said that he not only had never considered Seth's opinion about school, he was taken aback by her suggestion. A car behind them honked, and Jack gave the truck more gas than needed, zipping across the intersection as he cast her a disgruntled look.

"I'm not saying leave the decision to him. You have the final say as his parent, but you should feel him out. Don't make him promises or give him false expectations, just ask him general questions to gauge his interest and needs. Does he ever miss having friends his age to play with? Is he curious about books and learning how to write?"

"I think I know my son."

Jack's sarcastic tone stung, and she turned toward the passenger window. "I'm sorry. I was just trying to help."

Across the truck cab, she heard Jack groan. "No, I'm sorry. You didn't deserve that. I get…touchy when I feel like someone is second-guessing me. I make the choices I feel are best regarding the running of the ranch and raising my son, and when someone questions my intentions or decisions, I…" He huffed a sigh.

She swiveled to face him, studying the shadows in his expression. The crease in his brow said he had more than just their discussion about when Seth would start school on his mind. "Are you concerned about this banking business Big J asked you to handle?"

Jack flicked a startled look to her. "I—no, that's not… Well, maybe a little, but it's not the main thing on my plate at the moment."

She watched him fidget and drum his thumbs on the steering wheel for a minute or two, and finally asked, "Want to talk about it?"

He dented his brow and frowned at her. "No."

"Mmm, well…if you change your mind, I'm a good listener. I'll even promise not to offer any advice."

He snorted and sent her a skeptical grin. "Yeah, right."

She gave him a playful slug in the arm in return. Which was a mistake, because feeling the firm bulge of muscle under his sleeve only refreshed the tingle of lustful awareness she'd been trying to tamp down.

Jack parked his truck in front of the bank and sat staring out the windshield for a moment before cutting the engine. "Brett wants me to invest in horse breeding. He's found a stud he thinks we should buy to start a breeding program that Daniel would run. When I said no the first time, he went out lobbying investors to front the cash. I shut that down the other day, but I know he hasn't forgotten the subject. He thinks breeding cutting horses will make us a buttload of profit and entice Daniel to stay at the Lucky C instead of starting his own breeding business."

Tracy blinked. *You asked*, she thought.

She wet her lips and chose her words carefully, determined not to blow this opportunity. Jack had trusted her enough to confide his business worries, and she hated to jeopardize that by saying the wrong thing.

Before she got the chance to say anything, right or wrong, he aimed his thumb down the street. "There are clothing stores that way. Laura dragged me shopping with her a few times and had some luck at a few shops the next block down. If you turn down the block to the right there's a department store that way, too."

Tracy peered at the signs along the street and got a sense of her options. "And where do you suggest I get a pair of basic jeans for the ranch?"

Jack cracked an amused half grin. "Feed and seed store."

She hummed a wry acknowledgment, enjoying the more affable tone between them. "Where and when shall we meet?"

He lifted a shoulder. "Don't know. I could be an hour or more."

She pulled her cell phone from her purse. "What's your number?"

They exchanged mobile numbers, and he told her he'd text when he was finished with his bank business. Sliding her sunglasses on, Tracy climbed out of Jack's truck and started down the sidewalk. The June heat had already swelled to stifling levels, and made the fumes of exhaust from the many cars all the more suffocating. She did a bit of window shopping as she strolled, admiring artwork at galleries, tempting pastries at a bakery and sparkling rings and pendants at a high-end jeweler. When she reached a shop with cowboy boots and stylish Western shirts on the mannequins in the display window, she stepped inside, sighing in pleasure as the store's air-conditioning bathed her heated face.

She greeted the shopkeeper and began searching the racks of women's jeans and shirts, finding numerous items she thought would work. Most of the clothes she tried on were affordable, and from the clearance table she scored a great pair of no-frills boots that would be perfect for the ranch yard and stables. After paying for her purchases—two pairs of jeans, the boots and one Western button-down shirt—she headed back out in search of more bargains. Spending Cliff's life-insurance money always reminded her that soon she'd have to find a job. Not that she had a problem with that. But because Cliff had refused to let her work, she hadn't been in the workforce for a long time. She'd be playing catch-up, learning the latest technology and software wherever she landed.

As she strolled down the sidewalk, glancing in store windows, a strange sensation crawled up her spine. She knew the spiders-up-her-back feeling well, had fine-tuned the sixth sense during her marriage to Cliff. A premonition. A warning. She stiffened, and a chill washed through her, despite the muggy heat.

Someone was watching her. Maybe it was Jack, she thought, trying to be optimistic. Hadn't she felt an odd sort of connection to him? But her link to Jack didn't give her this creepy sensation.

Casting a surreptitious glance to the reflection of the busy street in the display window beside her, Tracy looked for signs of anything suspicious. She studied the reflection but didn't see Jack or anyone else watching her. Turning slowly, she lowered her sunglasses to better view the people on the street. The prickling sensation eased, and Tracy chalked the feeling up to lingering paranoia. Spending Cliff's life-insurance money brought the realities of her doomed marriage up from the recesses of her memory. His control over her had included their finances, and she'd had to account for every penny she'd spent. If her purchases didn't meet with his approval, she'd paid the price physically and in humiliation.

But Cliff was dead. She was free of his tyranny and cruelty.

Shake it off. She rolled the tension from her shoulders and wiped the sheen of sweat from her upper lip. Since Jack hadn't yet texted that he was finished with his business, she headed to the next block of stores and found a boutique with pretty shoes and fun jewelry. Not ranch attire, for sure, but intriguing to browse through. She found a pair of shorts she wanted and some pumps to replace the ones she'd ruined her first day at the ranch.

Her cell phone buzzed as she was signing the credit card receipt at the boutique, and Tracy glanced at the screen.

All done. Meet at truck.

Tucking her phone back in her purse, she thanked the shop attendant and bustled out onto the sidewalk, headed back to meet Jack with her purchases. She smiled to herself, satisfied with the success of the trip. From a block away, she spotted Jack's black cowboy hat. He was leaning against the front of his truck, his legs crossed in front of him in a relaxed pose as he waited for her. She thought of how her new shorts showed off her legs and wondered what Jack would think of her new acquisition. Her stomach bunched with a giddy thrill as she imagined Jack's green gaze studying her with a hint of heat and promise.

Tracy stopped at the street corner, waiting for the light to change and traffic to clear before she crossed. She couldn't wait to get in the—

A large hand struck her back. Shoved.

Tracy gasped as she reeled forward. Her arms windmilled, and her bags scattered as she stumbled off the curb. A car horn blasted. A bumper smacked her legs, and she heard brakes screech, tires squeal. She slammed to the pavement with a tooth-jarring impact.

Chapter 7

For several mind-numbing seconds, Tracy lay sprawled on the scorching concrete. She couldn't catch her breath. Couldn't hear over the whoosh of blood pounding in her ears. Finally, the fog of shock cleared, and she made a quick assessment of her condition. Her knees stung. Her hip throbbed. Her hands burned.

An engine roared. A car whizzed past, narrowly missing her head. She was in the street, blocking traffic. People had begun to gather around her, touching her shoulder, asking her questions. Was she all right? Did she need an ambulance?

She shuddered as adrenaline coursed through her. "I—I th-think I'm—"

"Tracy!" The deep voice reverberated through her, curling warmly inside her like a smooth shot of whiskey.

She blinked against the bright sun as she glanced up at the rugged face of the speaker looming over her. *Jack.* His dark eyebrows were knit, his eyes lit with concern.

"J-Jack…" She tried to stand, tried to dust the grit from her seared palms, but her legs ached and buckled when she attempted to rise from the pavement. A pair of strong arms caught her when she swayed, lifting her, cradling her against a broad chest.

"I've got you," he murmured against her hair. Someone had gathered her bags and handed them to Jack, hooking them on his fingers. He juggled both her and her purchases as he headed down the street.

Safe. The word flittered through her mind. The instant he pulled her close, a sense of security rolled through her that went beyond that street corner and her tumble into traffic. Her muscles relaxed, and her bones seemed to melt as she leaned into Jack's embrace. Her galloping pulse slowed to an even canter.

Jack moved away from the crowded corner and carried her toward his pickup. "Are you hurt?"

"N-no. Just shaken up. I don't know what happened. I—"

He chuckled softly. "Clearly, you tripped. Not surprising, given all these bags."

She flattened her hand against his chest, savoring the low rumble.

And then she remembered the hand at her back, the shove. Fresh adrenaline rushed through her. Her gut twisted, and her body shuddered. Someone had pushed her into traffic. Heartlessly. Viciously. Intentionally.

She gasped, and her fingers curled into Jack's shirt. "Oh my God."

"What?" Beneath the brim of his cowboy hat, his brow dented.

"I didn't trip. I—I was pushed."

He grunted. "Accidents happen."

"No." She shook her head as a chill crept through her. "I mean someone shoved me. On purpose."

He arched a dark eyebrow. "On purpose?" He gave a short, snorting laugh. "Paranoid much?"

His skepticism sliced to her core. In the wake of the warm comfort she'd experienced moments earlier, his doubt seemed all the more sharp and cold. "I'm not imagining things. I felt a hand push me. Hard."

They'd reached his F-250, and he shifted her bags, trying to open the passenger door.

"You can put me down. I can stand alone now."

He stooped to ease her legs to the ground, and she winced as her hip bore her full weight again. Jack didn't move away until she steadied herself and gave him a nod.

"You should see a doctor."

She glanced down at her scraped palms. While they stung and she was sure she'd have a nasty bruise on her hip, she didn't feel the injuries warranted a doctor's care. "No, I'll be all right."

Jack grunted and narrowed a scrutinizing gaze on her. "Why?"

She blinked at him as she took her bags back. "What?"

"Why would someone push you?" He flipped the bucket seat forward, then loaded her purchases on the backseat.

"I don't know. But…" Tracy paused and frowned. "You think I'm lying? Why would I lie about it?"

"I didn't say that. But maybe you mistook an accidental bump as a push. That makes more sense than someone gunning for you."

She blew on her palms, which throbbed more now that the adrenaline from her tumble had subsided. "I know what I felt."

"Well, I wasn't watching you the whole time, but…I

didn't see anyone specific come up behind you. If someone *had* pushed you, don't you think someone would have seen them and said something?"

"I saw him," a woman on the sidewalk said.

Tracy whipped her gaze toward the petite woman with glasses. "You did?"

"I did." The woman nodded and pushed wispy hair back from her face. "He was a big guy, but for his size he moved quickly. He pushed you, and in the hullabaloo of your fall, he disappeared."

Jack tapped the brim of his Stetson back as he faced the woman. "What did he look like?"

"Well…" The woman screwed her face up in thought. "It was an older white man." She twisted her lips as if unsure, then added, "I mean, I assume he was older. He had a lot of gray hair, anyway. The rest was dark. And like I said, he was really big. Not just tall, but big all over. Dark clothes. That's all I remember."

Tracy should have felt vindicated, having the woman's confirmation. Instead, her gut roiled and her apprehension grew. Someone had targeted her, tried to hurt her. Jack's question reverberated in her head. Why? Why would someone want to hurt her?

"I just came over to make sure you were okay," the woman said. She waved a finger toward Tracy. "You need to clean those scrapes so they don't get infected. Do you have hand sanitizer?"

Tracy tried to answer, but a belated reaction to the man's attack snaked through her and left her numb and trembling.

"I have a first-aid box in my truck, and I'm taking her to the ER, just in case." Jack's voice cut through her distraction, and he put a hand at her elbow to assist her into the truck.

She roused from her daze with a jolt. The ER? The urgent-care department at hospitals held too many memories of trips for injuries when she'd "tripped over the dog" or "slipped on the ice." Her most recent visit to the ER had been the worst. Laura had been pronounced DOA. Cliff had arrived in a separate ambulance, barely scraped. And Tracy had sustained a broken collarbone, bruising to her face and internal injuries that required a week's stay in a Denver hospital. She swallowed hard, forcing down the bitter taste that rose in her throat.

"No, Jack, please…no hospital," she pleaded.

"My brother works at Tulsa General. I'll call and have him meet us."

When she shook her head, a lightning-like streak of pain shot under her skull. She drew a sharp breath and raised a hand to her screaming temple.

"Humph," Jack grunted. "See? No arguments."

The ER. She hugged her arms to her chest as Jack circled the truck and climbed behind the wheel. Images flashed in her mind's eye, and whispers of ancient shouts hissed in her ear. Cliff's derision. His slaps. His fingers biting into her arm. She thought she'd escaped that brand of fear. Laura had died helping to free her.

Jack cranked the engine and turned the air conditioner on high. Reaching across her, he opened the glove box and took out a plastic box.

If Cliff was dead, who was the man targeting her today?

Jack handed her the first-aid kit. "Here. I keep this in here for accidents when I'm out in the pastures. You can waste a lot of time driving back to the house to treat every cut and scrape you get while ranching. This is a start, but I want Eric to check you for concussion." He started the engine, then paused, narrowing a hard look at her. "Tracy, what is it? You look like you've seen a ghost."

In a manner of speaking, she had. "I—I just can't imagine why someone would want to hurt me. Who would w-want to do this?"

Jack shook his head. "I still think you're making assumptions. You don't know you were targeted. The man that woman described may have bumped you, but that doesn't mean he singled you out, to harm you."

She angled her head to meet Jack's gaze, to reiterate her case, but stopped. His words said he didn't believe her, but his eyes were full of doubts and turmoil.

Over the next several minutes, she protested his decision to take her to the hospital many times, but Jack headed straight to the emergency room, where his brother Eric met them at the entrance with a wheelchair. She felt a bit self-conscious using the wheelchair, but when she tried to climb out of the truck, her body throbbed and she stumbled. Jack caught her arm and eased her into the seat.

"Missy, set them up in exam room three, please." At his bidding, a nurse scurried ahead of them down a side hall. Eric wasted no time hustling Tracy through the lobby. "What happened, Jack?"

Jack explained how she'd fallen into the street, leaving out her allegation that she'd been pushed, and outlined his concerns about a head injury and significant contusions. Eric parked the wheelchair in the room where the nurse was waiting, then lifted Tracy from the seat onto the exam table. Like his brother's, Eric's arms were strong and steady, his chest broad, but she didn't get the same deep-down sense of security that Jack's hold had given her.

"This is all unnecessary. Really." She tried again, but like his brother, Eric ignored her protest. While the nurse took her blood pressure, Eric began a meticulous examination of her pupils, the injuries to her hands and knees.

She sat quietly through the exam, giving Jack's brother her own brand of scrutiny. Though Tracy saw the obvious facial similarities, Jack's brother wore his lighter brown hair in a buzz cut instead of the shaggy style Jack did. Jack had introduced him as his younger brother, but Eric seemed older than Jack in several ways. Foremost was the fact that he had tiny creases around his eyes and bracketing his mouth. On someone else, the fine lines would have detracted from his appearance, but on Eric, the creases enhanced the chiseled intensity of his handsome face. Eric's Colton-green eyes had a much more serious look that reflected his gravitas as he treated his patient. With a gentle touch, he palpated her scalp, and she winced when he found a tender spot.

"Missy, will you arrange for a CT scan?" Eric asked, without looking up from his study of Tracy's injuries.

"Of course, Dr. Colton."

Tracy cut a glance to the nurse as she lifted the receiver on an in-house phone. Tracy noted that the nurse's attention never left Eric as she made the call. The young woman's expression was openly worshipful, leaving no question that she was smitten with the doctor. Not that Tracy blamed the gal. She'd yet to meet a Colton male who was less than drool worthy.

"Does this hurt?" Eric asked her as he flexed her wrist.

She shifted her attention back to Jack's brother, who seemed oblivious to the nurse's admiring gaze. "Not much. Just a—oh!" She gasped as a bolt of pain shot up her arm.

Eric grunted. "Let's get her wrist x-rayed, as well."

"Yes, Doctor." Missy all but swooned when he glanced at her.

Another nurse passed the open door to the exam room and did a double take as she glanced in. She pulled up short and stepped inside, pasting a smile on her lips. "Dr. Colton, I didn't know you were working the ER today."

"I'm not. I'm just helping my brother out with an emergency." Eric never glanced up as he cleaned and disinfected Tracy's scraped knee.

"Oh, can I do anything to help?" The nurse smiled and squared her shoulders in such a way that her ample bosom was thrust forward in a none-too-subtle move.

Eric either didn't notice or didn't care about the attractive woman's flirting. The scenario was repeated when a radiology tech arrived to take Tracy for her scans. The women postured and flaunted their wares, but Eric remained focused on his job, apparently immune to the women's attention.

Jack accompanied her to the X-ray lab, and when they were alone she whispered, "Do women always fall over themselves for your brother like that?"

He snorted. "Yeah."

"I can understand. He's quite handsome."

Jack gave her a disgruntled look, one that said he was irritated that she'd noticed his brother's appearance. "They're wasting their time. Eric is all about the job. He's probably the best trauma surgeon in the state, and he's not about to compromise that for a workplace romance."

Tracy had little time to puzzle over Jack's curious reaction to her comment before she was escorted back for her CT scan and X-ray. An hour later, she was discharged with a diagnosis of a strained wrist, which Eric skillfully bandaged with a brace, but no skull fracture. Eric gave her a low-dose shot of Demerol for pain and a prescription for Lorcet for her aches in the coming days, along with instructions to keep her scrapes clean and disinfected with over-the-counter ointments. Jack helped her to the hospital pharmacy to fill her prescription and buy a supply of antibiotic cream before heading for home.

The drive back to the ranch was largely quiet. Jack cast frequent side glances to her, until she finally muttered groggily, "I'm fine. Just woozy. The shot your brother gave me is making me sleepy."

"Good. You should rest. Close your eyes. I'll wake you when we get home."

She rocked her head from side to side, the drugs in her blood making it feel thick and heavy. "I can wait until we get back."

By the time they returned to the Lucky C, Tracy was physically and mentally exhausted. Jack helped carry her bags into the main house, dropping them on the marble floor at the base of the wide staircase. Before he left, he gave her a stern appraisal. "I can have Maria send a tray up with dinner."

"Not necessary. I don't want to be any more of a bother."

He arched an eyebrow, silently communicating his skepticism.

She bent to gather her bags, biting her bottom lip to hold back the grunt of discomfort, and wobbling from the painkiller. When she turned and contemplated negotiating the massive staircase, she couldn't help the fatigued sigh that escaped. Before she could take the first step, Jack wrapped his fingers around her good wrist and tugged the bags from her grasp.

"I'll come back and get those," he said, when she raised a startled look to him. He bent to catch her behind the knees and across her back, then scooped her up to cradle her against his chest.

Tracy gasped in surprise and clutched his shoulders for balance. "Jack, what are you doing?"

"I'd think that was obvious."

He started up the steps two at a time, and she had no choice but to lean into him and hold on. With her arms looped around his neck, she buried her face in his shoulder and inhaled the masculine scents of soap and leather that clung to him. As a little girl watching *Gone with the Wind*, she'd swooned when Rhett carried Scarlett up the grand staircase. But Tracy's girlish response to Rhett's act of passion paled now as her head swam dizzily over Jack's valiant gesture. His hold was strong and sure, his stride unfaltering. When he reached the top of the steps, he wasn't even breathing hard.

He swept down the hallway with her, hesitating only long enough to ask, "Which room?"

She raised her muzzy head from the soft fabric of his shirt and met his mesmerizing eyes. Her fingers curled into the shaggy hair on his nape, savoring the silky feel of the wisps against her skin. "Second door on the right."

Jack shouldered his way into the guest room and set her on the sleigh bed. Perhaps it was the drugs lowering her inhibitions, but as she released her grip on him, she allowed her hand to trail slowly from his neck along his shoulder, then linger briefly on his chest. She could feel the steady thump of his heart beneath her palm, and her own pulse answered with hard, clamoring beats.

Glancing up at him with a shaky smile, she shifted her touch to his upper arm, giving a small squeeze of appreciation.

"Thank you." Her voice sounded far too breathy and sensual, as if she were trying to seduce him, and she winced mentally. Clearly, he heard what she had, because his muscles tensed and something hot and hungry flared in his eyes. The predatory gleam in his gaze backed the air up in her lungs and doubled her heart rate. Her aching limbs and stinging wounds were forgotten as she held his stare for what seemed simultaneously an aeon and a flicker in time. Tracy couldn't tell how much of her light-headed buzz was Jack's effect on her and how much was the painkiller, but her head spun dizzily, nonetheless.

When she wet her dry lips, his focus dropped to her mouth, and his pupils grew to inky, fathomless pools. She both hoped and feared that he was going to kiss her. His desire was evident in the intensity of his stare and the quiver in his muscles as he hovered over her. A shiver of expectation sluiced through her.

In the end, though, he clenched his jaw and shoved away from the bed with an exhalation rife with frustration. Disappointment rippled through Tracy, and she sank deeper into the pillows, kicking herself for wanting things she shouldn't. How could she be lusting after her cousin's ex when she was still coping with the aftermath of her own late husband?

"I'll get your bags," Jack said as he stalked from her room, his tone deeper and huskier than usual. From unspent desire? she wondered. Within minutes, fatigue dragged her into a deep sleep and dreams of Jack carrying her through a swirling flood of black water.

The next morning, a thunderstorm woke Tracy. When a particularly close crash rattled the guest room windows, Tracy bolted upright in her bed and raked her hair back from her face. Her bedside alarm clock read 6:24 a.m. Knowing that the rest of the ranch residents were likely up and starting their day, Tracy tossed back the covers and staggered to the shower. Her muscles were predictably sore and stiff, and the hot water stung her healing scrapes. All in all, she knew she was lucky to be alive. If she'd fallen in traffic just as a vehicle sped by, she'd have a lot more than stiff muscles to worry about.

After her shower, Tracy joined Abra for breakfast in the formal dining room.

"I understand you had some excitement yesterday," Abra said.

So Jack had shared news of her accident with the family. Tracy rolled her sore shoulders. "You could call it that, just…not the kind of excitement one likes to have."

"But Eric got you all fixed up?"

"Yes, ma'am. He and Jack were both very helpful."

Abra smiled brightly. "I have no doubt."

Tracy passed the plate of scrambled eggs to her hostess. "What time will Greta be back today?"

"Somewhere around three this afternoon, I believe." Abra pulled a face and shook her head. "Honestly, I think she should go ahead and move to Oklahoma City, rather than commute back and forth as she plans the wedding. But she hates to leave her horses. Sometimes I think she loves the horses more than she does Mark."

Tracy grinned, assuming that Abra was teasing, but the crease in Abra's forehead said otherwise.

When Big J arrived in the dining room, he greeted Tracy with a warm smile. "You all right this morning, darlin'?"

She showed him her raw palms and wrapped wrist with a grimace. "A little dinged up, but nothing I can't handle. Still planning to make the most of the day."

He tipped his hat to her. "That's the cowboy spirit."

Abra invited Big J to join them for breakfast, but he only poured a cup coffee and took a piece of bacon with him as he left for the stables. Tracy sensed an awkwardness between them and recalled what Greta had said about Big J's indiscretion with Daniel's mother, and

Jack's comment that Abra had traveled most of his childhood. None of her business, Tracy told herself as she nibbled her bacon.

A loud clap of thunder shook the house hard enough to make the china coffee cups on the table rattle. Abra frowned, as if the storm was insulting her personally. "What plans do you have today? This weather looks to keep us inside for a while."

Tracy cupped her hands around her mug of java, savoring the rich aroma. "I brought a book to read, but if you have something I can help you with, I'd be happy to."

Abra lifted a shoulder. "No. I have a few calls to make for the wedding, thank-you notes to write."

After taking a gulp of coffee, Tracy pushed her eggs around her plate, wondering what Jack and his son were up to this rainy morning. "I'd like to spend some time with Seth today. Maybe we could play cards or a board game. Do you think Jack would bring him up to the house?"

Abra gave another mild shrug. "You're welcome to call him. Jack's house is number two on speed dial." She nodded toward the landline telephone on the kitchen wall.

"Oh, thanks, but I have his cell number on my phone."

Abra quirked an eyebrow, clearly intrigued and reading hidden meaning into that fact, but she made no comment.

Tracy managed to keep up a stilted conversation with Abra through the rest of breakfast, but when she finished eating, she excused herself to her room. As she walked along the upstairs corridor, she passed one of the mullioned windows that looked out over the front lawn and circular drive leading to the front door. She lingered long enough to enjoy the view, made all the more enticing when a golden ray of sun peeked through the departing rain clouds. On the lawn below, near a side door of the house, she spotted a familiar head of wavy brown hair and long willowy limbs.

Tracy blinked, startled to see Greta at the ranch. Had she gotten back early? Abra had said she wasn't expected until closer to three.

Tracy raised her hand to knock on the window and wave to Greta, but the woman below gave a furtive glance over her shoulder, then darted in the side door, out of view.

Odd. Maybe Greta's business in OKC had been cut short. Or, Tracy decided, noting how the decorative glass made slight distortions to the view, maybe it hadn't been Greta at all, but a member of the household staff who had a similar hairstyle.

Dismissing the incident, Tracy continued down the long hall to the guest room, where she cracked open the windows to enjoy the cool breeze and pattering of the last drips of rain. She put away the clothes she'd bought yesterday, setting aside a pair of jeans to wear to her riding lesson this evening with Greta.

Once the morning downpour cleared, leaving the air smelling sweet and clean, Tracy decided to enjoy her novel by the pool. She changed into shorts and a tank top, then trooped down to the patio and dragged a lounge chair into the sun near the deep end of the pool. As Tracy stretched out on the lounge chair, her muscles protested with a dull ache. She thought about the bottle of prescription painkillers on her bedside table but didn't like the idea of using the potent medicine unless she *really* needed it.

Leaning her head back, she closed her eyes behind her sunglasses and recalled the muzzy feeling the Demerol shot had given her last night…and the way her drug-muddled brain had led her to act. Her cheeks heated as she remembered how she'd draped herself over Jack, caressing his face and all but simpering for a kiss. Even now her head spun, thinking about the rough scrape of his day-end beard against her fingers and the hooded look of wanting in his eyes. How could she face him after her awkward advances?

Exhaling a cleansing breath, she tipped her head farther back and savored the warmth of the morning sun. She must have dozed off, because the next thing she was aware of was the slapping sound of running feet, then a loud splash. Fat drops of cold water rained down on her sun-baked skin, and she jerked upright with a gasp. Now fully awake, she shielded her eyes from the sun to bring the pool into focus. A small dark head broke the surface near her, and Seth grinned up at her, spiky lashes surrounding green eyes full of mischief.

"Did I splash ya?" he asked, with no sign of remorse.

She gave him a playful scowl and shook water droplets off her book. "You did. Scamp."

He wrinkled his nose. "What's a scamp?"

"A little boy who splashes unsuspecting ladies, then grins about it." She gave him a lopsided smile and a mock growl.

He laughed and padded away, calling, "Wanna swim with me?"

"Maybe later. I'm feeling kinda sore and stiff after my fall yesterday."

He grabbed the rail of the ladder at the deep end and cocked his head. "Daddy says you tripped and fell in the street. I bet that hurt. Did ya skin your hands and knees? I do that a lot."

Tripped, huh? She supposed the filtered version was better for Seth. Best not to worry the boy needlessly.

She held up her hands and bandaged wrist to show him. "A little scraped. But I've had worse. Just sore today."

Seth poked at a beetle floating in the water. "Daddy says the best thing to do when you're sore is work it out. Layin' round will just make ya stiff."

"Oh, he does, does he?" She could imagine Jack saying this to motivate his son to put away his video games or TV and get out in the fresh air. Hearing Seth parrot his father brought a secret smile to her lips that she bit her cheek to squelch.

Jack's son nodded. "It works, too. When I get sore from ridin' Pooh or mucking stalls, I take a walk, and I'm all better the next day."

She didn't bother to argue that his resilience probably had more to do with his youth than his father's prescribed walks. Instead, she nodded. "That's great, Seth. Maybe I'll try that later."

He hoisted himself out of the pool and padded to her, dripping. "Whatcha reading?"

She showed him the cover of her book. "A romance novel."

Seth screwed up his face. "Romance? Does that mean there's kissin' and stuff?"

Tracy chuckled at his look of disgust. "Yeah. Kissing is part of romance."

"Ew. Kissing is gross!"

She tweaked the boy's nose. "Not if you're doing it right."

With effort, she kept her thoughts from straying to her near kiss with Jack last night. She could well imagine he was an excellent kisser. Knowing how he liked to take control of every situation, she could guess he'd take command of a kiss and leave his partner breathless and satisfied.

"Brett says someday I'll want to kiss girls, same as he does," Seth said, bringing her out of her musing.

"He's right."

"Daddy says I got plenty of time before I gotta worry about kissing girls."

Tracy gave a lopsided grin. "He's right, too."

As if conjured by their discussion, Jack rode up to the back lawn astride Buck and gave a shrill whistle. "Seth, what are you doing up here? I thought you were going to help us sort the calves."

The boy's face brightened. "Oh, yeah. I forgot."

Jack tapped back the brim of his black cowboy hat to send Tracy an appraising scrutiny. She was prepared for him to grouse about her being alone with Seth without his approval, but instead he asked, "How are you feeling this morning?"

The thoroughness of his gaze and the piercing intensity of his eyes were as intimate as a physical caress. Goose bumps rose on her skin, and her breath hitched. She needed a moment to gather her composure before stuttering, "I'm, um, some b-better."

He jerked a nod. "Good." Turning toward his son, he added, "Let's go, Spud. You have to dry off and change clothes, and you're wastin' daylight."

When Seth scampered over to Buck, Jack took his foot from the stirrup, allowing his son to use it for a step up. Jack caught Seth's arm and helped swing him onto Buck's back.

Wrapping one arm around his father from behind, Seth gave her a wave. "'Bye, Miss Tracy. See ya later!"

She returned the wave, and her heart gave a giddy flutter when Jack tapped his hat brim and gave her a nod in parting. Dear Lord, the man was sexy enough without embodying every tough-guy cowboy ideal she remembered from movies. He had the strong and silent archetype down to a tee. Perhaps she couldn't understand Laura's leaving the Lucky C, but Tracy had no problem understanding why her cousin had fallen for Jack Colton to start with.

Chapter 8

"We can do this another day if you're too sore," Greta offered later that evening, as they led Mabel and Scout into the corral for Tracy's riding lesson.

"No, I'm game to give it a try." Tracy found that she'd been looking forward to her riding lesson, partly because she'd enjoyed her last time in the saddle and partly because she enjoyed Greta's company. "I'd wager aches and pains are all part of life for a rancher. If my hosts can work through the pain, so can I."

Greta laughed. "That's the spirit!"

After opening the gate to the corral, Greta tugged Scout's lead, and Tracy followed, guiding Mabel in the somewhat muddy space. "So did things go well in Oklahoma City?"

Lifting her shoulder in dismissal, Greta closed the gate behind them and patted Mabel on the rump as she walked passed. "Well enough. We were interviewed for the society page of the *Journal Record*. Mark was named one of Oklahoma City's most eligible bachelors a couple of years ago, so apparently it's big news that he's getting married." She grinned as she unhooked Mabel's lead and tossed it over a fence post. "Abra was thrilled when I told her about the article, but personally, I find all the attention our wedding is getting a bit overwhelming."

"Your mother did seem to be enjoying the limelight at your engagement party." Tracy shooed a fly that buzzed in her face.

Greta gave a snorting sort of laugh. "Yes, God love her, my mother is happiest when she's the center of attention. My wedding would be a bigger media circus than Prince William and Catherine's royal wedding if I let her have her way. The best thing to come out of this wedding so far is that I've gotten closer to my mother. Being her only daughter, I think she was hoping for someone a little less...well, *tomboyish* than I've been. Being allowed to help me choose a dress and flowers and china patterns has tickled her pink."

"Well, if there's anything I can do to help you with your wedding plans, please ask. I'd be happy to do anything I can."

Greta angled a startled look at her that morphed into a warm smile. "Thank you, Tracy. I appreciate that." She stroked her horse's flank, then sighed. "As much as I love my brothers, I've really missed having a sister. When I saw the camaraderie my brothers had, I always felt like I was missing out on something, not having a sister to share things."

Tracy nodded, swiping perspiration from her brow with the back of her hand. "I can understand that. I was an only child, and I wished I had siblings quite often, too."

"Well, enough of that!" Greta waved off the discussion, which was turning too serious. "Let's get you in the saddle, shall we?" She directed Tracy to a small platform with steps, telling her to walk Mabel up beside the three-foot-high deck. "It's easier for beginners and short people to mount from there."

"Oh." Tracy's cheeks heated when she remembered the intimate boost Jack had given her as she'd climbed into the saddle earlier in the week.

Once Tracy was astride, Greta instructed her to simply walk the perimeter of the corral, getting accustomed to using the reins to guide Mabel. Tracy had opted to wear the gloves Greta had offered, to protect her scraped hands, and she flexed her fingers a few times, loosening the fit. After the first few circuits, Greta joined her, falling in beside Tracy at an easy pace.

"So what's next on your agenda for the wedding? I meant what I said about helping."

"I'll remember that when the time comes to start addressing envelopes. We have hundreds to do!"

Tracy gulped. "Hundreds?"

Greta gave her a wry look. "Heaven forbid Abra leave out anyone she ever met. I told you this wedding was overwhelming." She huffed in frustration, then said, "Next up is a lot of tedious paperwork including the prenup and having our blood tests done for the marriage license. Hardly the fun part of getting married. I much preferred the day we sampled cakes and hors d'oeuvres with the caterers."

Tracy flashed a grin. "I guess so!" She sobered then, and Greta caught her scowl.

"What's that frown for?"

"Well, I guess it just bothers me to hear people talk about getting a prenup. I mean, I can understand why some people feel they're necessary, but…it seems to me if you're marrying someone, it's because you love and trust them. And if that's really the case, a prenup agreement wouldn't be needed." Tracy furrowed her brow. "Is that totally naive of me?"

"Well, I agree with your sentiments, but I didn't want to rock the boat when Mark suggested it. I really have no designs on his money, and when my father heard about the prenup, he was all for it and for protecting my interests in the Lucky C."

Tracy dropped her gaze and shook her head. "I shouldn't have said anything. It's not my business."

"Oh, it's all right." Greta flapped a hand in dismissal. "I know you mean well. After all, signing papers that prepare for a divorce isn't the most romantic way to prepare for a wedding." She pointed to a line of barrels at the end of the corral. "This time go to the left of the first barrel and weave through the others."

Tracy did as instructed, and Greta cheered. "Well done! You're a natural. Now let's pick up the pace." She showed Tracy how to use her legs and stirrups to keep from bouncing in the saddle.

When they paused for a breath, Tracy rubbed the achy muscles in her thighs and lifted a hesitant glance to Greta. She remembered Abra's comment about Greta loving her horses more than her fiancé, and couldn't shake the odd niggling that tickled her brain. "May I be presumptuous one last time?"

Her new friend sent her a wary look, then a wry grin. "Sure. The more candid the better."

"Be sure, before you say 'I do.'"

Greta's eyes widened and her cheeks paled. "What?"

"The voice of experience here. I had reservations before I married my ex, and I ignored the tiny voice in my head. I regretted my marriage almost immediately, but… it was too late."

Greta's face darkened. "Tracy? What—"

She raised a palm to forestall Greta's questions. "It's in the past. Cliff is dead, and I'm starting over. My point is simply to be sure the man you're marrying is the person you want to spend your life with. It's easy to get swept up in the wedding plans or the romanticism of a proposal and engagement, and shut out the doubts."

Jack's sister looked visibly shaken, and Tracy regretted having said anything. She may have had a bad marriage, but who was she to rain on Greta's parade? She ducked her head, ashamed of herself for her negativity. "Greta, forgive me. I shouldn't be such a downer. Just because I got into a bad situation doesn't mean I have the right to spoil your happiness."

Greta nudged her horse closer to Mabel so that she could put a hand on Tracy's arm. "Don't apologize for caring. You're absolutely right, and your frankness is refreshing." She squeezed Tracy's good wrist gently. "I hate that your marriage left you with scars, but…don't give up on the idea of love. Your prince is out there. I just know he is. You deserve someone who makes you happy." Greta shifted her hand back to the horn of her saddle and glanced out toward one of the pastures. "And you're right. Now is the time to think long and hard about what I want."

Movement in her peripheral vision pulled Tracy's attention to the stable yard, where a ranch hand in a black hat was checking the hooves of a gray horse. As the cowboy straightened from his task, he glanced toward the practice corral. Tracy's breath lodged in her throat as his eyes locked on hers.

Not a ranch hand. Jack.

He gave her a slow nod of greeting, and she twitched a smile, even as her heartbeat kicked up.

"Hmm."

Greta's hum of interest drew her attention, and she turned to see Jack's sister watching her with a knowing grin.

"What?" Tracy asked innocently, although the sting in her cheeks said her damnable tendency to blush gave her away.

Over the next several days, Tracy spent much of her time learning how to muck stalls, groom horses and feel more comfortable in the saddle. Her busy days learning ranch work left her exhausted at night, but the ache made her happy, made her feel productive and useful. She enjoyed working side by side with Seth as he did his chores and was amazed at how much the little boy knew about ranching. Not that she should be surprised, since Jack was such a good teacher.

True to his word, whenever she was around Seth, Jack was close by, keeping tabs on their conversation and interaction. At first she considered his hovering annoying, but before long, she found herself looking forward to Jack's presence as much as Seth's, but for wholly different reasons. Like a schoolgirl, she caught herself anticipating an accidental touch of their hands or an opportunity to spend time alone with Jack. She even looked for errands she could send Seth on to provide such one-on-one time with his father. And was it her imagination, or did Jack move closer to her, touch her more often and look into her eyes more deeply when Seth left them alone together?

On one occasion, when Jack sent his son to retrieve a pair of work gloves from his truck, she suspected Jack was using the same ploy. She'd even thought he might be ready to kiss her, when Seth scurried back into the stables shouting, "Hey, Daddy, your truck is locked."

Jack stepped back from her quickly and mumbled something under his breath. "Never mind, Spud. I'll get them later."

A couple of the ranch hands, a young fellow named Kurt Rodgers and an older, slightly pudgy man named Tom Vasquez, entered the stable then, sharing a laugh.

Tom slowed his step and gave Jack a funny look as they passed the stall where he and Tracy had been grooming Mabel. "Everything okay, boss?"

"Uh, yeah. Why?"

"Well, it just seems like you've been spending a lot more time than usual in the stable and pastures in the last few days. If we're not doing something right—"

"No." Jack raised a hand to reassure the man, and Tracy swore his cheeks flushed under his tan. "Y'all are doing fine. I just, um, wanted to show Tracy the ropes, you know?"

Tom flashed a knowing grin. "Oh, I think I know."

Kurt muffled a chuckle, and Jack shifted uncomfortably before asking, "Did Brett tell you two that the shipment of vaccines arrived? We'll start vaccinating the calves tomorrow."

Tom tugged on the brim of his hat. "Sure thing, boss. See ya, ma'am."

Tracy smiled and gave a little wave as they shuffled away.

"I want to help with the calves!" Seth said, bouncing on his toes.

"We'll see," Jack replied in the classic parental stalling technique.

But the next morning, Seth arrived at the main house just as Tracy was heading down to the ranch yard to see what she might help with today. Seth gave her a disgruntled pout and crossed his arms over his chest. "Daddy said I can't help with the calves getting shot."

"Shot?" Tracy echoed in shock, before she figured out his meaning. "Oh, getting their shots…the vaccines?"

He bobbed his head, frowning. "I'm big enough!"

"Well," she said, not wanting to contradict Jack, "for most things, but…I was hoping you'd take me on that walk you mentioned a few days ago."

Seth's face brightened. "I can show you the fishing pond and the old tree where Daddy made my tree house!"

When he grabbed for her hand and tugged, she laughed. "Now?"

"Sure! Why not?"

"Well…" She knew she needed to check with Jack before she disappeared with Seth into the surrounding fields. "I'll need to change shoes. These are my ranching boots, not my walking shoes." Nodding toward his bare feet, she added, "And you'll need to put shoes on."

He gave a negligent shrug. "I go barefoot all the time."

"Hmm. Just the same, if you're walking with me, I'd prefer your feet were protected."

He rolled his eyes as if she were the silliest female ever and groaned in capitulation. "Okay. Meet me at my house in a few minutes."

When he fetched a bicycle from the grassy lawn and pedaled away, she muttered, "I need one of those." Typically, she hitched a ride with Brett on a UTV for the two-mile stretch from the main house to Jack's home and the ranch's other outbuildings.

"Need what?"

She turned and smiled a greeting to Big J as he brought a glass of what appeared to be tomato juice out to the patio. Or perhaps a bloody Mary, she amended, noticing the celery stalk and ice cubes in his drink.

"I was coveting Seth's bike. Brett headed out early this morning, and I was dreading the walk down to Jack's house."

Her host chuckled and set his drink aside to reach in his pocket. "You're in luck. I have just the thing for you, darlin'."

Tracy slid her sunglasses to the top of her head as Big J pulled a ring of keys from his pocket. After flipping through the collection a moment, he wiggled one small key loose and dangled it on his index finger. "We keep a couple golf carts in the garage off the back wing of the house for Abra and the house staff to use as needed. This key works for the blue cart. Use it whenever you want for as long as you're here, my dear."

"Why, thank you!" She crossed the patio and took the proffered key. "That's very generous."

He pursed his lips. "Pshaw! You'll be doing me a favor. If they're not used regularly the batteries go bad, and Abra has no interest, most days, in going anywhere near the stables or other outbuildings."

Tracy repeated her thanks and hurried inside to change into more appropriate clothes for a walk. How would Jack feel about her going to the fishing pond with Seth? Was Jack going to be involved in vaccinating the calves?

If not, he'd likely insist on accompanying them. Secretly, she hoped he would, although the time alone with Seth would be welcome, too. She wanted to broach topics with Seth that she guessed Jack wouldn't approve of.

Ten minutes later she parked in front of Jack's house and tooted the tinny horn for Seth. As she climbed out of the golf cart, the boy burst through the front door, having donned a pair of tennis shoes.

When he skittered to a stop in front of her, she put a hand under the boy's chin to meet his eyes. "Is your dad home? Did you tell him where you were going?"

"He's working in his office. He doesn't mind me goin' places, s'long as I have an adult with me."

She twisted her mouth as if considering his assertion. "I think you should at least let him know where you're headed."

Seth rolled his eyes but trudged back to the house, opened the door and hollered, "Daddy, I'm goin' to the fishing pond with an adult!"

She heard a muffled reply from deep in the house, and Seth slammed the front door as he scampered back to join her. "Come on, I'll show you the shortcut!"

He took her hand and tugged her toward one of the pastures. She followed, jogging to keep up with the pace Seth set, and occasionally sidestepping to avoid cow patties. After crossing the pasture, Seth ducked through the fence and rambled into an area where a few trees dotted the landscape.

Tracy panted for a breath, winded from the sprint across the field. Pressing a hand to her racing heart, she gasped, "Seth, slow down! I thought…we were taking a walk! You've…done nothing but run…since we left the house."

"Oh." He curled his mouth in a sheepish grin. "Right. I forget old people can't run so good."

Tracy sputtered a laugh. "Who are you calling old?"

Seth's eyes twinkled devilishly. "You."

She scrunched her face in a mock scowl, swatting at him. "Why, you scamp! I'll show you who can run!"

Laughing, he took off with her at his heels. They darted through the trees until Seth pulled up short and pointed up in the branches of a large oak. "That's the tree house my daddy helped me build. Wanna go up in it?"

"Umm…" Tracy eyed the two-by-four wood scraps nailed in evenly spaced intervals leading to the platform fifteen feet up the tree. Under normal circumstances, navigating the homemade ladder would have been tricky for her. She'd never been especially athletic. But her sore muscles promised to make it even more challenging.

"It's easy," Seth said when she hesitated. "I'll show you." And off he went, clambering like a monkey up the wooden ladder to his tree house.

Not willing to let her cousin's boy down, especially when she had this rare opportunity to talk with him alone, she began an awkward ascent. One hand, one foot, hand, foot, hand, foot, achy muscles screaming, until she dragged herself into the fort next to Seth.

He grinned at her. "You did it!"

She cuffed him on the shoulder lightly. "You don't have to sound surprised." Even if she was a bit surprised at herself…and embarrassingly proud, as well.

He scooted to a window, cut from the sheet of plywood that comprised one of three walls, with the trunk of the oak making the bulk of the fourth wall. Peering out the window herself, she saw that the outside of the wooden walls had been reinforced with corrugated sheets of metal, spray painted with green-and-brown camouflage.

"Fancy." She flashed Seth an impressed look. "Very sturdy. And camouflaged, too?"

"Yep. It was my idea to paint the camo so it was hidden. Do ya like it?"

She hugged his shoulders and nodded. "It is the best tree house I've ever seen!"

Her opinion clearly pleased him, and he settled on the

small homemade wood bench that sat against one wall. "Did you ever have a tree house when you were a kid?"

She joined him on the tiny bench, suppressing a grunt as her leg muscles throbbed and her knees creaked. Though she felt battered and sore from her scalp to her toenails, she wouldn't trade this chance to visit with Seth for all the world or an ache-free body. "No. I grew up in an apartment in Denver. I didn't have a yard. If I wanted to play outside, I had to go to the park a few blocks from my building."

"No yard?" Seth gaped at her, his tone truly astonished.

"Afraid not. I'm a city girl through and through."

He wrinkled his nose as he mulled over this news. "Gosh, I'm glad I'm not a city boy. I love playin' outside and helpin' with the cows and horses."

"And from what I've seen, you are very good at it." She tweaked his nose, and he chuckled. "You'll make an excellent rancher when you grow up."

He puffed up his chest, and a broad grin spread across his face. He fell silent then and picked at the loose rubber at the toe of his muddy tennis shoe. "Ms. Tracy?" The quiet, almost reluctant pitch of his voice told her his thoughts had grown serious.

"Yes, sweetie?"

"Was my mom a city girl?"

Her pulse skipped. Jack's warnings about what she could and couldn't tell Seth about his mother echoed in her head. Her own resolve not to lie to Seth surged to the surface, and she drew a deep breath. "Sort of. She grew up in the suburbs."

He tipped his face up to hers. "What's a sub-burp?"

She sputtered a laugh. "Not burp. Burb. Suburb."

He laughed at his mistake, and predictably, because

he was a boy, he forced a burp. She pulled a face to show him she didn't find his belch funny, and he lowered his gaze in remorse.

Tousling his hair, she explained, "A suburb is a neighborhood close to a city. Your mom had a nice yard growing up, as I recall, but she was something of a girlie girl."

"What's a girlie girl?" He scooted closer to Tracy, soaking up what she told him like a sponge.

"She loved girlish things. She liked dolls and tea parties and dressing up in hats and jewelry."

He sneered. "Ew!"

"And her room was pink and frilly, and she had lots of Hello Kitty stuff and *Barbies*," Tracy said with relish, enjoying the way he cringed in disgust. "I loved to go to her house because we could play with her Barbie camper and her Barbie pool and her Barbie beauty shop…"

"Ugh!" He covered his head with his arms as if to deflect the girl cooties. "Stop!"

She tickled him under the arms. "What's the matter, Seth? Don't you like Barbies?"

"No! Barbies suck!"

She gasped at the harsh word that sounded all the more crude coming from a five-year-old's mouth. His eyes cut up to hers, and he wrinkled his nose in dread.

"Oops. Don't tell my daddy I said that, or I'll get in trouble."

She arched an eyebrow. "Where did you learn that word?"

"Daniel said it. But he said I couldn't or Daddy'd get mad." Seth's face sobered, and he grasped her sleeve. "You won't tell him, will you?"

She pursed her lips as if considering the matter. "Tell you what. If you promise never to say that word again, I'll keep this little slip as our secret. Deal?"

He released a big breath and smiled. "Deal." He wiggled around on the bench to face her. "Tell me more stuff about my mom."

Tracy's heart pattered. Here was the opening she'd been looking for. But now that she had the chance to talk to Seth about Laura, what should she say?

Chapter 9

"Seth?" Jack stuck his head in the family room, where he'd last seen his son playing video games. He'd reached a stopping place in the bookkeeping files and had noticed the house was quiet. Too quiet. Where was Seth? The television was still on, but the game remote lay abandoned on the coffee table.

"Seth?" He called louder, glancing over the breakfast bar into the kitchen. Also empty.

He turned off the TV and was headed upstairs to check his son's room when a knock sounded on the front door. Turning to go back downstairs, Jack called out for his visitor to come in.

Brett poked his head inside, peering around the door, his expression unusually serious. "Got a minute?"

Jack eyed his brother in concern, imagining something having gone horribly wrong in the barn or in the fields.

"Sure. What's up?"

"It's Daniel." Brett removed his hat and cocked his head.

Jack frowned. "What about Daniel? Did something happen to him?"

"I overheard him talking to Kurt Rodgers a little while ago. He's gettin' real serious about this breeding program. He's been in touch with someplace called Kennedy Farms about their breeding program, and he's all hyped up about it."

Jack groaned. "Brett…"

"And it doesn't help matters that his assistant, Megan, came here from a large horse breeding ranch in California."

"Is this about buying that stud—what's his name—Geronimo?"

"Yes. No. I…" Brett huffed in frustration. "I'm telling you, Jack. If you don't let Daniel develop his horse-breeding business here as part of the Lucky C, he'll take it somewhere else. We'll lose both Daniel and the potential profits."

"We already had this conversation, and I made my position clear. I won't pressure Daniel to stay here if he feels led to go somewhere else. I won't guilt him into staying just because horse breeding is profitable—"

"Damn it, Jack!" Brett interrupted. "Why are you being so stubborn about this?"

He ignored him and continued, "What's more, I don't want to dilute the focus of the ranch from our tried-and-true business model. Big J entrusted me with the running of the ranch, and I take that responsibility seriously."

"Tell me about it," his brother grumbled, looking away.

"What's that mean?"

Brett squared his shoulders and turned fully to face Jack. "It means you used to be willing to take risks. You rode the wildest bulls at competition and took gambles in business most people wouldn't have the guts for. You weren't afraid to lose a few dollars in pursuit of a high-dollar payout."

"That's different. I was risking my own money, not the ranch's."

"You worked hard, drank hard and rode hard," his brother continued, getting more worked up. "You weren't afraid to try something new. What's happened to you?"

Jack huffed a quiet laugh and shook his head. "You know what happened. I became a father. I had to settle down to raise my son, especially after Laura walked out on us."

Brett looked unconvinced.

"And I took the reins as manager. That means something to me. I won't let Big J down by screwing up his legacy or running the ranch into the ground."

Brett shook his head, giving Jack a narrow-eyed look. "Naw. I don't buy it. The change in you is more than a factor of new responsibility. Your spark is gone, man. You just don't seem…happy anymore."

"I'm plenty happy, Oprah. I have a good life and a great kid." He waved off that conversation. "What does this have to do with Daniel and the breeding program?"

Brett blew out a long breath, making his lips buzz. "Nothing, I guess. Only that ten years ago you would have been all over this horse-breeding venture. I know you would have."

"Maybe so. But that was then, and this is now. I hope I've made my point. I'm really not interested in debating this again."

Brett continued staring at him speculatively. "It's Laura, isn't it?"

"What?"

"That's when the big change happened. Not when you

became manager or when Seth was born. You changed when Laura left."

Jack swiped a hand down his face as he groaned. "Don't you have something better to do than psycho-analyze me?"

"Why don't you date?"

Jack jerked his head up, sputtering a laugh. "What?"

"When's the last time you slept with a woman or so much as had a dinner date?"

Stomping down the last few steps, he crossed the foyer and yanked the front door open. "Goodbye, Brett."

"I know she hurt you, but you gotta stop living in the past, man."

He gritted his back teeth and gave Brett a warning glare. His history with Laura, and especially their divorce, was his absolute *least* favorite topic.

"I could fix you up with someone if you want," Brett said, undaunted by his brother's glower. "Or…hey, that Tracy McCain's a hot little number. I've seen the way she watches you. I think she's into you, bro."

The air in Jack's lungs stilled briefly, and a ripple of heat streaked through his veins. He'd been trying hard all morning to keep visions of Tracy's sleek legs, her wide blue eyes and her bowed lips out of his head. "I don't need dating advice, Brett."

His tone was darker than he intended, but the coil of lust that tightened inside him every time he thought about Tracy made him grumpy. Maybe he did need a night of no-strings sex with someone, just to work off the tension pounding through his blood. But not Tracy. Anyone but Tracy. He would not, could not get involved with Laura's cousin, of all people. For cripes' sake!

"Speaking of the lovely Miss Tracy…" Brett flashed a

simpering grin. "I saw her head out toward the bull pasture about an hour ago with Seth."

Jack stiffened. "What?"

He'd told her she wasn't allowed to be alone with Seth. And what was Seth doing, taking off somewhere without telling him? The heat of anger filled him and kicked his pulse up.

"You ought to head out there and spend a little *quality time* with her," Brett suggested with a waggle of his eyebrows.

"Oh, I'm going out there after them, all right," he said with a growl as he reached past his brother to retrieve his Stetson from the hat rack by the door. "If you'll excuse me…" He pushed his brother out the door as he exited. "I have to go collect my son and have a word with Miss McCain."

"Will you at least think about underwriting Daniel's horse breeding program?" Brett called after him.

"No!" Jack stomped down the porch steps and set off at a jog. "The subject is closed!"

I told Seth his mother died shortly after he was born. That's the story you need to stick to. Telling him anything else will only hurt him. It will lead to questions about where she's been, why she left…

Tracy dug her fingernails into her palms as she gazed at Seth's expectant face, and she swallowed hard. She searched for truths she could tell the boy that wouldn't violate her agreement with Jack. "Well…she was my cousin, and even though we were estranged for a number of years—"

Seth's head tilted, and his nose wrinkled.

Before he could ask, she said, "Estranged means we didn't get to see each other or talk to each other."

"Why not?"

She balled her hands tighter. *Because my husband was a selfish, controlling bastard.*

"Because…we, uh, both got busy with our lives and, uh, well…"

"Ms. Tracy?"

She stroked his hair, thankful for the reprieve from that question. "Yes, sweetie."

"I hope we don't get *stranged*."

Her insides turned to goo, and she pressed a kiss to the top of his sweaty head. "I hope not, too."

He picked at his tennis shoe again and murmured, "How did she die?"

Visions of shattered glass, crumpled metal and a tumbling landscape flashed in Tracy's mind's eye. She heard screams—Laura's and her own—smelled the leaking gas, tasted the tang of blood, felt again the pain that had streaked through her. And she remembered Laura's lifeless eyes, the wrenching realization that her cousin was dead.

Tracy drew and released a deep, cleansing breath. "She died in a car accident, sweetie."

Seth blinked and frowned as he scratched his arm. "Oh."

Tracy covered his hand with hers and squeezed. "Seth, the most important thing you need to know about your mom is that she loved you."

He raised a wide-eyed look to her as if this was news to him.

Tracy sighed with disgust. Of course it was news to him. Jack wouldn't have told him that, and obviously, none of the gifts or messages Laura had sent to her son had been delivered.

Tracy cupped his chin in her hand and met his bright

blue eyes evenly. "Your mother always wanted the best for you. She sometimes made bad choices, but her choices never changed the way she loved you. You were very important to her, and she was so very proud to be your mommy."

His eyes filled with tears, and Tracy pulled him close for a hug.

"I wish I knewed her," he said, his voice muffled against her shoulder.

She fought down the spike of pique toward Jack that swelled inside her. It served no purpose for her to hold a grudge against him for the past. Instead, she kissed Seth's head again and patted his back. "I wish you had known her, too."

Pulling out of her embrace, Seth swiped his arm over his eyes and nose and rose to his feet. "So, um, do you wanna see the fishing pond now?"

She knuckled away a tear from her own eye and flashed a smile. "Lead on, good sir!"

After fumbling down the ladder, a task that gave her a scraped knee and a splinter for her trouble, she followed Seth back through the wooded area. Once again, he set a brisk pace that forced her to jog to keep up. As she batted limbs out of her way, she kept an eye out for spiderwebs and snakes, certain such creepy crawlies were about somewhere.

A short distance later, they reached a stream, gurgling slowly toward a small pond before continuing its journey through a lower pasture. As they stumbled to a stop, Seth laughing while she wheezed and fought for a breath, she noticed hoofprints in the mud along the bank of the stream. "Is this…part of another…pasture?"

"Yep. The cows like to drink here. See? There's one."

She turned her gaze the direction he pointed and found

a rather stern-looking bull glaring at them. "Oh. Uh, that's a bull, not a cow. He doesn't look too happy to see us. Maybe we should move on?"

She took Seth's hand, and they started down the stream. Tracy picked her way carefully across rocks, trying to avoid the muck, and Seth traipsed contentedly through the shallow water, getting his shoes wet and muddy. Hearing a rustling noise in the trees near them, Tracy paused and glanced toward the trees. Two more bulls wandered in the shade of the wooded area, flicking their tails. Her heart kicked. *Hoo-boy.*

Distracted by the bulls, she stumbled a bit over a rock, and Seth squeezed her hand. "Careful, Miss Tracy. Don't hurt yourself. You're too heavy for me to carry home if you fall."

She snorted a chuckle, amused by his childlike bluntness. "So now I'm old and fat?"

He giggled. "Not fat. Just big like a grown-up."

"Okay." She ruffled his hair and had it on the tip of her tongue to ask him about his favorite TV shows when she spotted another impression in the mud. A footprint—man-sized.

"We shoulda brought fishin' poles with us. Have you ever been fishin', Ms. Tracy?"

"Nope. I'm a city girl. Remember?"

"Gol-ly!" Seth dragged the word out in dismay. "Never? In your *whole life*?"

Tracy grinned at the emphasis he put behind the question, as if she was ancient and the omission from her life was nothing short of tragic. "Not that I recall. But I—"

A loud cracking sound cut her off. She was hyper-aware of the bulls around them and paused to look for the source of the sound. Though it wasn't quite right to be a limb breaking under a bull's hoof, the noise was definitely out of place and sent a tingle up her spine. If a bull charged them, what would she do? Where would they go?

Seth hadn't waited for her when she'd stopped to listen, and now she hurried over the creek bank to catch up to him. "Wait for me, Seth. I—"

She gasped as her foot slipped on the wet, mossy rocks, and she went down. In the same instant, a loud, echoing bang shattered the calm. The gravel just past her hand scattered like shrapnel. For a stunned second, she simply stared at the spot where a large shiny rifle bullet gleamed in the sun.

"Miss Tracy! Are you okay?" Seth's frightened voice reached her through her shock as he scurried back to her. "That was a gunshot! And it was close!"

She shook herself from her momentary stupor, now fueled by adrenaline. By panic.

She reached for him, needing to feel him close to her, assure herself *he* was safe. "Yeah, I—"

Another cracking sound rode the wind, and she knew immediately what it was. A rifle cocking.

"Seth!" She grabbed his shirtfront and jerked him to her. Just as she threw them both down in the mud, another blast rang out. She screamed. Seth hollered. A bull bellowed and ran away, hooves thundering.

This time, Tracy didn't squander any time on shock and disbelief. The simple truth blared in her brain. Someone was shooting at them. On purpose. Someone was trying to kill them.

Jack trudged through the bull pasture, headed toward the pond where Seth liked to fish, fuming to himself about Tracy's defiance, Seth's disobedience and Brett's continued challenge to his business decision. He wasn't against making money. He wasn't against breeding horses at the Lucky C. He just didn't want to force Daniel's hand or guilt him into staying at the ranch if he felt a calling to go elsewhere. If Daniel came to him and said he wanted—

The blast of a rifle brought Jack's head up. The nearly simultaneous scream sent a chill to his bones and jacked his heart rate into overdrive. A fist of panic squeezing his throat, he spun to race in the direction the scream had originated.

"Miss Tracy!" he heard Seth shout.

"Run, Seth!" she answered, her voice taut with fear.

Another gunshot rent the air, reverberating in Jack's chest.

Tracy yelped. "Seth! Hurry!"

Horror punched Jack's gut as a frightening realization dawned. The shots were being fired *at Tracy. At his son.* Jack darted into the line of trees, scanning the area, desperately searching for Seth. His hand went to his hip, where he found only his cell phone. He thought of the handgun back at his house, cursed the fact he didn't have it with him. He glanced at his phone as he ran through the maze of trees and underbrush, thumbing the speed dial for Brett's cell.

Another shot was fired. He heard the terrified whimper of his son.

Brett answered his phone, and as he sped toward the creek, Jack panted, "Shots fired…bull pasture…call cops…bring my gun."

Chapter 10

Tracy seized Seth's hand as she scrambled for cover. Her feet slipped on the slick creek stones, and her ankle wrenched to an awkward angle. She ignored the bolt of pain in her shin. Her only thought was of protecting Seth. Finding shelter. Getting them to safety.

"Run!" She towed the boy behind her as she stumbled toward the trees. His frightened whimpers broke her heart, but they had no time for comfort. Her brain clicked in fast-forward, trying to find the best plan of retreat, the safest place to hide. A ditch? A tree? She discarded these ideas in rapid succession, even as she squeezed Seth's hand and clambered up a muddy bank and into the trees. Another shot whizzed past them, so close she felt the heat of the bullet just before it splintered the bark of a tree beside her.

Another scream slipped from her throat, and she dropped to the leaf-strewn ground, dragging Seth with her as she scuttled behind the tree.

"Miss Tracy, I'm scared!" Seth whispered, his voice shaking as much as her hands were.

"I know, sweetie. Me, too. But we're gonna be fine." She prayed she was right about that.

Groping in her pocket, she felt for her cell phone. Could she get a signal out here to call 911? Or should she call Jack? He was closer.

But her pocket was empty. She'd lost her phone somewhere when she fell or as they'd scrambled for cover.

As she gulped in air, her gaze searched the thin line of woods that bordered the pasture. If only they were nearer to the outbuildings or an old shack or... Her breath caught. "Your tree house!"

"Huh?"

"Come on, Seth. We gotta get to your tree house. It's the only shelter we have out here."

His eyes were round with fear, but he gave her a trusting nod. Shoving herself to her feet, she led him at a sprint through the tangled weeds and branches. Thorns clawed at her, limbs slapped her cheeks and her injured ankle throbbed. But she plowed on, determined to get Seth to the relative safety of his fort.

She could hear the rustle and snap of foliage behind them as their assailant pursued them. Another gunshot fired and another. She tried to weave as she ran, making herself and Seth harder targets to hit. Finally, they skidded to a stop at the base of the homemade ladder. She lifted him up the first several rungs, strengthened by the rush of adrenaline coursing through her. "Go!" she rasped. "I'm...right behind you!"

Seth scrambled up, and she placed her feet on the first rung. Her legs shook, her hands trembled and her heart beat so hard she could barely catch her breath. In her haste, her feet fumbled once, making her slide back down a rung and sending a fresh wave of pain through her twisted ankle.

Another blast of gunfire accompanied something hot searing her back near her shoulder. She cried out, frightened more than hurt. She knew she'd been hit, knew the next bullet could hit home, knew her next breath could be her last.

"Miss Tracy!"

"Seth, stay down!" She shook off the buzzing in her ears and put one hand, one foot after the other. Climbing. Hurrying. Praying.

As she reached the floor of the tree house, she rolled away from the ladder, hunkering low and away from the wall nearest the assassin. Seth clutched at her, hugging her and crying. She pulled his head to her chest and kissed his hair as she panted for oxygen. "It's okay. We're…safe."

A bullet pinged as it hit the corrugated metal and cracked the plywood. The walls of the little tree house would protect them only for a short while. They needed help. Rescue.

Jack.

Weaving through the underbrush at full speed, Jack spotted the flash of a muzzle. He skidded to a stop and used a tree for protection as he narrowed his sights on the area where he'd seen the flare of light. Approximately fifty yards ahead, he made out the hulking form of the shooter, a lever-action rifle lifted, and his attention focused on his target. Jack's mouth dried as he spotted Tracy at the foot of the ladder to Seth's tree house. He drew a deep breath to shout a warning to her but stopped it in his throat. Rather than draw attention to himself or distract Tracy in her escape, he needed to concentrate on the man with the rifle. He had to take the bastard down.

Moving with the stealth and silence he'd learned through years of hunting, years of hiding from his younger brothers, years of exploring these very woods, Jack crept closer to the gunman. He edged one careful step at a time, moving from tree to tree, avoiding anything in his path that would give his presence away. His footfalls were quiet, but the thump of his own heartbeat in his ears sounded loud enough to wake the dead. Holding his breath, Jack slipped to the last bit of cover he'd have before making his move on the shooter.

And, as if sensing Jack's approach, the gunman whirled around. Jack lunged. He shoved the barrel of the rifle up with his left hand, even as he swung at the man's jaw with his right fist.

The shooter's head snapped back from Jack's punch, but he recovered quickly. With a two-handed grip on the rifle, he jerked the weapon from Jack's reach, then swung it in an arc that crashed into Jack's head with a blinding force. Skull throbbing, Jack staggered and fell to his knees. From his peripheral vision, he saw the man level the weapon at him. The click of the lever cocking echoed in his ears, and rolling to his butt, he swept a leg toward the back of the shooter's knees.

His opponent swayed, and though the man didn't fall, the move bought Jack the time he needed to surge to his feet. Grunting, he plowed a shoulder into the trespasser's gut. They stumbled together, Jack shoving the man until his back came up against a cottonwood tree. When the shooter tried to reaim his weapon, Jack wrapped both hands around the rifle and jammed the fore stock against the man's throat. He held the gunman trapped against the tree and struggling for a breath.

"Who are you?" Jack barked. "Why are you here? Why are you shooting at Tracy and my son?"

The man gasped for a breath but made no effort to answer. He narrowed a glare on Jack while fighting for the leverage to push the rifle away from his neck.

Jack shoved harder, snarling at the man. "Who the hell are you? Who are you working for?"

His prisoner bit out a pithy and vulgar slur. Jack silenced him by shoving harder on the rifle, until the man's face grew red from lack of air.

"Help!" Seth cried from his tree house, the fear in his tone drawing Jack's attention.

That split second of distraction was all his opponent needed to lift a knee, land a glancing blow to Jack's groin, and shove the gun away from his throat. The groin strike hurt but wasn't incapacitating. As the man twisted away, he rammed an elbow into Jack's ribs.

In return, Jack swung a fist into the gunman's jaw. And they continued to trade blows until the shooter managed to break free of Jack's grasp and fled. Though winded from their fight, Jack gave chase. He followed the man through the knee-high grass of the bull pasture to a section of cut fence. There, the gunman mounted an ATV and sped away.

Jack bent at the waist, sucking in deep gulps of oxygen as his quarry escaped.

As he hurried back across the pasture, eager to check on Seth, a prickling awareness crawled through him. Tracy was sure she'd been targeted, been pushed when she fell into traffic earlier in the week. Now a gunman had sneaked onto Lucky C property and fired at her. Two incidents in one week. This was no random act of violence. Someone was determined to kill Tracy. But Jack was just as determined to find out why…and keep her safe.

* * *

"Miss Tracy, you're bleeding!" Seth's face was unnaturally pale as he gaped at the crimson smear on his fingers.

Tracy glanced over her shoulder to the spot on her upper back that stung like fire.

No shots had been fired in several minutes, but she kept Seth pinned down, her body protecting his until she could be sure the danger had passed.

For the past several minutes, she'd been singing to him in a whisper, trying to keep him calm…and ease her own nerves.

She could hear some sort of ruckus a short distance from them, but she didn't risk giving away their position or getting shot by stealing a peek. Taking slow breaths and struggling to stay calm, she examined her wound as best she could from her vantage point. She had a growing red stain on her shirt, but she gave Seth a half smile through her pain. "It's just a graze. I'll be fine. Are you hurt?" She ran a hand over his arms, turning him to check for injuries.

He shook his head, tears blossoming in his eyes. "I want my daddy."

Me, too, sweetie. She stroked a hand over his back and closed her eyes. "We're going to be okay, Seth. I promise."

She knew she had no right to make promises that were beyond her control, but she fully intended to protect Seth, even if it cost her her own life. They huddled together for long minutes while the wind soughed in the leaves and birds twittered overhead.

Laura's little boy sniffed and clung to Tracy, then jerked his head up. "Did you hear that?"

She shook her head. "Hear what?" Tracy had been focused on her own prayers that they'd survive the attack, and on the quiet sounds of nature.

Seth wiggled away from her, and she gasped, reaching for his shirttail to stop him. "Seth, no! Stay down!"

"I heard my dad." Before she could stop him, he cupped his hands to his mouth. "Help!"

"Seth!" she whispered, tugging his sleeve. "Get down! The shooter will see you!"

"But I heard my daddy. I know I did!" The earnest plea in his eyes broke her heart.

"Seth, you—"

Then she heard what the boy had. Voices. One was definitely Jack's. A staccato beat thumped in her chest.

"Stay down." She emphasized her order with a firm hand on his shoulder. "Let me look."

When she peered over the top of the tree-house wall, she carefully scanned the woods and pasture. In the distance, she spotted two men struggling, heard the harsh tones of arguing, saw the long-barreled gun that had no doubt been the one fired at them.

Identifying Jack was easy. His tall frame, shaggy hair and tightly muscled body were as familiar to her in just a few short days as if she'd known him for years.

The second man was also large. Frighteningly so. His hair was dark, heavily streaked with gray and cropped shorter than Jack's. A shiver raced through her, and as she watched, horrified by the scene, Jack's opponent broke free and ran. Within seconds, Seth's father was in pursuit.

While she couldn't be sure the shooter didn't have an accomplice, she knew she needed to get back to the ranch and get help. For her bleeding shoulder and for Jack. He might have been ably handling the gunman, but things could turn bad quickly.

"Okay, Seth." She pressed a hand to her stomach,

where acid churned. "We need to make a run for it. Get back to your house and find help." She didn't consider herself especially brave or heroic—after all, she'd cowered at her husband's intimidation for years—but to protect Seth, she'd mine every ounce of steel in her resolve that she could.

"I don't need to see a doctor. I just need to disinfect the wound and—"

"Too late. I've already called both Eric and Ryan to meet us here."

Tracy sighed, though she appreciated Jack's concern. He and Brett had showed up at his house a few minutes after she and Seth had. Once he'd seen for himself that Seth was safe and given his son a lingering hug, he'd been on the phone to Ryan at the Tulsa Police Department, then left a message for Eric at the hospital. While Brett had taken Seth into his bedroom to distract him with a video game, Jack had helped clean Tracy's bullet wound and given her the fifth degree. Who was the shooter? Did she recognize him? What had happened, and how did they escape?

She'd tried her best to answer all his questions, knowing she'd have to repeat everything for the police when they arrived. As they waited for his brothers, Jack held a sterile bandage over the injury to her shoulder, and with constant pressure to the ragged flesh, most of the bleeding had stopped. Tracy gripped her cell phone in her hand. Jack had handed it to her when she and Seth turned up back at the house, and she assumed he had found it in the woods.

His phone buzzed with a text from Eric saying he was headed into surgery and couldn't come.

"Good," Tracy said. "He won't be wasting a trip out here."

"Then we'll meet him at the ER again."

She growled in frustration. "Jack, I don't need a trauma surgeon for a little cut. You're the one who should be getting medical help!" She met Jack's gaze in the bathroom mirror. Already his right eye was purpling from a bruise, and his jaw and knuckles had swollen. Lord only knew what other injuries he hid under his T-shirt.

He waved her off. "I've had worse and survived. Don't worry about me."

"I've had worse, too," she told him, and his gaze darkened with understanding.

A deep voice called down the hall from his front room. "Jack? Where are you?"

"We'll be right there," he called back, still holding her stare. "That's Ryan." When Jack finally tore his lingering gaze away, he jerked open the cabinet and took a tube from the shelf. "Let me apply some antibiotic before we go out there."

She nodded and turned her injured shoulder to him. He dabbed the cool cream on her wound with gentle strokes, pausing to blow on the sting when she winced in pain, much the way she'd doctored Seth's wound more than a week ago.

When they met his brother in the living room a few minutes later, she took a seat on the sofa and carefully recounted the events of the afternoon. After she was finished, Jack gave his statement, detailing his description of the shooter.

"I'll arrange for a sketch artist to meet with you later today so we can get a composite together for the department," Ryan told his brother.

"Jack," Tracy said, a tremor low in her belly, "your

description sounds a lot like the one that woman gave of the guy who pushed me in town last week."

His jaw tightened and his eyes narrowed on her. "I thought of that."

"Whoa," Ryan said, eyeing them both. "What guy? Was there another incident like this?"

Taking a deep breath for patience and calm, Tracy explained to him about the man who'd pushed her into traffic. "And before you ask, I don't know why he would have done it. Jack already asked all those questions last week, and I have no answers."

Jack stroked his sore jaw and divided a look between Ryan and Tracy. "Whether she knows why or not, she's become someone's target. Someone wants her dead."

Tracy's already pale skin grew even more ghostly white. She closed her eyes slowly, and her shoulders drooped. Her nod was subtle and defeated, and Jack's gut wrenched. The urge to swallow her in his embrace and chase away the shadows of vulnerability in her expression nearly knocked him over.

"Sounds that way. In law enforcement, we don't believe in coincidence," Ryan said, folding his arms over his chest as he planted his feet in a wide stance. "I'll do everything I can to find out who is behind this and why, but I'll need your complete honesty and cooperation."

Tracy raised a startled look to Ryan. "I *have* been honest."

"But have you been completely forthcoming? I get the feeling there is something you are not telling us."

Jack had had the same sense many times with Tracy, but he didn't voice that opinion now. He simply watched the fragile-looking woman shrink farther into the cushions of his couch.

Tracy twisted the ring on her right hand with her left,

staring at her lap in silence for several minutes. Ryan said nothing, in turn. He let Tracy stew and the silence drag on. Jack was familiar with the interrogation technique. Eventually, the pressure of the quiet, the expectant and patient stare his brother had mastered, would crack even a hardened criminal.

Finally, she sighed and said softly, "The car accident that killed Laura happened when I was fleeing my marriage, running away from my husband."

"Running away?" Ryan repeated. "Why?"

But the truth was obvious. Jack had suspected it from the day he'd met Tracy and questioned her in the barn about her motives regarding Seth.

"He was violent. And…verbally abusive."

Even though he'd been expecting this truth, hearing it confirmed sent a blaze of fury and disgust through Jack. His hands fisted, itching to slam into a man he'd never met but loathed just the same.

"Laura had finally convinced me to leave him," Tracy continued, in a voice that shook with shame and regret. "She'd promised to help me find a new place to live, get a job and change my name." Tracy paused for a breath and knuckled away the moisture at the corner of her eye. Jack called on all his inner strength not to scoop her into his arms and kiss the tears away.

"But Cliff found out what was happening…somehow. He came home from work early. He showed up at the house just as we were leaving. Laura was driving. He chased us, and we ended up on a twisty road in the foothills not far from our house. He forced us off the road, then his car crashed into the guardrail. He was unconscious until the cops revived him and arrested him. Laura…was killed instantly."

"And you?" Jack asked, feeling tension vibrate in him like a tuning fork.

"I had a broken collarbone and internal bleeding. The air bag left bruising on my face." She frowned and waved her injuries away as if they were nothing. "My injuries don't matter, not compared to the price Laura paid to help me." She dropped her face to her hands, and her shoulders shook as she sobbed. "My only comfort is knowing she didn't suffer. The coroner said her neck broke. She died instantly. But it's my fault. She was saving me from a marriage I should have left years earlier."

"I'm not sure I see how this is relevant to what happened today," Jack said. "You told me Cliff was killed in prison."

"He was."

He flipped a palm up. "Then it clearly wasn't him who was shooting at you today."

She tipped her head, conceding the point. "No, but you asked what I had been keeping from you." She twisted her fingers together, fidgeting. "I didn't want to tell you about my marriage when I arrived because I wasn't looking for sympathy. And, to be honest, I'm still a little ashamed that I stayed with Cliff as long as I did. More ashamed that Laura died helping to free me from him."

Jack and Ryan exchanged a look.

"And?" Jack prompted.

Her brow furrowed. "And what? That's it. I've been completely open and truthful about everything else."

Ryan tapped a pen against a small notepad, his gaze hard and probing. "If someone is targeting you, as we believe, then there must be something in your past—"

"No," she said, shaking her head vehemently. "I really can't think of anything."

Jack paced to the window with a growing sense of

disquiet roiling through him. Knowing that somebody was trying to kill Tracy was bad enough, but not knowing who was gunning for her, not knowing where the threat was coming from, made the situation all the more untenable. Jack didn't do uncertainty. He hated feeling exposed. And he loathed the idea of someone innocent being harmed on his watch.

The primitive instinct to protect Tracy that had been simmering inside Jack since he met her roared to life. Despite any qualms or doubts he might still have about her, he knew he had to step up the safeguards around her, and he couldn't delegate the job of protecting her to anyone else.

"There's no one who has a personal beef against you or a legal dispute?" Ryan pressed, and Jack turned back to the room, eyeing the petite woman on the couch with renewed determination to keep her safe.

Tracy sat straighter, meeting his brother's gaze evenly. "I'm not the sort of person who goes through life making enemies at every turn. In fact, before today, I'd say the person with the most animosity toward me was you, Jack."

Ryan raised his dark eyebrows and shot his brother an openly questioning glance. "What's this?"

Guilt tripped through him, and Jack waved off his brother's curiosity. "My issues with Tracy have nothing to do with the shooter today. Just…personal business." He narrowed a hard look at Tracy, not quite ready to believe she wasn't still protecting a secret. "Is there anyone with something to gain if you were gone?"

"No. No one. Nothing," she repeated firmly, as she shook her head again.

"When Cliff died, did you inherit a large estate?" Ryan asked.

Her shoulders sagged, proof that she was growing weary of their questions. "He had a life-insurance policy, and we had some savings, but not enough that I would think it was worth murdering me over."

"So you don't think his family might be behind this?"

"Well," Tracy said, then hesitated, "there was no love lost between me and his parents. I think Cliff poisoned them against me soon after our marriage. They didn't think I was good enough for their little boy. In fact, his mother made many comments about how she thought Cliff would be better off without me." Her tone and expression made clear how this opinion hurt her. "But...I can't see Mrs. Baxter as a murderer."

"And his father?" Jack asked.

"I—" Tracy rubbed her forehead and closed her eyes. "I don't know. What would he have to gain from hurting me? This is all just so bizarre to me."

"Well, we can certainly start with Cliff's parents. I'll contact the Denver police department and have the Baxters questioned." Ryan flipped his small notebook closed and stashed it in his shirt pocket. "If you think of anything else let me know."

Tracy nodded wearily. "I will." With what seemed a tremendous effort, she pushed to her feet, swaying slightly. "So...it looks like you win, Jack. Clearly, I can't stay here if my presence is going to bring the threat to Seth and the rest of your family. I'll go back to the main house and pack my things to leave."

An uneasy thrumming started low in Jack's belly. "Sit down."

She angled a startled glance at him. "Wh—"

He aimed a finger at the couch. "You're not going anywhere."

Chapter 11

Tracy blinked at him, incredulous. "Excuse me?"

"I can't in good conscience let you leave the ranch knowing that there's a threat against you. In fact, I don't want you staying at the main house any longer. I want you where I can keep an eye on you." When she lifted an eyebrow in consternation, he added, "In order to protect you, not because I don't trust you."

"Does that mean you trust me now?"

Jack glanced away as if weighing his words. "Let's just say…I believe you have Seth's best interests in mind. He told me how you protected him when the shooting started, how you sang to him to calm him."

She flipped up a palm. "He's a little boy. I did what anyone would do."

"Maybe. But you took care of him, even at your own risk…" He tightened his mouth and held her gaze. "And I don't take that lightly."

Jack moved to the coatrack and took down his Stetson.

"When you're ready, I'll go back up to the main house with you and help you move your things."

"Jack, I'm not your responsibility." Tracy shook her head, surprising him with the starch in her back and the defiance in her tone. "I really think the best thing would be for me to leave the Lucky C. I don't want to put anyone in danger."

He glanced at Ryan, who lifted his eyebrows and gave him a mild this-is-your-fight-not-mine look. Jack's returned glare said, *Thanks for nothing, man*.

When Jack faced Tracy, he tried to maintain a calm, reasonable tone. "By leaving, you'd put *yourself* in danger. Is that what you want?" He shoved his hat on his head, then slid his fingers into his front jeans pockets. "Here on the ranch, you have a whole staff of ranch hands, not to mention Brett, Big J, Daniel and myself. There's not a one of us Coltons that's not a top-notch marksman." Surely she couldn't argue with that logic.

Tracy looked from Jack to Ryan and back again. "I appreciate everything you're doing for me, and I'll do anything I can to help catch the shooter. But I couldn't stand it if something happened to one of you because of me. Especially if something happened to Seth."

"It's my job to protect my son, and that's what I'm going to do." Jack infused his tone with the finality that ended arguments with his son, but Tracy persisted.

"We got lucky today, and he wasn't hurt. But if that man comes after me again…" Instead of finishing the thought, she nibbled her bottom lip and creased her brow.

Jack squared his shoulders, trying to ignore the heat that threaded through him as he watched her abuse her lip. He wanted to taste that mouth and knew he could distract her from her worries with a deep, lingering kiss. Clearing his throat, he growled, "If anyone comes after you again, I intend to be there. I'm making it my business to keep you safe until the shooter is caught." He paused and narrowed his gaze. "If you'd done as I asked about not spending time alone with Seth, I'd have been with you when the shooting started."

He knew he sounded peevish, but he didn't care. He'd been scared out of his wits earlier today when he'd thought about something happening to Seth. That same fear curled through him when he thought of the shooter gunning for Tracy, of the vicious ape returning to finish the job.

Her shoulders drooped in defeat, and she lowered her gaze to her lap. "All right, I'll stay."

Ryan opened the front door to leave.

"But—"

Ryan paused, and Jack groaned internally. He should have known she'd have conditions. He was in no mood to bargain, but he rested his hands on his hips and turned back to the couch. "But what?"

"As you said, Brett and Big J are skilled marksmen, and at the main house, I'll have them *and* the staff for protection. I'm settled there. There's no need to move me."

Except that *he* wanted to oversee her protection. Jack felt an overwhelming personal link to her, a duty to keep her safe, and a strange premonition that if he didn't take charge of her protection, something awful would happen to her. He didn't want to delegate this to his aging father and womanizing younger brother. Jack gritted his back teeth.

Ryan cleared his throat, and his eyebrow lifted as he moved out the door. "Jack, Tracy, I'll leave you two to figure out the logistics of your lodging. Meantime, I'll be down at the station making arrangements for a sketch artist and calling my Denver contacts." His gaze focused on Jack. "Meet me at my office soon as you can. We have work to do, and if I can arrange it with Denver, I'm going to fly up to assist with interviewing the Baxters."

Jack stiffened. "Tell me when you get that arranged. I'll go with you."

Ryan shook his head. "This is a police matter. You don't need to go."

"Maybe I don't need to, but I am going."

Ryan grunted. "If anyone should go with me, Tracy should. The Baxters are her in-laws."

Jack turned and narrowed a hard look on the fragile woman sitting on his couch. "You're right. We'll both go."

Tracy jerked her head up, her eyes wide with dismay, as his brother grated, "Hell, no. That wasn't my point. I wasn't inviting her to go."

"Maybe not, but she should be there. She may be able to give us valuable information during the interview, help us redirect our questioning or tell us when they are flat out lying."

Ryan poked Jack in the chest with his index finger. "What's all this 'us' business? Did you not hear me say that this is a police matter? The last time I checked, you don't carry a badge."

"Ryan, that sonofabitch took a shot at my son, on my property. I am going. And considering somebody seems to have a beef against Miss McCain, I intend to bring her with us. Not only will she be helpful during the interview, I can do a better job of protecting her if I keep her close."

"Excuse me," Tracy said, rising to her feet and sounding more than a little miffed. "Don't I get a say in this?"

Jack shot her another hard look. "Of course you do. The question boils down to whether you want to be of assistance catching the shooter like you said…or not."

She raised her chin a notch and pressed her lips in a thin line. "You know I want him caught."

"Then I guess you are going with me to Denver."

"Jack—" Ryan began, his face dark.

"Are you going to lock me in a cell down at the police station, Detective? Because that's the only way you're going to stop me. You have my word that I won't interfere with the official investigation, but I need to be there."

Ryan held his glare for several taut seconds. Finally, with an exasperated sigh, he shook his head and said, "Fine. Fly to Denver if you are so damn determined. But so help me, if you step one foot across the line during this investigation, I *will* lock you in a holding cell. *Capisce?*"

Jack jerked a nod. "Yeah, I understand."

After Ryan left for the police station, Tracy stayed at Jack's house. Even though he had already treated the wound on her shoulder and she had no good reason to linger, the thought of returning to the main house with all its cold marble and numerous large empty rooms left her oddly out of sorts. Brett wouldn't be back from the pastures yet and Greta was out of town, and she didn't look forward to sitting alone in the vast mansion. She much preferred the warm decor and cozy feel of Jack's ranch house. And if she were honest with herself, she felt safer being close to Jack. The crack of the shooter's rifle still echoed in her mind, sending rippling chills to her core.

Using the excuse that she felt a bit dizzy, she'd stayed to rest on the couch in Jack's family room. She managed to take a short nap, though her rest was fitful and filled with dreams of wild animals chasing her through the woods, their large teeth flashing and snapping at her.

When she woke, her forehead was damp with a cold sweat. She sat up and found that a lightweight afghan had been laid across her legs. The mantel clock read 6:30 p.m., and the scent of roasting beef told her Jack had already started dinner. Folding the crocheted blanket and draping it over the back of the sofa, she went in search of Seth and his father.

The tinny music and beeps of a video game led her to the living room, where Seth was engrossed in a cartoon car race, his thumbs flying over his game controller like a teenager texting gossip to his best friend. On the couch next to him, the barn cat—Sleekie, Seth had called her—slept curled into in ball. As she watched, Seth reached over and gave Sleekie a pat, and the feline woke to roll on her back and stretch, showing her fuzzy belly.

Tracy couldn't resist rubbing the cat's furry tummy, then ruffling Seth's hair. Sleekie chirped a greeting, but the little boy didn't even look up. Quirking a lopsided grin, she found her way down the short hall to Jack's study. She knocked softly on the door frame, and he lifted his head from his perusal of his laptop screen.

"Hi. Did you sleep okay?" Jack leaned back in his chair and laced his fingers together as he rested his hands against his chest.

"About as well as can be expected, I suppose, considering someone tried to kill me this afternoon." She stepped into the office and let her gaze take in the wood paneling and wall of bookshelves. Jack's desk sat in a corner of the room by a window, outside of which the early summer sun was sinking low on the horizon, casting the world in a golden glow. A highball glass with about an inch of amber liquid and ice sat on the corner of his desk near where he worked. The glass sweated, and condensation rolled down to puddle on a coaster.

"Are you hungry? I put a meat loaf in the oven a little while ago, and you're welcome to stay and eat with us."

Meat loaf was far from her favorite food, but sharing a meal with Jack and Seth sounded better to her than anything she might find to eat at the main house. She nodded and sent him a grateful smile. "Thank you. I'd love to. Is there anything I can do to help get dinner ready?"

"Now that you mention it, I was going to make a salad, but I got engrossed with what I was doing here."

"One salad coming up," she said, glad to have something useful to occupy herself.

"You should find all the vegetables you need in the refrigerator crisper." He told her where to find a chopping board and the knives she would need, then checked his watch. "The meat should be done in about twenty minutes. Give me a shout if you need any help."

Tracy returned to the kitchen and had a salad full of fresh summer vegetables ready ten minutes later. She peeked in the oven, checking on their entrée, before she went back down the hall to Jack's study.

She paused in the doorway and watched Jack sip his liquor for a moment without calling attention to her presence. Even small details about this man mesmerized her, enchanted her. He was every inch a man's man. His Adam's apple bobbed as he swallowed, drawing her attention to the muscled column of his neck and the small whorl of dark hair at the open V of his shirt. His long blunt-tipped fingers curled around his glass, and she imagined them stroking her. After he sipped his drink again, he licked a drop from the corner of his mouth. The sight of his moistened lips, his agile tongue, stirred more erotic images in her brain, and she caught a groan in her throat, stifling her lust.

But Jack must have sensed her attention, because without preamble, he said, "I've been doing a little checking on your ex in-laws."

"Oh?"

He waved her into the office and pointed to a chair, directing her to take a seat.

Wiping her palms on the legs of her jeans, she stepped into the room and perched on the edge of the high-backed chair he indicated. She clasped her hands in her lap and angled her head to see the computer screen. "Anything interesting?"

"I'll say. Did you know that Cliff's parents have business ties with Tony Rossetto?"

Tracy crumpled her nose in confusion. "No. Is that significant?"

"You don't know the name?"

"Should I?"

Jack laced his fingers behind his head and leaned back, making springs in his chair creak. "Maybe not, if you've been living under a rock recently."

She pulled a face and sent him a you're-not-funny glare. "Just tell me who he is. Why is it significant that Cliff's parents have ties to him?"

"Tony Rossetto stood trial in federal court last year for extortion, fraud, tax evasion, intimidation…and those are just the charges they could prove. I'm sure they wanted to try him for murder, money laundering and God knows what else. In short, he's a real bad dude, and even a preliminary search of public records shows that Cliff's parents were invested in a number of business operations that Rossetto also had his fingers in."

Tracy stared at Jack for a moment, trying to come to grips with what she was learning. "Th-that doesn't mean anything. Lots of people have the misfortune of investing with partners who prove to be bad apples. It doesn't make them criminals."

Jack snorted a humorless laugh. "Tony Rossetto is more than a bad apple. He's organized crime."

Chapter 12

Organized crime. Tracy's mouth dried. "You mean, like, the Mafia?"

He arched a dark eyebrow. "Not all organized crime is Mafia, but you get the gist." When his cell phone buzzed, he unclipped it from his belt and checked the caller ID. "It's Ryan. Hang on a minute, while I tell him what I've found, okay?"

She nodded numbly, too stunned by Jack's revelation to do more than gape. The Baxters had links to organized crime? She'd known they were wealthy and powerful in the business world, but she'd never imagined their sphere of influence came through illicit means. And while Cliff had been aggressive and cruel to her, she had a hard time imagining her ex-husband, who was so scrupulous about obeying traffic laws and abiding by neighborhood ordinances, being so bold as to flout the law in business matters.

You really are naive, aren't you? she could imagine Cliff saying with a sneer. A shiver ran through her, and she balled her hands into fists.

While Jack conducted a conversation in low tones with his brother, Tracy gathered her composure and forced herself to face facts. Cliff had not been the man she'd thought he was when she married him, and clearly, his parents had been just as deceitful.

Knowing how blind she'd been, a weighty sense of defeat pressed down on her. She slumped back in the chair and pressed her thumbs against her closed eyes. Was it possible that Cliff's parents were behind the attack on her yesterday? A greasy ball of guilt churned in her gut. She could never forgive herself if something happened to one of the Coltons from a danger she'd brought to the Lucky C.

"Tracy?" Jack's voice seeped through her thoughts on some level, but it wasn't until he grasped her wrist and shook her arm with a loud, "Tracy!" that she jolted from her fretting with a gasp.

"What?" She lurched upright in the chair, her gaze flying to Jack's worried frown.

"Are you all right?"

"I…yeah."

He leaned back, propping his elbows on his armrests and pressing his fingertips together. "Where did you go just then? I've been trying to get your attention for a full minute."

"Nowhere good," she mumbled, letting her shoulders slouch. Tipping a side glance up at him, she braced herself for more bad news. "What did Ryan say?"

"He's looking into the connections I found and will do more digging into the Baxters' business associates.

For now, you and I need to work out some ground rules to keep you safe."

"I still say, if there's a threat against me, I should leave the ranch. How can I stay on, knowing I could be putting the rest of you in danger?"

He drew a deep breath and expelled it slowly through his lips, allowing his cheeks to puff out. He lifted his glass for a sip before saying, "Try to see things from my point of view. How can I let you leave the ranch knowing you're in danger? That'd be like sending a lamb into a forest full of wolves. I'm not that callous."

"Jack, I appreciate your wanting to protect me, b—"

"Good." He set his drink on the coaster again, and the ice rattled as it settled. "Then we'll consider the matter closed." His level gaze brooked no resistance, and she was secretly relieved to acquiesce. Though she didn't like Jack's high-handedness—she'd had quite enough of that with Cliff—she hadn't been looking forward to going it alone while there was a killer stalking her. A jittery sense of unrest danced through her. She'd thought she was free of Cliff. Hadn't Laura paid the ultimate price in order to win Tracy freedom from this fear? The notion that her poor choice of husband could still be haunting her, putting other people at risk, was more than a little unsettling.

Unable to remain still, she rose to pace Jack's office. Distraction. She needed to think about something other than Cliff's disapproving parents, the crack of the shooter's rifle and the heart-wrenching sound of Seth's frightened sobs. Swallowing hard, she waved an unsteady finger at the room in general, asking, "Mind if I take a look around?"

He shrugged and bent over the laptop. "Knock yourself out."

With an encompassing glance, she cataloged the decor, the items Jack chose to surround himself with as he worked. She wanted to build a better mental image of who he was. As expected, he had numerous pictures of Seth at various ages scattered around the room, and she lifted one of a laughing toddler. Touched, she grinned back at the cherubic face. "Seth was a cute baby."

Jack gave a quiet hum that she took as agreement. When she glanced his way, she found his attention locked on the computer screen. His intent focus on the device reminded her of Seth's single-minded attention to his video game. *Like father, like son.*

As she moved on around the room, she trailed her fingers lightly over dusty book covers with titles by John Jakes, agriculture manuals and basic reference books— a dictionary, a thesaurus and a Farmer's Almanac—all with well-creased spines. She found the bottle of Kentucky bourbon, no doubt what he was drinking now, on a tray with an ice bucket and extra highball glasses.

"Help yourself. I'm sure after the day you've had, a drink might help calm you."

She shook her head. "Thanks, but I took something for pain. I'd best not add alcohol to the mix."

She continued her tour and found that his bookcase held a few rodeo trophies. Also not surprising. She recalled him mentioning his early start in the rodeo when they'd watched Daniel teaching Seth to ride around barrels.

She read the plaques at the base of the trophies. First Place, Bull Riding. First Place, Calf Roping. Second Place, Bull Riding. Her heart skipped as she imaged Jack in a rodeo arena, astride a bucking bull or charging after a calf on his horse, lariat raised. Dusty chaps and well-worn boots. Faded jeans and sweat…

Her mouth dried, and she shook her head to clear it. *Don't go there*, she warned herself. *You came to get to know Seth, not to fall for his father.*

Moving on, she noticed knickknacks made from re-purposed horseshoes, and a small box decorated with Magic Markers and glued-on macaroni. A formal framed portrait of all of the Colton siblings, minus Daniel, also held a prominent spot on the bookshelves. Her heart gave a sympathetic tug for Daniel, remembering how hurt he'd looked at Greta's party when Big J had excluded mention of him. Poor Daniel. She sighed as she studied the handsome faces, the similar smiles, the matching green eyes—although Greta's were much more hazel than her brothers'. The family dynamic was none of her business.

A tingle on the back of her neck told her Jack was watching her, even before he said, "That was taken three years ago as a Christmas present for our mother. She wouldn't have appreciated Daniel being in the shot."

She whipped her head around, startled that he'd so clearly read in her expression or body language where her thoughts had been. While his explanation gave the why behind Daniel's exclusion, it didn't soften the sympathetic ache for Jack's half brother.

"Daniel would be the first to tell you he's not looking for sympathy. He knows we count him as one of our own, regardless of Abra's opinion," Jack said, again reading her mind. But having seen Daniel's downcast face last week, she wondered how well Jack really knew his half brother's feelings about his place in the family.

Deciding it wasn't her place to argue the point, she gave Jack a nod of assent and strolled to the other side of the room as Jack got back to work. A glance at her watch told her the timer on the oven should be dinging in another two minutes.

She approached a glass-topped wood cabinet with ornate carvings on the face of the drawers, and she spied another picture that caught her eye. She picked up the small photo for a closer look. The man in the photo wore a white protective outfit and had a helmet with a face screen tucked under his arm. At first she thought the man was Ryan, due to the short hair, but upon closer inspection she realized it was Jack. The clothing seemed familiar, and she groped mentally to figure out what she was seeing. She turned back to Jack. "Do you keep bees?"

He raised his gaze, his forehead dented in confusion. "Bees?"

She angled the photo for him to see what she'd found. "Isn't this a beekeeper's protective suit you're wearing?"

He arched one eyebrow and chuckled softly. "No. It's fencing gear."

Jack couldn't have surprised her more if he'd tried. "Fencing?"

"You've heard of it, right?"

"Well, yeah. It's a sport. It's…sword fighting."

A disgruntled noise rumbled from his throat. "Maybe in the broadest terms. Sword fighting is about battle. Strength and physicality. The biomechanics of how to disarm and maim your opponent before they slice you up."

She winced at the brutal-sounding descriptive, and her bullet wound gave a throb of protest.

"Fencing," he continued as he pushed his chair back and crossed the floor to her, "is more civil. It's about subtle movements and skill." He took the picture from her and studied it himself. "This was taken at a tournament in New Hampshire. I was seventeen."

She'd started her prowl of the office hoping to learn

more about Jack but never thought she'd uncover such an intriguing tidbit. She lifted the corner of her mouth in amazement. "How in the world did a cowboy like you get interested in fencing?"

"Oh, I didn't care a fig about fencing when I started." Down the hall, the timer on the oven buzzed. He aimed a thumb toward the hall. "But I guess that story will have to keep."

She caught his arm as he turned to leave the room. "No, please. I want to hear it now. Dinner will keep a few more minutes."

"All right, but if your meat loaf is dry, remember... you asked."

"A risk I'm willing to take." She sent him a lopsided smile and leaned her back against the glass-topped cabinet.

Jack set the picture down and rubbed a hand against his stubble-dusted chin. "Well, let's see. When I was a kid, I wanted to be a pirate."

Startled by his explanation, she gave an indelicate snort of a laugh, earning an arched-eyebrow glance from him. "I'm sorry." She waved her fingers, indicating he should continue. "You were saying?"

"It started when I was ten, and I watched an Errol Flynn movie with Big J." Jack's deep voice warmed to his subject, and Tracy realized she was getting a rare peek beneath the tough surface of the normally taciturn cowboy. "All that swashbuckling appealed to the rambunctious kid I was. I spent months battling my brothers with plastic swords and broomsticks...pretty much anything I could find. Our nanny got tired of the inevitable roughhousing that would result— Eric and Ryan both thought wrestling was the best way to deal with my pirate obsession—so she told Big J to find me a better outlet for my new interest. Thing is, public schools in Oklahoma just don't teach sword fighting, and the closest he could come was fencing. Even then he had to drive me to Oklahoma City for private lessons. Like I said, fencing is similar to sword fighting, but it didn't quite satisfy me."

"Not swashbuckler-y enough for you, huh?"

"Something like that. I was looking for something more physical, more challenging. Well, Big J could tell I'd never really given up my first love, my real interest, so when he found these at an auction—" He nudged her aside with his hip and stepped up to the cabinet. Thumbing a latch open, he lifted the glass top "—he bought them for me."

Tracy peered down into the chest, where a pair of ornate swords were nestled in a red velvet bed, their blades crossed. She drew a sharp breath. "Oh, my word! Those are beautiful!"

She angled her head to glance up at Jack, and an unquestionable pride gleamed in the eyes. "Eighteenth-century small swords. They're from France. See the inscription here?" He tapped the engraved hilt of one sword, and she leaned closer for a better look.

"*L'Honneur ou la mort*," she read aloud. "Honor in death?"

"Close. Honor or death."

"Oh, right. My high school French is rusty."

"Anyway, the guy selling the swords asked Big J if he was a collector. Big J explained my interest in sword fighting, and the guy hooked me up with a friend of his who had trained in actual sword fighting."

"And you were able to take lessons from him?"

"For a while, yes. Meanwhile, I'd also gotten involved in the rodeo."

Her gaze traveled to the trophies on the shelf next to the horseshoe art.

"Bull riding and calf roping," she said, remembering the inscriptions on the awards.

His eyes widen briefly in surprise. "How did you—?" Without finishing the question, he turned and let his eyes follow hers. "Oh. Right. Anyway, rodeo started taking most of my time. For one thing, it had practical applications on the ranch. And that's where my friends all spent most of their time, and—" he cut a quick glance at her, his expression sly "—that's where the buckle bunnies were."

She wrinkled her nose. "I'm sorry? Buckle bunnies?"

His lips twitched. "Women. Rodeo groupies." He lifted one of the swords from the case, resting the blade carefully in one palm, the grip in his other while he stroked a thumb along the hilt. "When you're a testosterone-driven teenager, one thing always trumped all, and the buckle bunnies were happy to oblige."

Tracy felt her cheeks sting with a blush. "Took advantage of the admiring fans, did you?"

His eyebrows dipped. "Depends on what you mean by 'took advantage.' I was hellion in the past, no doubt about it. But Big J raised me to respect women. To know *no* meant *no*. I never preyed on a girl's vulnerabilities." He paused and handed her the sword. "But I never lacked for a date when I wanted one, either."

As she accepted the antique weapon, something deep inside Tracy squirmed uneasily at the thought of Jack with all those other women. Laura had told her Jack had been rather wild and sowing his oats before they married. As much as Laura had been suffocated by ranch life, Jack had chafed at the confines of marriage early on. Jack's attitude had changed when Seth was born.

Tracy kept these tidbits of insider information Laura

had shared to herself, though she found it hard to reconcile the image of Jack as an adrenaline-loving, risk-taking womanizer with the quiet, doting father and responsible rancher/businessman. Greta had said Laura broke Jack's heart, but had their divorce also broken his spirit?

"All of this work was done by hand, by an artisan in Paris around the time of the French Revolution." Jack's voice pulled her out of her thoughts as he waved a finger to the scrolled knuckle guard and elaborate engraving on the hilt.

She weighed the weapon in her hands. "It's heavy. Hard to imagine anyone wielding something like this as a weapon."

"But they did. The chinks here and here—" he pointed to the spots on the blade he meant "—are signs of use." He furrowed his brow as if in deep thought. "I like to imagine the circumstances of the battle or duel that put those chinks there." He scoffed lightly in dismissal. "Oh, well... That meat is getting drier by the minute."

He lifted the sword from her hands and placed it back in the velvet bedding.

"Have you ever used them? You know, for fun. A mock duel or whatever?"

"Not these. They're too valuable. But I have another small sword I use when I have time to indulge my hobby."

"Thank you...for showing these to me. They really are magnificent." She shook her head and grinned. "I'd never have guessed you had an interest in something so...unusual."

He lowered the top of the cabinet and paused with his hand resting on the display glass. "I'm not sure if I should feel insulted or complimented." He cast a side glance and cocked one eyebrow. "Are you saying you thought I was mundane?"

Hearing the teasing note in his tone, she laughed and curled her hand around his arm. "No…gosh, no! I'd never say that about you. I only meant…you were largely a mystery to me when I arrived, and what I've discovered about you this week has been…surprising."

He cocked his head. "As in, still waters run deep?"

His voice was as smooth and intoxicating as aged whiskey, and it rolled through her with a heady warmth. "Something like that."

When she started to remove her hand from his forearm, he covered it and wrapped his fingers around hers. "I have to admit, you've surprised me a bit, too."

Tracy was so startled by his touch, so enthralled by the scrape of his calloused palm against her skin, that she needed a moment to catch her breath. Heart thrashing in her chest, she croaked, "Oh? How?"

"You're tougher than I gave you credit for." His thumb stroked her wrist with the same gentle fondness he'd employed when he'd admired the decorative hilt. A low buzzing sounded in her ears, the sound of her blood pumping harder, faster in response to his mesmerizing touch and rumbling voice. "My first impression of you was that you were fragile. Like a doll that would break under pressure. But I realize now I was judging your character based on your appearance."

She forced her throat to swallow despite her rapidly drying mouth and worked to flash a smile that didn't tremble. "Now I'm not sure if I should feel insulted or complimented. You thought of me as a doll?"

He tugged her hand to bring her closer as he faced her and raised his free hand to her cheek. "A china doll, yes. Because you have that sort of delicate beauty. Big, innocent blue eyes and skin so pale I can see your veins." He tracked one of those veins in her throat with a fingertip, then lifted the same finger to brush her lips. "And a rosebud mouth."

Jack's voice had grown even softer, and his eyelids lowered as he focused on her lips. He dipped his head toward hers, nudging her chin up with a thumb as he cradled her cheek. Tracy's breath stuttered from her. She canted toward him, drawn to him by a force more powerful than common sense. She felt the moist heat of his breath as he exhaled a sigh of resignation, and angled his head—

"Dad?" Seth bellowed a fraction of a second before he crashed through the office door. "When's dinner? I'm starving!"

Tracy gasped and stumbled guiltily back a step. Disappointment speared her. Of all the bad timing! Or maybe it was providential that Seth had interrupted when he did. Becoming involved with her cousin's ex had never been part of her plan when she came to the Lucky C.

"We'll be in there in a minute. Meanwhile, you wash up and set the table." Jack's tone held none of the irritation or frustration that vibrated through her for their lost moment. When she turned a side glance to him, only the hint of color in his cheeks and dark pools of his pupils gave any indication how close they'd come to kissing.

Seth divided a look between the adults, then shrugged. "Okay."

"Hey! Turn the oven off, too. Okay, Spud?" Jack called as Seth trooped out.

Finally catching her breath, Tracy moved toward the door, pressing a shaky palm to the swirl of jitters and unsatisfied lust in her belly. "I'll help him."

But Jack caught her arm, stopping her. "There's something else you should know about me, Tracy."

She met his heated gaze, and her heart flip-flopped.

He drew her close again with a firm grip on her arm and a guiding hand at her hip. "I finish what I start."

With that, he captured her lips with his.

Chapter 13

Jack pulled her body flush to the whipcord strength and lean muscle of his, and Tracy's knees buckled as desire stampeded through her. Only his arm around her waist, cinching her to him, kept her upright. Once the shock of his kiss faded, heady sensations rolled through her and pooled low in her belly. A tiny mewl of pleasure escaped her throat, and she slid her arms around his neck, relaxing in his embrace.

Her fingers curled into the hair that brushed his collar. The silky wisps tickled her palm, while the stubble of his chin scraped lightly against her cheeks. His kiss tasted like the bourbon he'd been sipping, and his skin smelled like sweet hay, mellow leather and sensual man.

Jack took command of the kiss, holding her head pinioned with one hand splayed at her nape. While her body wallowed blissfully in his skill and seduction, a small voice in her head whispered a warning. Cliff had been demanding, unyielding, overbearing. His tyranny had become the source of her terror. *Don't make the same mistake*, her brain whispered.

Jack must have sensed the shift in her thoughts, because he broke their kiss and peered down at her. "You can tell me to go to hell if this isn't what you want."

"No, I—" Her voice cracked, and a tiny tremor shimmied through her. "You just…surprised me."

"Did I?" His fingers pushed a lock of her hair that had escaped her ponytail behind her ear. "Are you going to tell me you haven't felt the undercurrent of heat between us since the day you showed up at Greta's party?"

"I—" She swallowed audibly. She wasn't going to lie to him. Especially since she'd so obviously enjoyed his kiss. And because she desperately wanted his trust. "I have. I just…didn't want my purpose for being here, my wish to know Seth, to get tangled up in what I was feeling toward you."

"And I didn't want my desire for you to cloud my judgment of your purpose. But you showed me today—" he whispered as he trailed kisses along the line of her jaw and throat "—that you have an incredible core of strength. No matter how fragile…your appearance, you proved…you are no pushover."

Though his compliment warmed her heart, her gut tightened. She squeezed her eyes closed, feeling like a fraud. "I didn't feel strong," she admitted. "I felt horribly vulnerable." She tightened her grip around his shoulders as the chilling horror of those moments washed through her again. She buried her head under his chin, her ear pressed to his breastbone and shivered. "I did what I had to to protect Seth, but…I was scared to death."

Beneath her cheek, a hum of acknowledgment rumbled in his chest, and his arms tightened around her. "Fear doesn't determine your courage and inner strength. What you do in the face of fear does."

He angled his body away and tipped her head up with a hand under her chin. "Based on what you've said about your ex, I'd say you also showed that inner strength by breaking away from him."

She gave her head a little shake. "I couldn't have done it without Laura. She helped me get away, in so many ways. Not just by driving the car that day..." She let her voice trail off. The usual roil of unrest swirled through her, remembering Laura's death in the car accident, the high-speed chase that precipitated the wreck. But today, here, wrapped in Jack's arms, she felt safer than she had in months. In years.

He stroked the back of his hand along her cheek. "I stand by my assessment. What you did today— and when you left Cliff— took courage." He paused, his penetrating gaze locked on hers. "And I thank you for protecting Seth."

"Jack, I—"

He silenced her with another deep, toe-curling kiss, and Tracy forgot what she'd planned to say. She forgot everything but that cozy office and the cowboy holding her snug against him. She leaned into the kiss, parting her lips when his tongue sought entry to her mouth.

Falling for Jack may have been the farthest thing from her mind when she arrived at the Lucky C, but life was nothing if not full of surprises. She'd have never guessed a madman would track her to Tulsa and try to kill her, either. The dizzying speed of events, taking her life in directions she couldn't have predicted, left her mind spinning, the ground shifting beneath her feet.

Or was it the thorough, sultry way Jack took charge of

their kiss that made her legs rubbery and her head light? Some of each, probably.

"Now...how 'bout that supper?" he said, when he finally raised his head, and Tracy sucked in a shuddering breath. He gave her shoulders a squeeze before stepping back from her, his gaze still dark with desire.

With her heart drumming wildly, she nodded, not trusting her voice. Later, Tracy couldn't have said anything about the meat loaf, potatoes or salad that comprised their meal, because her mind kept straying to Jack's office, to his kiss. She didn't miss the intimate sense of family as they shared the meal. She savored the chance to watch Seth and Jack interact. To be included in the conversations about the ranch and Seth's video game. She marveled at Jack's loving reassurance when Seth mentioned the shooting, his ability to say just the right thing to calm the boy's fears without lying or evading.

He then explained to Seth about the plan to fly to Denver in the morning.

"Can I go?" Seth asked, his eyes wide with the excitement of a possible trip to a new city.

"This is business. You'd be bored. I've asked Brett to keep an eye on you."

Seth drooped in his chair, clearly disappointed.

"I want you to mind Brett and help him with chores. Understand?"

Seth nodded. "Yes, sir."

"Good boy. Now take your plate to the sink and get in your pajamas. I'll be up in a minute to read you a book."

"Can Tracy read to me tonight?" Seth asked, casting her a hopeful glance.

She consulted Jack, who dipped his chin in agreement, before sending Seth a broad smile. "I'd love to, sweetie."

Her heart clenched knowing that if Jack had his way,

she'd be living under the same roof with the father and son, sharing more dinners, more bedtimes, more familial moments in the coming days. How wonderful it would be to feel this warmth, this bond, the peaceful routine that was family life every day. A poignant longing tightened her chest, and she did her best to shove it down.

Before she could dream of home and hearth, she had to rid herself of the menace that had invaded her life. Her priority had to be keeping Seth and the rest of the Coltons safe from the assassin bent on killing her.

Early the next morning, Jack, Ryan and Tracy disembarked at the Denver airport and took a cab straight to the Denver PD station. The Baxters were being brought in for questioning, and according to Ryan's contacts in the department, the couple had immediately called their lawyer to meet them at the station.

"Interesting," Jack said, arching an eyebrow when Ryan relayed this tidbit.

"Actually, not so interesting. The Baxters are on a first-name basis with their lawyer. They don't scratch their noses without asking Mr. Rampart's legal advice." Now Ryan arched a dark eyebrow. "Are they paranoid or do they have something to hide?"

Tracy shrugged. "I don't know. Honestly, I tried to avoid spending much time with them. They're not exactly pleasant people to be around. But you'll see that for yourself soon enough."

Jack and Ryan exchanged a look but said nothing. As their taxi approached downtown Denver, Jack called Brett to check on Seth. While Edith would likely manage most of Seth's care while he was gone, Brett had promised to oversee Seth's protection in light of the gunman's attack. If there was trouble, Jack knew Brett could handle it.

"We're playing Sorry, and Seth is kicking my tail. Your kid is merciless, man!" Brett said, and Jack heard Seth's laugh in the background.

Jack tugged his cheek up in a half grin, and chuckled softly. "If you're gonna play, you might as well play to win." Assured that Seth was fine and all was quiet at the ranch, Jack signed off and clipped his phone back on his belt. He caught Tracy looking at him with a bemused expression and asked, "What's that look for?"

She blinked as if startled to have been caught staring. "I…uh, nothing." A tantalizing pink flush stained her cheeks. "I just…so rarely see you smile."

He wasn't sure what he'd expected her to say, but not that. He glowered at her. "I smile." He watched as Tracy and Ryan exchange a look and realizing his current countenance contradicted his assertion, he grumbled, "When it's warranted."

The taxi pulled up in front of the police department at that moment, and the subject was put on hold for the moment. But as Tracy swept past him into the bustling police station, she leaned close and said, "Perhaps you should consider what warrants a smile more often. Yours is quite stunning."

Her compliment was unexpected, and it rattled him. Discomposed was not a good state for the business at hand, but he couldn't deny the warmth that settled in his core as she tossed him a sideways grin and sashayed inside.

Was he really as dour as she made him sound? Granted, he didn't smile much. He'd found it hard to smile after Laura ditched him, Seth and the ranch, and perhaps he'd made little effort in more recent years. Seth had been his only source of real joy, his only reason to smile in the past few years.

Ryan showed his badge at the front desk, and a few minutes later, a plain-clothes detective with auburn hair and friendly smile appeared from the back offices to meet them. Ryan introduced the man as Detective Ron Hunnicutt, and Jack and Tracy both shook the detective's hand as Ryan gave their names. Genial questions about their flight and formalities concerning signing in to the police department and acquiring visitor tags were dispensed with in short order, and the group filed back toward the interrogation rooms.

"So here's how this will work," Detective Hunnicutt said as they walked, "I will question Mr. and Mrs. Baxter separately. Detective Colton will sit in and is free to ask any questions he has. My understanding of your case is you haven't any evidence they are tied to the shooting at your ranch. You are just looking for any information that might be helpful?"

Ryan nodded. "That's right. Ms. McCain had a contentious relationship with her in-laws before her husband died, and they are the only people she could think of who had any kind of beef with her."

The detective directed his next statements to Tracy. "So you understand, your in-laws are not under arrest. They are here voluntarily for questioning and are free to leave at any time. Without any evidence of their involvement, we have no legal grounds to hold them."

"It's a fishing trip, for sure," Ryan added, "but we have no other leads except the sketch of the suspect Jack helped us draw up last night."

"You're the only one saw the shooter?" Hunnicutt asked Jack.

"I saw him, too," Tracy volunteered, "but only from a distance. I had nothing to add to Jack's description that would be helpful."

Ryan paused long enough to open a satchel he'd brought with him and took out a file. Flipping the file open, he extracted a stiff sheet of paper. "I faxed this to you last night, but this is the original if you'd like to make copies."

Hunnicutt stopped walking and turned his attention to the sheet Ryan passed to him. Jack glimpsed the surly face of the man in the sketch the police artist had composed with his direction, and his gut soured. With his thumb, he stroked the still-sore and swollen knuckles of his opposite hand, remembering the hatred in the shooter's eyes. A killer's eyes. Jack had no doubt the man harbored no compunction for his crime, would feel no guilt for murdering Tracy and anyone else who got in his way.

He glanced at Tracy, whose face had paled since Ryan had produced the police sketch. "You don't recognize him at all? Have you thought of anything since last night?"

She tore her gaze from the image to face Jack. "No."

"You've never seen him before yesterday? You're sure?" Hunnicutt asked, handing the sketch back to Ryan.

She shook her head. "Never. I'd remember that face, those eyes. He looks...evil."

Tracy chafed her arms as if chilled, and the Denver detective twisted his mouth in thought. "Well, let's see if your in-laws recognize him."

"Ex-in-laws," Tracy corrected.

"You divorced your husband before he died?" Detective Hunnicutt asked.

"Well, no. But I'd left him...and since Cliff died, they've wanted nothing to do with me and vice versa."

A uniformed officer poked his head out of one of the doors along the corridor where they stood and announced, "We're ready when you are, Ron."

Hunnicutt nodded to the officer, then to Ryan. "Shall we?" Turning to Tracy and Jack, he aimed a finger further down the corridor and said, "There are some chairs down the hall where you can wait."

Jack squared his shoulders. "No."

Detective Hunnicutt blinked and angled his head. "Excuse me?"

"We came to observe the interview."

The Denver detective glanced at Ryan, whose jaw tightened.

"I'm sorry, that's not—"

"The interrogation room has an adjoining area where we can observe, doesn't it?" Jack interrupted. "We don't want to interfere with the questioning. We just want to observe."

Hunnicutt propped his hands on his hips and twisted his mouth again, dividing a look between Jack and Ryan.

"I told him before we left he wouldn't be allowed access to the interview room, but he insisted on coming."

Detective Hunnicutt appeared to be looking for the most tactful way to tell him to take a hike, when Tracy said, "Isn't it possible that I could have information that would assist in your interview? Or something they say may trigger a memory I'd forgotten, something that might help the investigation."

"If this were an official interrogation, my hands would be tied. I couldn't—" Hunnicutt fell silent and nodded a greeting as another officer passed them in the hall. When they were alone again, he finished. "You can watch from the observation room, but you may not do or say anything to influence the interview of either interviewee. And you will have Officer Grunnel in the room with you at all times." He marched to the next door and opened it.

"Got it." Jack placed a hand at the small of Tracy's back to usher her inside. "Thank you, Detective."

If the enticing presence of Jack's possessive hand at the base of her spine weren't unsettling enough, the sight of her former mother-in-law sitting behind the small table in the interview room, scowling, shook Tracy to the marrow. Irene's hair, a golden brown with subtle highlights, thanks to the help of her hairdresser, was worn swept up in a loose, stylish twist, and she'd accented her aqua silk pantsuit with chunky turquoise jewelry. Despite her advanced years, her cheeks were facelift-smooth and her makeup impeccably painted on. For all her style and attention to her appearance, she radiated a coolness that went beyond her glacial gray eyes.

The balding man in the crisp business suit next to her was equally menacing with his hard jaw and heavy brow over dark eyes. She'd met the Baxters' lawyer on more than one occasion, and each time she saw him, he seemed more intimidating than the last. Hovering at the edge of the crowd at her wedding, meeting with Cliff in their home behind closed doors and reading the terms of Cliff's will after the funeral. She remembered thinking at one point during her marriage that Rampart made Ebenezer Scrooge seem warm and cuddly.

Icy tingles nipped her neck as the ghostlike images flickered in her mind's eye. By sheer force of will, she held the flood of nightmarish memories at bay.

Wiping sweat from her palms onto her slacks, she moved closer to the one-way window.

She could imagine Jack and the uniformed officer in the observation room were both watching her closely, as if she were the suspect with something to hide. Taking a breath and digging up courage, she focused on the activity in the next room.

Detectives Hunnicutt and Colton entered and shook hands cordially with both Irene Baxter and her attorney, Joseph Rampart.

Once introductions were made, Joseph Rampart asked, "Would you mind telling us what this is about? Why have you dragged my clients down here?"

"Certainly. As I explained to Mrs. Baxter when I called her home, there was an incident at a ranch just outside Tulsa, Oklahoma, that we feel Mr. and Mrs. Baxter may be able to help us with."

"I haven't been to Tulsa in years, and neither has my husband! Whatever happened down there, you're barking up the wrong tree," Irene said, then pressed her mouth in a taut line of disapproval.

"I didn't say we thought you were there. As for your husband, we'll let him talk for himself when we interview him."

"About that," Irene snapped, "this business of separating us for questioning, like we were common criminals. It's insulting! I don't see why we couldn't be *interviewed* together." She infused the term with disdain.

"Standard procedure, ma'am. No insult intended," Hunnicutt replied with a patient smile. Hunnicutt pressed a button on the recording device on the table, then pulled out a chair and sat. Ryan remained standing, leaning against the wall by the door with his arms folded over his chest.

"Do you know a woman named Tracy McCain?"

Irene blinked, glanced to her lawyer for a nod of permission to answer, then narrowed her eyes with suspicion. "You know I do. That information is easy enough to obtain."

Tracy shook her head in disbelief. Irene was seeking guidance from Rampart about a question as basic as her acquaintance with her former daughter-in-law?

Hunnicutt rolled up a palm. "Again, just standard procedure. We need your response stated for the record."

Mrs. Baxter shifted her gaze to the recorder and wrinkled her nose in distaste as if the device were a foul-smelling baby diaper. "Tracy was my son's wife." She paused a moment before adding, "Though apparently the marriage meant so little to her, she didn't deign to keep my son's name after he died."

Tracy tensed. Irene was partially correct. Tracy had reverted to her maiden name after Cliff's death, but not because she didn't respect the sanctity of marriage. She had simply wanted a fresh start. She hadn't wanted the reminder of the years of agony that Cliff had put her through.

She glanced at Jack and found him watching her. She opened her mouth as if to defend herself, but before she could, Jack muttered, "Charming woman. Guess I'd change my name back and disassociate myself from her, too."

An odd warmth spread through Tracy's midsection. Jack had probably meant the comment as a throwaway, but Tracy appreciated the support underlying the snark. Pressing a hand to her swirling stomach, she returned her attention to the interview room.

"When's the last time you spoke with Tracy?" Hunnicutt asked.

Mrs. Baxter frowned, glancing to Rampart again. When he inclined his head, she wrinkled her brow in thought. "I don't know. Probably Cliff's funeral. Why?"

Hunnicutt flashed her a wry smile. "Mrs. Baxter, the

way this works is this—I ask the questions, and you give me concise honest answers. All right?"

Rampart sat forward and waggled a finger at Hunnicutt. "There's no need to be patronizing, Detective."

Hunnicutt raised a hand and flashed a quick smile. "My apologies. No offense intended."

Irene lifted her nose and gave a haughty sniff. "Fine. Get on with it then. I don't have all day."

Beside her, Jack grunted.

"Told you," Tracy said softly without looking at the imposing man beside her. Bad enough that his distractingly virile scent filled her nose and teased her with memories of their kiss.

"How would you characterize your relationship with Ms. McCain?" Ryan asked, drawing Irene's hostile gaze.

After consulting Rampart again, she said, "I wouldn't say we have a relationship at all. We were never close when she was married to my son, and I haven't spoken to her since his funeral. As I just said."

Hunnicutt laced his fingers, rested his arms on the table and leaned forward. "Would you say that the two of you are on good terms? Was there any bad blood between you?"

Irene, predictably, glanced to Rampart before she answered. He hesitated, then gave a subtle flick of his fingers. When she spoke, it was clear she was choosing her words carefully. "It was…indifferent. I know that sounds harsh, but—" she shrugged "—I really had very little chance to get to know her before Cliff was murdered." The hand Irene rested on the table fisted, and she drew her shoulders back. "I really don't know what you want me to say, Detective. I can't characterize our relationship because I really had none with her— good or bad."

Hunnicutt made no comment but kept a level gaze

fixed on Mrs. Baxter. When it was clear Irene would add nothing else, Ryan stepped forward and joined the group at the table, straddling a chair he'd turned backward.

"Mrs. Baxter," Ryan said, "yesterday afternoon, someone shot at Tracy McCain while she was visiting my family's ranch outside of Tulsa."

Chapter 14

Tracy swallowed hard, her eyes locked on Irene, and tried to interpret every subtle facial expression and gesture the woman made.

Mrs. Baxter's sculpted eyebrows shot up. Tracy would have sworn she saw the tic of a smug grin at the corners of Irene's mouth, but it was gone so quickly, she couldn't be sure. Or perhaps she was seeing what she expected to see.

Irene sat back in her chair, her eyes darting from one detective to the other before she pressed a hand to her chest, as if remembering the proper response to such news was shock or grief. A deep V furrowed her forehead, and she made the appropriate sounds of dismay in her throat. "Oh, dear. That's terrible! Have you caught the man responsible?"

Ryan kept his expression neutral. "I didn't say that the shooter was a man."

Irene flinched, then glaring at Ryan, snapped, "Surely you're not implying that you think I did it! I told you I haven't been in Tulsa for years. I was home all day yesterday. You can ask my husband."

Hunnicutt nodded. "We will. Were you with your husband all day yesterday?"

"Yes." Once again, Mrs. Baxter stiffened in the chair and lifted her chin. "We are well-respected members of this community," she added tapping the table top with a salon-perfect French-manicured fingernail. "It is preposterous to think that either of us could be responsible for anything as heinous as murder."

"No one is accusing you of murder, ma'am," Ryan said calmly. "In fact, I never said Ms. McCain was killed."

Irene shifted nervously on the chair, dividing a confused look between Ryan and Detective Hunnicutt. "Yes, you did."

"No," Ryan said shaking his head, "I said someone shot at her."

"I—" Mrs. Baxter shot a dubious glance to her lawyer.

"We can rewind the recording," Hunnicutt said, nodding to the gadget on the table, "and play it back for you, if you'd like proof." He scratched his chin and pulled a face that said he was intrigued. "I do find it interesting, though, that you assume that she was dead."

Irene turned back to glare at the two detectives, her chest heaving with indignation. "Do not play word games with me, Detectives, twisting everything I say, or this *interview* is over!"

"I've also noticed she has yet to ask how you are, how badly hurt you might be," Jack said, voicing Tracy's thoughts. He cut a side glance to her, and she met his gaze. Even in the dimly lit room, his eyes held a bright gleam that stole her breath.

"I know. Should I be offended that she doesn't care?"

In the interrogation room, Irene divided a hard look

between Ryan and Detective Hunnicutt. "So? Is she or isn't she dead?"

This time it was Officer Grunnel, in the observation room with them, that scoffed and muttered under his breath. "Cold."

Tracy shivered. She'd never known just how unfeeling and selfish Irene Baxter was until today. She shouldn't be surprised. She was Cliff's mother, after all. She felt more than saw Jack shift closer to her. She welcomed the warmth as his body heat wrapped around her in the confined, overly air-conditioned room.

"She survived the shooting," Ryan said cryptically, leaving it to Irene to inquire—or not—about Tracy's exact condition. Her eyebrows twitching and her mouth pinching slightly, Irene chose the latter.

Under normal circumstances, Tracy might have been hurt by the indifference, the lack of compassion shown by her late husband's mother. But things being what they were, she'd expected no more from Mrs. Baxter.

Detective Hunnicutt flipped open the file folder he'd brought in with him and pulled out the police sketch of the shooter. As he slid the sheet across the table, he asked, "Do you recognize this man?"

Irene dragged the picture closer for a better look, and Tracy noticed the woman's hand was shaking. Her ex-mother-in-law schooled her face as she examined the drawing. "I've never seen that man before in my life."

"Are you sure?" Hunnicutt asked. "Take your time."

"I said I don't know him." She shoved the picture back across the table and folded her arms across her bosom, shaking her head. "This is a waste of my time. Why are you asking me about this?" She focused her attention on Detective Colton, her thin eyebrows dipping low. "What did that girl say about us that brought you all the way up here?"

"By 'that girl,' may I assume you are referring to Ms. McCain?" Ryan asked.

"Of course, Tracy! Isn't she the reason we're here? Because someone tried to kill her?"

"Once again, ma'am," Ryan said, "you're putting words in our mouth. Why do you assume the shooter was trying to kill her?"

Mrs. Baxter's lips pursed, and she shifted in her chair, clearly growing agitated. "A natural assumption, gentlemen. Why else would someone shoot at her?"

Ryan lifted a shoulder. "There are as many reasons for a person's actions as there are people on this planet, ma'am. Maybe he simply wanted to scare her. Or he could have been a hunter who mistook what he saw and fired recklessly."

Mrs. Baxter's nostrils flared as she took a deep, aggrieved breath. "If you want to dicker over semantics, Detective, I suggest you do it on your own time. Either charge me with something or let me go home."

Hunnicutt rocked back in his chair and raised both hands. "Hey, like I said, you're not under arrest. You may leave any time."

"Good." She turned to her lawyer with a nod. "Joseph."

Irene and Rampart rose to their feet, and Tracy's heartbeat scrambled. "That's it?" She jerked a panicked look to Officer Grunnel for confirmation. "But they didn't—"

"Of course," Ryan said in the interview room, drawing Tracy's attention back to the one-way window. "I'd have thought you'd be more interested in helping find the person responsible for firing on a member of your family."

Irene paused, her hand on the strap of the purse she'd hung on the back of her chair.

"I know I want him caught and locked up. See—" Ryan leaned forward, his expression grave "—the man put my nephew at risk, too. Seth is only five, and I love him like my own son."

Tracy sensed the tightening of Jack's muscles as he drew his spine taller and his breath caught. A quick side glance to the spasming tendons at his jaw confirmed the tension gripping him. Without really thinking about what she was doing or why, Tracy reached for his hand and curled her fingers around his. He gave her a brief startled look before squeezing her hand and returning his gaze to his brother.

"I want the man responsible for the shooting," Detective Colton was saying, "if only to make him pay for scaring Seth and endangering an innocent little boy."

Irene's knuckles whitened as she gripped the back of the chair, as if she were realizing how callous she'd appear if she dismissed Seth's involvement in what had happened. Even if she could discount Tracy's. "You didn't mention the little boy before. Was the boy hurt?"

Ryan shook his head. "Not badly. A few scrapes as they scrambled for cover. Tracy protected him, for which my family will be eternally grateful."

Jack angled his head toward Tracy, and she met his gaze. His eyes were softer, reflecting a warmth that said he echoed his brother's sentiments. He gave her fingers another pulse-like squeeze, and something airy and magical fluttered in her chest. After being on the receiving end of Jack's hard-edged suspicion for days, this kinder, gentler Jack touched a part of Tracy that had been left raw and aching after Cliff's abuse.

"Not that Ms. McCain deserved to be frightened or put at risk herself," Ryan added. He waited a beat then stood like the others in the interview room. "We still need to talk to your husband, of course. If you would be so kind as to wait here, we'll let you know when we are through questioning him."

After whispering something to his client, Rampart straightened his tie and followed Hunnicutt to the door. Ryan and Rampart trailed out behind Hunnicutt, leaving Irene by herself. She pulled the chair back out and dropped into the seat with a huff and a glower at the closed door.

"I want to watch the interview of Mr. Baxter, too," Jack said, cutting a look to Officer Grunnel. "Will they question him in this same room?"

"No, I'll take you to the new observation room across the hall in a minute. Detective Hunnicutt didn't want the Baxters to see you or know you were on the premises."

"All right." Jack slipped his hand from Tracy's and moved it to her back, as if to show her out to the hall.

But Tracy's gaze stayed locked on Irene, fascinated by the woman's behavior once she thought she was alone. Mrs. Baxter rubbed her temples, her face puckered in an angry sneer. "Of all the incompetent..." she muttered before letting her hand drop to the table with a grunt of frustration.

Incompetent? Tracy puzzled over Irene's grumbled word choice. Who did she think was not performing up to standard? Rampart? Detectives Colton and Hunnicutt?

With an eerie sense of intuition, a chill slithered through her and pooled in her gut. "The shooter."

Jack hesitated by the door and turned back to her. "Did you say something?"

Tracy's throat felt dry, and she had to force herself to swallow before she could speak. "I said, 'the shooter.'" She flattened her hand over her jittery stomach. "After your brother and Detective Hunnicutt left the room, Mrs.

Baxter mumbled something. It sounded like she said, 'Of all the incompetent…'"

Tracy paused to draw a shuddering breath, and Jack walked back to her, his eyes narrowed and gleaming with an intensity that arrowed to her core. "And?"

"Well, I was trying to figure out who she could be talking about. It seemed unlikely she meant Mr. Rampart or the detectives. And when I thought about her reaction to the news that I hadn't been killed, I just…I don't know."

Jack angled his head to glare through the one-way glass at Mrs. Baxter.

"I'm just speculating, of course, but I had the weirdest feeling come over me, this odd insight that she meant the shooter." She rubbed the spot at her temple where her pulse was pounding, a throbbing headache building.

Officer Grunnel stepped closer. "Are you sure that's what she said?"

"Well, no. Like I said, she was kind of mumbling." Tracy glanced through the window to the interrogation room again. Mrs. Baxter continued to frown and tap her fingers restlessly on the tabletop. "But it sure sounded like that. I'm almost sure I heard her say 'incompetent.'"

Jack faced Grunnel. "Can we use this?"

"Not officially. It would be considered hearsay. But I'll let the detectives know what she heard, and perhaps they can use it to guide the conversation in new directions." Officer Grunnel returned to the door and stuck his head into the hall. He glanced back at Tracy and Jack and held his hand up. "Wait here a moment."

The officer stepped into the hall, closing the door behind him, and Tracy chafed the goose bumps that had risen on her arms.

"How are you holding up?" Jack asked, moving close and rubbing his wide palms along her arms. Rather than calm the jitters in her gut, his touch simply transformed the uneasy jangle. She flashed back to the last time he'd held her close—to the evening before, when he'd kissed the breath from her.

"I'm all right." She walked into his embrace, wrapping her arms around his waist. He pressed a light kiss to her forehead. "This is all just so surreal. Could Cliff's parents really be behind the attacks? Is it about money? I'll gladly give them Cliff's life insurance and savings. I don't want it."

Rather than answer her rhetorical questions, Jack tucked her under his chin and rubbed her back in small circles. A calm sank into her slowly, lulled by his caress and the security of his arms around her. After a moment, he moved a hand to her cheek and angled her face up to his. His intent blazed in his eyes, even before he dipped his head.

Heat curled through her blood, and she rose on her toes to meet his kiss. The hum of the busy police department beyond the closed door faded as she centered her attention on Jack. On his fingers threading through her hair. On his skillful lips possessing hers.

"So, new plan of attack," Ryan said as he burst through the door, then stopped short when he found his brother in a lip-lock.

Tracy tensed and would have jerked out of the embrace if not for Jack's firm grip cradling her skull with one hand and the small of her back with his other.

Lifting his eyebrows, Ryan sent them an amused grin. "Should I come back later? Or perhaps rent you a hotel room?"

Jack released Tracy and met his brother's quip with a scowl. "Save the jokes. What's the new plan?"

"In light of what Tracy heard the missus say, we're

going to go fishing again with her but using new bait," Ryan said, still eyeing his brother with a speculative gleam.

Movement in her peripheral vision caught Tracy's attention as Hunnicutt entered the interview room and took a seat at the table. "I've just talked with your husband and, well…I have one or two more questions for you, ma'am."

Mrs. Baxter gave Hunnicutt a peeved glare. "What now?"

The Denver detective made a show of shifting uncomfortably in his chair. "Well, you see…" He rubbed his temples and sighed.

"What is it? What did my husband say?"

Tracy stepped closer to the one-way glass to follow the exchange with rapt attention. She felt more than saw Jack step up behind her.

In the next room, Hunnicutt bowed his head and groaned. "I tell you, ma'am, there are a lot of things about my job that I don't like, but the two worst have to be making that house call to let someone know their loved one has died, and letting someone know a trusted friend or relative has betrayed them."

Irene flinched, and her face visibly paled. "What are you saying? What did my husband tell you?"

Hunnicutt shifted awkwardly again and sent her a frown. "Before we get into what your husband is saying—" he paused and gave Mrs. Baxter an almost apologetic look "—is there anything else you'd like to tell me about Ms. McCain or the attacks on her?"

Irene blinked rapidly and clutched her purse to her chest like a shield. "He's blaming me, isn't he?" Her face darkened. "That rat bastard… How dare he?" She raised a shaking hand to her throat. "I-I may have made the arrangements, b-but it was *his* idea."

A chill ran down Tracy's spine. Had Hunnicutt just gotten a confession?

Beside her, Tracy heard Ryan chuckle. "Brilliant."

"What?" Jack asked.

"Her husband's being even more tight-lipped than she was. Hunnicutt never said her husband rolled over on her, she just assumed that from his little speech and his little uncomfortable act. He played on her guilty conscience…"

"What was his idea?" Hunnicutt asked.

"Hiring someone to get rid of her." Irene's expression soured, and she leaned toward Hunnicutt, clearly caught up in defending herself. "She's the reason our Cliff was murdered. If the ungrateful bitch hadn't left him, the car accident would never have happened, and he wouldn't have been in that miserable prison where he was murdered. An inmate may have killed Cliff, but it was all Tracy's fault…and she has to pay!" Irene's deep, agitated breathing matched the thudding beats of Tracy's heart as she stared through the one-way glass in disbelief.

Hunnicutt nodded sympathetically and slid the picture of the gunman back toward her. "Okay. Is this the man you hired to get rid of Ms. McCain? Who is he?"

The woman barely glanced at the sketch. "You'll never find him. We hired him because he's the best. He stays under the radar and always completes his assignment. He's stealthy and thorough and very lethal."

"His name?" Hunnicutt repeated.

Irene lifted a shoulder, her voice bolder now as if she were relieved to have the confession off her chest. "I don't know. That's part of how he operates. No one knows his name. Our meeting was arranged through…" She cleared her throat. "Mutual associates."

Tracy cut her glance to Jack, and his expression said his thoughts were where hers were. The connections to organized crime Jack had discovered through his digging into financial holdings and public records.

"I simply think of him as The Wolf," Irene said.

"The wolf?" Hunnicutt repeated.

"Well, look at him." She flicked a finger toward the sketch. "Don't you think it fits?"

Hunnicutt didn't respond. Instead, he leaned forward and narrowed his eyes on Mrs. Baxter. "Can you have your…'mutual friends' arrange another meeting? To call off the hit? It would go a long way toward winning favor with the powers that be."

As if realizing for the first time that she had incriminated herself, Irene's eyes widened, and she sat back in the chair, once again clutching her purse against her as if it could protect her. "I've said too much. I want my lawyer, and I want to cut a deal."

Hunnicutt's chin dropped to his chest as if knowing he'd gotten all he'd get from Irene for the time being.

"I'll tell you what you want to know," the woman added, "but I want a guarantee of no jail time."

"Bingo," Ryan said. "If you'll excuse me, I need to make a call to the Denver district attorney." He exited the observation room, spilling light from the corridor into the dark space.

Tracy shivered, and Jack enveloped her in his warm arms from behind, whispering into her ear. "We'll get him, Tracy. I won't rest until we catch the man who shot at you, and I promise that the bastard won't get near you again."

"You won't stop him. I can't stop him." Upon learning his wife had cracked, George Baxter had started pouring out his guts, as if competing to be more forthcoming and win the better plea deal. "The Wolf will not stop until Tracy is dead. I have no way to reach him, and since he wasn't going to get the final payment until the job was done, he's all the more motivated to finish his assignment."

His assignment. Jack's gut churned. Meaning to murder Tracy and anyone else that got in his way, including little boys.

He glanced to Tracy, who had her arms wrapped around her middle as if to hold herself together. "Come on, Tracy. Let's get out of here."

She sent him an anxious look. "But they're not finished questioning the Baxters."

"Ryan will fill us in. We know the worst of it. Let me take you home." He held his hand out to her, and after a brief hesitation, she placed her cold fingers in his hand.

Her icy fingers worried him, because they spoke to her mental state, the stress and fear she had to be experiencing. Once the shock of learning her in-laws were behind the attack on her had passed, she'd grown increasingly pale and distraught looking.

Not that he could blame her. Knowing a professional assassin with connections to organized crime was gunning for her had shaken him to the marrow as well. And though Hunnicutt and Ryan had been grilling Irene and George Baxter for hours now, their story hadn't changed. The Wolf was invisible, unreachable, in the wind. And he wouldn't stop until he'd killed Tracy.

Chapter 15

Over my dead body. As he escorted Tracy out of the Denver police-department building and hailed a cab, Jack gritted his teeth. He swore silently to do whatever was necessary to keep Tracy safe. The Baxters might not know how to reach The Wolf and call him off, but he had faith in Ryan's detective skills. He and his team at the Tulsa PD would find this ghost and bring him in. And until they did, Jack would protect his family.

A jolt rippled through Jack when he realized that he included Tracy in that category. His *family*. She was Seth's cousin, so that made her family of sorts, but…

He balled his fists and exhaled deeply. Who was he kidding? The kiss they'd shared last night had rocked him to his roots. He hadn't felt a connection to a woman this strong, this pure and life changing since…since… hell, *ever*.

He was in unchartered waters, and that scared the hell

out of him. Because if loving Laura and having her leave him had hurt as badly as it had, how much would it cost him to lose Tracy? And how had he grown so attached to her in such a short time?

On the drive from the Tulsa airport back to the Lucky C, Jack revisited the idea of her moving from the main house to the old family house with him and Seth.

She nodded, too tired to fight him on the topic any further. "I'll move. In the morning. Tonight I just want to crawl into bed, pull the covers over my head and sleep for about twenty hours."

Jack reached for her hand and rubbed his thumb over her knuckles. "I know that today has been mentally and physically exhausting, but in light of what we've learned about who's after you, that he's a professional killer, I want somebody I can trust with your safety close to you at all times."

She massaged the growing headache in her temple with her free hand. "Don't you trust Brett for that?"

"Yeah, but I talked with Brett while you were in the ladies' room at the airport. He has Seth down at the bunkhouse, and he plans to sleep down there. Apparently Abra was complaining about the noise Seth was making, and she asked him to get Seth out from under foot."

Abra's attitude startled her, and she sent Jack a questioning look.

He shrugged. "This is the woman who spent most of my childhood in Europe, leaving me to be raised by nannies and Big J. She loves her family in her own way, but she has a very low threshold for noise and energetic children."

Tracy had suspected as much of Abra, and she experienced another pang of sympathy for Seth. He truly lacked a maternal influence in his life.

"If I have to," Jack said, leveling a hard stare at her, "I'll come in and pack you up myself. But I want you where I can protect you. Starting tonight."

She should have been annoyed by his high handedness, but in this case, Tracy appreciated Jack's concern and determination. The idea of the man they called The Wolf hunting her chilled her to the marrow. If she were honest, she was more than a little nervous about staying in the large mansion. The two miles from the main house to Jack's might as well have been one hundred. It was too far for him to reach her in time if there was trouble.

Jack parked his truck in the circular drive in front of the main house, and together they headed in to collect her belongings. The house was quiet and dark, evidence that Abra and Big J had already headed to their rooms for the evening. Greta was still in Oklahoma City, and Edith generally kept to herself after dinner, so the church-like silence wasn't surprising. But it did feel lonely…and somewhat eerie.

As Tracy trudged upstairs, keeping one hand on the railing for balance and putting one foot in front of the other with effort, she was glad Jack had insisted she move to the old ranch house tonight. The mansion, for all its grandeur, didn't have the warmth and sense of security that Jack's house did.

The throb of fatigue and stress that pounded in her skull turned her thoughts to the medicine bottle of Lorcet on her nightstand. Though she'd generally avoided taking the stronger painkillers Eric had prescribed, tonight she thought she might need the more powerful drug. The wound on her shoulder ached, and she was still sore from horseback riding and her tumble into the street earlier that week. But she couldn't complain. Not only was she still alive after two attempts on her life, but she was blessed to be getting to know Laura's son and his family. Lucky to have Jack's protection.

Despite the threat that hovered over her, she was free of Cliff's brutality. Laura had paid the highest price to give her that freedom, and Tracy could never take it for granted.

Jack placed a hand low on her back, as if he sensed she was struggling to mount the long flight of stairs. She recalled the last time they'd taken these stairs together, the way he'd swept her into his arms and cradled her to his broad chest. The memory caused a sweet quiver to race through her, and in response, Jack's fingers pressed more firmly against her skin.

"Tracy?"

She gave him a quick smile. "I'm fine. Just…not used to so many stairs."

When they reached the guest room, Jack slid her suitcase and toiletries bag out from under the bed. He handed her the smaller bag. "I'll start on your clothes while you pack in the bathroom."

She took the travel case from him and glanced to the small table beside the bed. Her novel was there, along with her hand lotion and a glass of water. But no pill bottle.

Tracy frowned. Had she moved the Lorcet to the bathroom and forgotten? Moving into the adjoining bathroom, she set the toiletries case on the counter top and scanned the area around the sink for the painkiller. She began packing her toothpaste, makeup and skin cleansers but still didn't find the bottle of Lorcet. She was puzzling over this when she noticed the small bag of jewelry items she'd brought with her was unzipped and had clearly been riffled.

Scowling, she checked the contents and discovered a

few of her better pieces were missing, including the two-karat diamond engagement ring Cliff had given her—no loss sentimentally but still quite valuable.

"Jack, have you ever had an issue with Edith stealing from the family?" she asked as she returned to the bedroom.

He raised his head from his careful work tucking her socks in the corners of the suitcase. "Edith? No. She's like family." He drew his eyebrows lower. "Why?"

"Well…some of my things are missing."

"Missing?" His expression darkened. "Like what?"

"Jewelry. And my Lorcet pills." She bit her bottom lip. "I'm not accusing her, but…well, who else could have taken them?"

He inhaled and slowly released a deep breath, stepping close to her. "I don't know, but I promise we'll get to the bottom of it in the morning."

After pressing a kiss to her forehead, he moved back to the dresser and opened the top drawer. Where she kept her panties and bras. An awkward flash of heat swamped her, and her pulse danced a nervous jig.

Jack, too, seemed caught off guard, and he stood for a moment simply staring at the collection of colorful lace bras and plain cotton bikini undies. Not until he reached for one of the frillier bras did it register that the undergarments were in an unkempt tumble.

"Jack," she said, catching her breath.

He paused with the pink bra dangling from his fingers and sent her a gaze, dark with desire.

She had to swallow twice to work loose the tangled knot of apprehension and lust that made strange bedfellows in her throat. Talking to him while he held her delicates in his callused hand left her off balance, but…

"My clothes…I—" she pointed at the rumpled disarray

"—I always keep things folded and in neat stacks. Someone's been rummaging in there. I'm sure of it."

Her first thought was that The Wolf had been in her room, searching for something or laying a trap. Planting a threat.

Clearly that was where Jack's thoughts went, as well, because he dropped the bra in order to conduct his own search of the drawer. After digging through the pink satin, lilac silk and white cotton garments, he turned a narrow-eyed look toward her. A muscle in his jaw twitched as he gritted his teeth and clamped his hands on her shoulders. "I assure you, whoever did this was not part of the house staff. Big J screens the help carefully, and most of them have been with the family since I was a kid. I don't know how anyone got up here unseen, but this only confirms my decision to get you out of here. I want you in the old house. With me."

With me. The emphasis he placed on the last words was underscored by the blaze in his blue eyes. His intensity stirred a tremor at her core. Before she could gather a coherent reply, he dragged her closer and crushed her mouth under his.

Her body reacted instantly, a fiery yearning flooding her limbs and melting her bones. When her knees buckled, she leaned into him, clutching his arms to steady herself. Her fatigue fled as he repositioned his lips to draw more deeply on hers, tracing the line of her mouth with the tip of his tongue.

A half whimper, half moan escaped her throat, and he answered with a hungry growl. Sliding his hands to her thighs, he lifted her so that her aching sex rode the thick ridge under his fly. In a couple of shuffling steps, he was at the edge of the guest bed. He hesitated briefly, giving her time to protest, then glancing at the door as if check to make sure it was closed.

Whether her defenses were low after the shocks and terror she'd experienced in recent days or whether Jack's kiss simply had her passionately mesmerized, a need burned in Tracy's blood unlike anything she'd experienced before. She wanted Jack Colton. Needed him. Here. Now.

She plowed her fingers into his thick, unruly hair and kissed him with a fervor that left no doubt what she wanted from him. Placing an arm across her back, he supported her as they tumbled to the mattress. She hooked her legs around his hips and gasped as he flipped up her skirt and simulated the sex act despite their clothes. The scrape of his jean-clad erection against her sensitized skin shot firebrands through her.

Jack slipped a hand under her bottom and squeezed. His intimate touch spun tendrils of pure pleasure through her, electrifying every nerve ending. His kiss was alternately demanding, then tender. He'd nip her bottom lip, then caress the fragile skin with a soft caress of his tongue. She'd never been kissed so thoroughly, so seductively. Her head spun, and she curled her fingers into his back. She had the sense of falling, of hurtling at a gallop over a cliff, and she clung to Jack for dear life.

When he skimmed his hand under her loosened blouse to her back, his fingertips strumming her ticklish spine, she sucked in a sharp hissing breath through her teeth. "Jack…"

"Tracy…I promise you," he murmured against her lips, "my intentions for taking you to my house are to protect you, not to get you into my bed." He feathered nibbling kisses across her cheek and down her throat, pausing at the V of her collar. "If this isn't what you want, tell me now. " He glanced up at her with eyes hooded with desire and a bright sincerity. "I would never take advantage of you."

His consideration was so unlike Cliff's merciless domination of her, she couldn't speak for a moment. Tears prickled her eyes, and her heart swelled with affection for her cowboy protector. "Yes. I want this. I want…you."

Rather than fumble for the words, she raised her mouth to his and anchored his head close with a splayed hand at his nape.

With a groan of satisfaction, Jack stroked his hand up her torso, setting her skin on fire. When he reached her bra, he dipped his fingers under the silky cup and covered her breast with his palm. She arched her back, savoring his touch and begging silently for more. His thumb flicked her nipple, while his mouth ravaged hers. While he rocked his body against hers, she groped with the buttons on his shirt, the zipper of his jeans.

Over the drumming of her heartbeat in her ears, she heard a loud thump from the wall behind them. Jack seemed not to notice, so she dismissed the sound and fought Jack's shirt out from his jeans. She found the hot, smooth flesh of his back and scraped her fingernails lightly over the ridges of muscle and sinew.

More noises reached her through the wall. A female voice. Abra's. Made sense. Abra's master suite was the next door down from her guest room.

Tracy tried not to let the voice distract her, but…

Something in Abra's voice disturbed Tracy. Although the words were indistinct, Tracy heard something in Abra's timbre that woke old demons. A note of confusion. Of *fear*. The word rippled through her as if an apparition had just passed through her. When a chilling sense of premonition choked her next breath, she stiffened and pulled away from Jack's kiss.

He lifted his head and frowned down at her. "Tracy? What's—"

A shriek rent the stillness. The sound of shattering glass. Abra screamed again, louder, her voice more horrified. "No! Please, no!"

Chapter 16

Jack shoved off the bed in an instant, scrambling to right his clothes.

Flashes of memory turned Tracy's insides to liquid. She saw Cliff hovering over her with a wine bottle raised. She felt the crashing blow of the decanter, saw the crimson liquid spread around her, mixing with her blood. She smelled the sweet port…

As Jack dashed for the door, more noises came from Abra's suite, shuffling and crashes.

"Mother!" Jack shouted as he disappeared into the hall.

Tracy's breath panted shallowly, panicked.

Past and present tangled. Adrenaline pounded in her ears, and she battled down the surge of bile that climbed her throat.

"Mother!" Jack's voice rang with agitation and dark concern, jolting Tracy from her paralyzing memories. Smoothing her skirt and blouse into place, she ran to the hall where she met Big J. His bathrobe loosely tied around him and hair mussed from sleep, he lumbered from his bedroom and scrubbed a hand over his face. "What the devil is going on out here?"

"It…it's Abra." She swallowed past the constriction blocking her windpipe. "Something's happened to her. I—"

"Call an ambulance!" Jack shouted from Abra's room, and Tracy watched the color leak from Big J's face.

"Abra? What—" Big J pushed past Tracy, hurrying into his wife's suite. "Abra!"

Tracy sucked in a reviving breath, knowing she'd already wasted precious seconds with her private fears and hesitation. Adrenaline fueled her feet as she hurried back to her room to find her phone and, hands trembling, tapped the screen to call 911.

Phone to her ear, she rushed to Abra's room and gasped when she saw the destruction. Abra's room had been violently trashed, mirrors broken, drawers emptied, furniture toppled and pillows slashed and gutted. In the midst of the chaos, Abra lay crumpled on the floor, face down, with blood pooling next to her head. Jack knelt beside her, gentling probing the wound on her head, pressing a strip of bedsheet to the gash on her scalp to staunch the flow of blood.

The emergency operator answered, asking for the nature of her call and her location.

"We need an ambulance. At the Colton ranch…the Lucky C…" Tracy's voice cracked when she spoke. She racked her muddled brain for the address until Big J snatched the phone from her hand and bellowed into the phone.

"My wife's been attacked! She's dying! Get someone out here. Now!" He spouted the address then demanded again that the ambulance, the police…anyone available, needed to hurry.

Spiders of dread skittered down Tracy's spine. Abra had been attacked. In her own bedroom. Ice filled Tracy's veins. Was no place safe? Was there no place sacred, private, secure…

A new horrifying thought occurred to her. Could the assailant still be there? The master suite was on the second floor, and they'd seen no one in the hallway…

Tracy swept her gaze around the room. She searched the vast room and every shadowed corner. No one was lurking there, but the French doors to her balcony stood ajar. The sheer curtains rippled in the warm night breeze.

Abra's suite was next door to her guest room. Had she been the real target and The Wolf entered the wrong room? Or had Abra discovered the assassin as he made his way toward Tracy's room and paid the price for the chance encounter?

Tracy knew the odds that this was a random attack were low. Nausea swamped her along with the guilt of having brought this calamity on her hostess.

"Abra!" Big J's pained tone shot to Tracy's core.

She held her breath as she crossed the floor to join the men. Abra lay motionless, her head bleeding and red marks swelling where she'd clearly been savagely struck.

"Tracy!" Jack's grave tone tripped through her. "Wake Edith. Speed dial five. Have her call the bunkhouse and alert Brett that there's an assailant on the grounds. And tell her to call Eric and have him meet us at the hospital." He shoved his cell phone at her, and she noticed the tremble in his hand. Not that she blamed him. Her whole body shook.

Tracy's heart contracted with the notion that she could be the reason her hostess had been hurt.

Big J glanced up at her. "Did you see anything? Who did this?"

"I don't know. I was in my room—" *About to make love to Jack...* A fresh wave of guilt rolled through her, and she took a shuddering breath. "I heard her talking to someone. She sounded upset. Then she screamed and—"

"And?" Big J prompted, his face pale. He still held her cell to his ear, his grip on the phone so tight his fingers were bloodless.

Tracy shook her head. "I don't know." She tried to swallow, but her mouth had grown arid. "I'm sorry. This is my fault. It must have been The Wolf...coming for me...I—"

Jack jerked his chin up and shook his head. "Don't blame yourself."

But how could she not? Every fiber of her being, her every instinct told her the attack on Abra had been intended for her.

"A wolf? What the hell are you talking about?" Big J asked.

"I'll explain later," Jack said.

The whine of distant sirens pierced the night, and Big J turned his stormy blue eyes to Tracy. "Will you go out front to meet the ambulance? Show them up? I don't..." He drew a shuddering breath. "I don't want to leave Abra."

She gave him a tiny nod and hurried to the stairs. Meeting the EMTs was the least she could do considering her certainty that her presence at the Lucky C had brought the lethal threat of The Wolf to the ranch residents. For that, she could never forgive herself.

Jack held Tracy against him, absorbing her tremors as Abra was put in the waiting ambulance. She flinched as the bay doors were slammed closed. He had to admit, the attack on his mother had him rattled, too. But he couldn't believe this was the work of a professional assassin. A pro like The Wolf would have no reason to search Tracy's or Abra's rooms, to steal from them and risk leaving trace evidence that would lead back to him. The Wolf would have realized quickly Abra was not Tracy and gotten away unnoticed. Wouldn't he?

But what he'd told Tracy was the truth. The household staff was trustworthy. This theft and attack must have been an outside job. But who? And why? Who would have a reason to hurt Abra, to steal Tracy's painkillers and jewelry and search for Lord-knows-what in Abra's suite?

Leading her by the elbow, Jack pulled Tracy back into the house and off to a corner of the foyer, away from the buzz of police officers searching the premises. He smoothed a loose wisp of her hair back from her face, tucking the silky strands behind her ear. "I think I'm going to fix myself a stiff drink. Can I get you something?"

She shook her head slowly, looking dazed, devastated.

Framing her face with his hands, he kissed the bridge of her nose. "This wasn't your fault."

"But I—"

"This *wasn't* your fault," he repeated, firming his grip. "Even if it turns out The Wolf did this, you can't blame yourself. Blame the cretin who attacked my mother. Blame the Baxters for hiring the bastard. Hell, blame *me* for being so focused on making love to you that I didn't realize what was happening in the next room until too late."

He paused and inhaled slowly, his gut quivering at the memory. The sweet taste of her kisses, the satiny feel of her skin and tantalizing whisper of her panting breaths had entranced him. Worked him to a fevered frenzy, wanting only to bury himself inside her. Even now his body quaked with unspent passion and need that he forced aside in deference to the more serious matters at hand. He rested his forehead against hers and said in a rasping murmur, "But do *not* blame yourself."

She bobbed her chin in agreement, but her expression said she was unconvinced. The bleak look in her eyes and uncharacteristically wan color of her cheeks told the story of her fatigue and stress. The sooner he could get her away from the main house for some rest, the better. But they'd been warned not to leave the area until the police dismissed them.

"I'm going to get that drink now and call to check on Seth. Why don't you sit down in the living room? You look ready to drop."

Her eyes widened and her lips parted at his mention of Seth, but before she could say anything, a police officer approached them and cleared his throat.

"I was told you two were the first on the scene. We need to take a full statement from each of you for the report."

Reluctantly, Jack released her, and he nodded to the officer. "Yes. Fine."

But he wasn't fine at all with letting Tracy go. He wanted to hold her until the pink glow returned to her cheeks, until the fear left her eyes…until he could be certain she was completely safe. As she followed the officer into the next room, she cast a glance over her shoulder that said her wishes echoed his.

The two of them were separated for questioning, much the way Irene and George Baxter had been earlier today. Basic procedure, he knew, but he didn't like it.

Ryan had arrived shortly after Jack's interview started, but his involvement, for now, was limited to observation. Jack could see Ryan's edginess, though. He sensed his brother's desire to dive into the investigation from the way he paced the floor and gritted his teeth, fire leaping in his gaze.

The police interviews lasted about thirty minutes, and when they were allowed to leave, Jack wasted no time collecting the last of Tracy's possessions from the guest room and trundling her down to the old homestead.

Eric had called from the hospital to report that Abra's condition was dire. Her doctors had decided to put her in a medically induced coma, giving her body time to heal the head wound while protecting her brain from further stress and damage. Eric had tried to get Big J to return to the ranch and rest, but he'd refused. Brett, too, had stayed at the hospital at Abra's bedside.

Due to the late hour, Seth was allowed to finish the night sleeping in Edith's quarters on the first floor of the main house.

After parking behind the house and unloading Tracy's suitcases from the truck bed, Jack led her in the back door, through the mudroom, piled high with Seth's dirty clothes and boots, and into the kitchen.

"Can I get you anything to eat?" He waved a hand toward his refrigerator. "We never got any dinner earlier."

"No," she said, her voice little more than a sigh. "I just want to go to bed." She heard the sudden catch in his breath and knew immediately where his thoughts had gone. Despite the tragic turn of events tonight, her mind had not strayed far from thoughts of the intimacy she'd shared with Jack in the guest room. Or where things would have led if Abra hadn't been attacked.

And now they were alone in his house...

"Jack, I…" She wet her lips, not sure what she wanted to tell him, but knowing something should be said about the new direction their relationship had taken. Did she want to sleep with Jack? Yes. Definitely.

Could she give herself to him and not put her heart at risk? Definitely not. Was Jack worth a broken heart? She studied the rugged lines of his square jaw, met the concern for her that burned in his bright green eyes and remembered the loving devotion he showed his son. A tender ache flowed through her, twisting a knot in her chest that stole her breath. Oh, yes. Jack was worth any pain she might experience down the road.

Drawing her shoulders back, she tried again. "About what happened earlier…when we…"

Dropping her bags with a thump, Jack closed the distance between them in two steps. He cradled the back of her head with one large splayed hand and angled her head up. Whispering her name, he bowed his head and kissed her gently. His lips were warm, their caress toe curling and sweet. Then he released her and stepped back, lifting her suitcases again.

"Follow me." He turned and strode toward the stairs.

Follow him? Oh, yes. To the ends of the earth. She was in deep. So deep it frightened her a bit. Jack Colton was so…very…

He was just *so very*.

Her pulse thundered in her ears and, moving like an automaton, she fell in step behind him. He showed her upstairs to a room at the far end of the hallway and laid her suitcase on top of a four-poster double bed with an ivory eyelet bedspread. Tracy sent an encompassing glance around the surprisingly feminine room and set her purse on the oak dresser.

"You should like this place. Laura decorated it, and I never saw any point in changing anything," Jack said.

Tracy jerked a startled glance toward Jack. She shouldn't be so surprised to learn that Laura had put her fingerprint on the guest room. What surprised her was that Jack hadn't seen fit to erase the traces of his ex. She cast a fresh eye to the room appreciating the feminine touches. A sky-blue and mint-green quilt was folded at the foot of the bed and small pillows trimmed with coordinating ribbons adorned the top. Sheer ivory curtains framed the windows, and dried flower arrangements sat atop the chest of drawers and bedside table. A set of pictures featuring turn-of-the-century women enjoying a picnic hung on one wall and a mounted piece of needlepoint in a floral design was displayed next to the window.

Tracy felt a tug at her heart, and a lump swelled in her throat. Standing in that bedroom, seeing all of the personal touches her cousin had chosen, she felt closer to Laura than she had in many months. "It's lovely. Thank you."

Jack gave a small nod of acknowledgment before striding to the door. "If you need anything, if there's...*trouble*, my room is across the hall."

Trouble. An image of Abra's body, blood puddling under her head flashed in Tracy's mind. The warmth she'd felt, being surrounded by the pretty things her cousin had chosen for the guest room evaporated in a chill. The terror of being hunted like an animal shimmied through her.

The Wolf will not stop until Tracy is dead. George Baxter's words reverberated in her head, in her heart. Jack was right. She stood little chance of surviving on her own. She'd thought staying on the ranch, having Jack's protection would be enough to keep her safe until The

Wolf was caught, but the attack on Abra changed things. How many more people would be hurt before The Wolf was caught? Was her death the only thing that would save the rest of the Coltons from the assassin's murderous mission?

The next morning, after helping Jack and Kurt Rodgers with ranching chores, Tracy accompanied Jack to the hospital to visit Abra in ICU. Though she wasn't allowed into the room with Jack's mother, she watched through a large window as Jack placed a chaste kiss on his mother's bandaged head.

"I hate seeing her like that."

She turned to find Big J standing behind her clutching a cup of coffee. Dark circles under his eyes stood out from his unnaturally wan skin and haggard expression. The man who'd seemed so robust and jocular when she'd met him at Greta's engagement party a couple weeks earlier, seemed to have aged ten years overnight.

Tracy touched his arm in sympathy. "I'm so sorry. Is there anything I can do?"

He heaved a weary sigh. "Just…pray."

She nodded. "Of course." When he continued to stare blankly through the glass to his wife's bed, Tracy asked quietly, "Big J, have you been here all night?"

He nodded weakly. "I can't leave her. She's…fragile. I have to take care of her…"

Her heart broke for him, knowing there was nothing he could do and how desperately he must have wanted to help her. "I know you want to be close to her, but…you need to rest, too."

He didn't react to her comment. He just stared into near space, swaying on his feet.

"Big J? Do you want to sit—"

"She wasn't happy here, you know. She never really loved the ranch the way I do."

Tracy blinked, not knowing how to respond.

"She spent most of her time in Europe when the boys were small. Recuperating." He sighed forlornly. "She spent more time at home with us after Greta came, but she…wasn't happy. I'd hurt her…with Daniel's mother… but her doctors had her depression under control…and Edith helps manage her on her worst days…"

Tracy shifted her weight, uncomfortable with the deeply personal nature of Big J's comments. He was overtired, rambling, feeling guilty and grief stricken.

Jack emerged from Abra's room and divided a glance between Tracy and his father. "Big J? Are you all right?"

The older man raised a hand and shook his head. "I'm not going home, so don't even start on me."

Tracy gave Jack a worried look that was reflected in Jack's eyes.

"Her doctors have said they intend to keep her in this medically induced coma for several days at least. She won't be coming to—"

"But she'll know if I leave!" Big J insisted. "I won't let her down by leaving her alone." He shuffled toward the window and pressed his hand to the plate glass. "Case closed."

Jack raked his hand through his rumpled hair and blew a deep breath through pursed lips. "Have it your way. I'll let Eric know you're staying, and he can check on you from time to time."

Big J lifted a gaze that flashed with emotion. "I'm not the one who needs attention. Your mother is!"

Jack opened his mouth, then snapped it closed. He jerked a nod and motioned for Tracy to follow him. "If anything changes with her condition, call me at the ranch office. I'm backlogged on paperwork and plan to be there most of the day."

Tracy fell in step beside Jack as he started for the elevator. "That's it? You're going to leave him here?"

"Coltons have their own brand of stubbornness and determination, Tracy, and Big J has Colton obstinacy in spades. I wasn't going to convince him to leave her once he'd made up his mind."

She cast another concerned glance over her shoulder as they arrived at the bank of elevators. "Maybe I should stay with him. He's—"

"No." Jack's tone brooked no argument. "Have you forgotten there's a hired killer after you? You're not leaving my side today."

"But—"

The ding of the elevator bell signaled its arrival. As the doors parted, Greta stepped off, and seeing Jack, she threw her arms around her brother and heaved a broken sob. "Oh, Jack! I got here as fast as I could. Why didn't anyone call me last night? How is she? What happened? Was the intruder caught? What did Eric say about her injuries?" she asked, not even pausing to take a breath.

After giving her a firm hug, Jack gripped his sister's shoulders. "There was nothing you could do last night, so Brett and I decided to wait until this morning to call." He summarized what had happened with the attacker, the police investigation into the break-in and assault, and the doctor's assessment of their mother's condition.

"I'll sit with Big J," Greta said, swiping a tear from her cheek. "I still wish you'd called me last night."

They left the hospital in silence, each absorbed in worrisome thoughts about Abra's condition and the killer who was on the loose, lurking somewhere in the area of the Lucky C. And if Jack's theory was correct, and the person who'd attacked Abra wasn't The Wolf, then there was *another* threat to the Colton family to worry about.

Chapter 17

Tracy leaned her head back, watching the ranch and farmland outside of Tulsa whiz past the passenger window of Jack's truck, and she rubbed the bridge of her nose. "What are you going to tell Seth?"

Creases of fatigue bracketed Jack's eyes and worry lined the corners of his mouth. "I don't know. The truth, but a scaled-down version of it. I don't want to scare him. He's only five, after all. But I won't lie to him, either."

"What does he know now about what happened and where we went this morning?"

His cell phone rang before he could answer. After checking his caller ID, Jack said, "It's Ryan." Lifting the phone to his ear he answered the call with, "Please tell me you have good news."

Tracy studied Jack's reactions for clues to what his brother was saying. The disgruntled twist of his mouth said his hope for good news was unmet.

"Hang on, I'm going to put you on speaker. I'm with Tracy. We're in the truck, headed back to the ranch after seeing Abra. No, no change. Greta's with Big J. Yeah, hang on." He handed her the phone to hold as he thumbed a button to switch the call to speaker mode. "Okay, whatcha got?"

"We've got some prelim test results back on the infant skeleton y'all found," Ryan said. "The baby was a male. Died approximately six years ago. Was African American."

Tracy snapped her chin up in surprise, her pulse kicking.

Jack's eyebrows drew together sharply, and he gave her a puzzled look as if asking if she'd heard what he did. "Come again?"

"A black infant boy. Five to seven years post-mortem." Ryan's tone was flat and matter-of-fact. But then he'd had time to digest this unusual bit of information.

"Why would he be buried in our family cemetery?" Jack gave his head a little shake. "That makes no sense."

"Which, in and of itself, is a clue. It's likely the bones weren't buried here originally. We're checking to see if any local cemeteries have reported a grave robbery or a theft from a medical school or lab."

"Are you thinking someone from the ranch stole the baby's bones and buried them out there? What would be the point in that?" Tracy asked. She clutched the phone tighter, this strange twist making her uneasy. How did this fit with the attack on Abra? With the Baxters' hiring an assassin to kill her?

"We haven't gotten as far as identifying who could have dug the grave," Ryan reported. "There were dozens of fingerprints on the handle of the shovel. I'm guessing everyone on the ranch has used it in the last couple weeks, so it's not proving helpful."

"So someone dug that grave and left the bones there for us to find… Why?" Jack asked, "To scare us? To send a message?"

"That's yet to be determined but…unofficially—" Ryan paused "—that'd be my guess."

"Who would do that? Why? That's…sick! It's just…" Tracy shuddered.

"Tracy," Ryan said with low, scoffing sigh, "ninety-nine percent of what I deal with in my job is sick and deranged."

"What else do you know?" Jack asked. "Anything new about last night's break-in and the attack on Mother?"

"Not much. Considering some jewelry and prescription drugs were stolen, we have to explore the possibility that this was a simple robbery gone bad. Abra was just in the wrong place at the wrong time."

"But—" Jack started, and Ryan interrupted.

"But…considering what we know about The Wolf and the contract on Tracy, we're definitely not dismissing the possibility this was a premeditated act."

Jack tapped his thumb restlessly on the steering wheel. "Keep us posted," he said, his tone grave.

"Of course. And Tracy?"

Her heart beat a little faster when he addressed her. "Yes?"

"I know you don't like being cooped up with Jack and feeling like you're under his thumb, but considering the circumstances, I think it's what's best. Listen to Jack and do what he tells you. I know my older brother's bossy, but if I had to choose one person to watch my back, it'd be Jack. He'll keep you safe."

Jack cut a startled glance toward his phone and arched one eyebrow, as if his brother's assessment of his skill surprised him.

Tracy didn't bother to explain that under Jack's roof was exactly where she wanted to be or that she agreed with Ryan's appraisal of Jack's capacity to protect her. Instead she simply said, "Thank you, Ryan, for all you're doing." She swiped the screen and disconnected the call.

Jack clipped the phone back on his belt, then signaled his turn onto the long drive leading to the main house.

Seth must have been watching for them, because he bolted out the front door as soon as they entered the circular drive.

Edith emerged from the house at his heels. "How is your mother?"

"No change," Jack said, as he slid out of the truck and crouched to greet his son.

"Dad!" Seth cried as he threw himself into Jack's arms. "What happened to Grandmother? Why is she in the hospital?"

Jack stroked his son's head and clutched him tightly. Finally, he sighed, and lifting Seth as he stood, he carried his boy inside the main house.

Tracy followed, not really wanting to return to the site of last night's vicious assault on Abra. The cold marble and formal decor of the main house didn't welcome and warm her the way Jack's house did, and she found herself longing for the homey, safe comfort of the old homestead.

After sending Edith to gather Seth's things, Jack sat down on the living room couch with Seth on his lap. "Well, Spud, she hit her head. And because it hurt her brain, the doctors put her into a deep sleep, so that her head could heal."

Seth wrinkled his nose in thought. "How did she hit her head? Was she playing too rough? Like when Brett and I wrestle, and you say to be careful 'cause someone could get hurt?"

Seth's youthful innocence twisted in Tracy's chest with a bittersweet pang. She grinned sadly, imagining a scene where Seth roughhoused with his uncle and Jack called them out.

"No, she wasn't playing," Jack said.

"Then what?" Seth's eyes, so like his father's in color, shape and attentiveness, widened in dismay and curiosity."

Jack raised a glance to Tracy that asked for her help. This was where the explanation got dicey.

"She was in her bedroom," Tracy volunteered, "and no one in the family was with her, so we don't really know, for sure, what happened."

Jack's face said the vague, dodging answer would suffice. He gave a curt nod.

Tracy exhaled a cleansing breath and sat beside Jack, taking Seth's hands in her own. "The important thing for you to know is, your grandmother has the best doctors taking care of her. She's in good hands, and she just needs time to get better." She prayed that was the truth. Until the doctors said otherwise, she intended to stay optimistic about Abra's prognosis. The answer seemed to satisfy Seth, who tucked his head under his father's chin and muttered, "Can we go home now?"

Edith returned with a Spider-Man backpack and a half-empty bottle of water. "Can I get either of you anything to eat? Greta called to say she and Mr. Colton would be at the hospital through lunch, but if either of you would like a sandwich or a reheated plate of brisket—"

Having no appetite, Tracy shook her head at the same time Jack said, "No. Thank you, Edith, but I'll wait till I get back to the house to eat something. I just want to get this little guy settled in at home and catch up on returning phone calls. I'll find something to eat after I see what's been happening with the ranch this morning."

Once they reached the old homestead, Jack parked in his usual spot behind house. As the three of them trudged into the house, Tracy glanced across the ranch yard, her attention snagged by a flash motion near the corner of one of the outbuildings. She caught a quick glance of a tall woman with dark brown hair just as the woman ducked into the shadows behind the bunkhouse.

Had she not known that Greta was at the hospital with her mother, she would have sworn that was who she'd seen. Remembering that she'd seen someone who looked like Greta from the upstairs window of the main house the week before, she asked, "Jack, do you have a lady on staff who is tall and dark-haired like your sister?"

He gave her a puzzled look. "I'm sure we have several people who fit that general description. Why do you ask?"

"I keep seeing someone around the ranch who looks like Greta."

"Maybe it is Greta."

"No. It's always when I know Greta isn't here. Like just now. I saw the woman in question out by the bunkhouse as we came inside, but I assume Greta's still at the hospital."

Jack's brow dented in concern. "Spud, why don't you build a spaceship for me out of your Legos?"

Seth gave his father a long uncertain look. "Will you help me?"

"I'll help you," Tracy volunteered. "I think your dad has work to do."

He ruffled his son's hair. "Tell you what, pal. You start working on that spaceship with Tracy, and I'll check on you in a few minutes, okay?"

After giving his father one last wary look, Seth took Tracy's hand. "Come on. I'll show you my room."

Jack strode back to the door he'd just locked behind them. "It's probably nothing, but I'll go have a look, just in case. Relock the door behind me."

She nodded and did as he directed, then let Seth tow her upstairs to his toy-strewn room. Half an hour later, Jack joined them, answering her unspoken question with a shrug. "I didn't find anyone and none of the hands saw anything."

A prickle of apprehension scraped down her spine. "I know I saw someone."

"You sure it wasn't one of the hands? Ralph Highshaw is kinda slim and has dark hair."

Tracy huffed her frustration. "No. I saw a woman. I'm almost sure…"

"Almost sure?" Jack's direct gaze questioned her, and her own wording had her doubting.

Had she seen a woman? It made more sense that it had been one of the hands. She'd never met this Highshaw person. But the figure's dark hair had been to the shoulders like Greta's.

"Look, Daddy. It's a fighter spaceship. See the guns?"

Seth's enthusiasm as he showed his father the creation he'd been building chased most of the odd jitters from Tracy's bones. She had enough to worry about with The Wolf, the Baxters' hired assassin, hunting her without conjuring mysterious women lurking on the ranch.

"Hey, that's impressive, Spud." Jack settled on the floor next to her, his arm draping loosely around her shoulders as they spent the next several minutes listening to Seth explain the design of his fleet of Lego aircraft. If she closed her eyes and pushed her doubts and worries aside, Tracy could sink completely into a domestic fantasy where Jack was her husband and Seth their son. She could pretend this life was hers and no one was trying to kill her. The peaceful tranquility of that moment, and the childish excitement in Seth's voice as he teased with his father warmed her heart. She longed for the boy's resilience from his recent traumas, clearly based in his complete faith that his father would protect him. That once the danger had passed, he had nothing to fear, nothing to doubt in his life.

Reaching for that same level of confidence and trust in Jack, Tracy snuggled closer to the green-eyed cowboy. She leaned her head against his shoulder, and he gave her a reassuring squeeze.

That night, Tracy reveled in the chance to assist in Seth's bedtime ritual. After Jack assisted with his son's bath and the boy was in his pajamas, Tracy cuddled next to him on his bed to read several books together. The barn cat, Sleek, had sneaked inside at some point that afternoon and was curled at the foot of the bed. Tracy used her bare toes to rub the cat's cheek and elicit a purr while Seth stumbled through reading *Go, Dog, Go*. She took many opportunities to kiss Seth's head and inhale the fragile scent of his freshly shampooed hair. When the books were put away, she knelt with him beside the bed and listened to his innocent but earnest prayers.

"Dear God," he said, eyes clenched shut and hands clasped tightly, "thank you for my Daddy and Pooh and Sleek. Thank you for my house and our food and my Legos. Help Grandmother get well and please make Ms. Tracy my real mom. Amen."

Tracy's heart swelled to bursting and with tears in her eyes, she raised a startled look first to Seth, who climbed back into bed, oblivious to her surprise, and then to Jack, who looked as poleaxed by his son's prayer as she. Gathering her composure, she tucked Seth in, wished him a good night and waited in the hallway while Jack did the same.

"Oh, Jack," she whispered as he came out and closed Seth's door. "I promise I never said anything to him about—"

"Shh." He touched a finger to his lips and motioned with a jerk of his head for her to follow him farther down the hall. When they stood between his bedroom door and the one to the guest room, he faced her. Putting a hand at her waist, he drew her close and threaded his fingers through her hair.

"I never said anything to him about being his mother. I swear!" she finished in a hushed tone.

He lifted one dark eyebrow as he caressed her cheek. "Are you saying you wouldn't want to?"

Her eyes widened. "No! I—I'd love to be his mother." Realizing how that sounded and not wanting to appear pushy, she backpedaled. "I mean…Seth is a great kid. Anyone would be lucky to have a boy like him to call their own."

Jack's cheek hiked in a lopsided grin. "I'm not accusing you of anything. But I'm not blind. I see the rapport you have with him. You'll be a great mother someday."

His compliment wound through her, warming places left cold and dead by Cliff's heartlessness and insults. She lowered her gaze, her pulse racing like a wild stallion on the open range. She tried to reply, but forming a cohesive thought was hard while Jack was touching her.

When she flattened her palm against his chest, she felt the strong, drubbing beat of his heart, and that steady, life-affirming thud was one of the sweetest, sexiest things she'd ever experienced. Because it was Jack. Because his powerful presence was reassuring. Because she remembered so vividly having that pounding heartbeat pressed tight against her own just last night.

"About last night," he started, as if reading her thoughts. And why wouldn't he know what she'd been thinking? She'd always been told her face was an open book. But more important, she'd sensed from her first day on the ranch that she and Jack had a unique connection. A link that went beyond the spark of passion that crackled when they were close.

"Jack…" she whispered, and he silenced her with a soft kiss.

"I haven't forgotten where we were, what we'd started when…" he left his sentence trail off.

When Abra was attacked and left for dead. The unspoken words hung between them, and a shiver raced through her. His arms tightened around her, pulling her closer, chasing away the chill of fear.

"Do you remember what I told you earlier this week… in my office?" he whispered, his breath a warm tickle in her ear.

"You said a lot of things in your office." Her lips twitched with a teasing grin.

"Let me help you remember, then." He trailed light kisses along her cheek to the tip of her nose, and her breath snagged in her lungs. "I said that I finish…" he nibbled at her lips. "…what I start."

His meaning dawned on her as he deepened his kiss, and her heart jolted. He caught her tiny gasp with the caress of his mouth on hers. Even as her body melted against his, the heat and sweet tension of desire coiling in her core, her head rebelled. How could she make love to Jack and not end up with a broken heart? He hadn't said he loved her. He'd made no promises beyond protecting her until the Baxters' assassin was stopped. How could she deepen the bond she felt for him, give him her body, and not lose her heart to him?

But, oh mercy, she wanted him. She knew she'd regret it if she didn't seize this chance to be held and loved by this tender and passionate man. Every woman should know how it felt to be cherished and fully aroused by a loving man at least once in her life. Shouldn't they? And she'd certainly never had that kind of gentle intimacy with Cliff.

As if sensing her hesitance, Jack lifted his head and peered deep into her eyes. "Tracy?"

She swallowed hard and listened to the whisper of her heart. "Yes, Jack. Make love to me."

In the days that followed, the home-like family atmosphere the three of them shared and the lack of disturbance to the ranch's routine made it easy to picture herself as part of Jack's family. By day, she helped nurture Seth, cooked their meals and shared the ranch chores. By night, she slept with Jack, made love to him until they were both spent, then slipped back into her own guest bed before dawn, so that Seth wouldn't find them together should the boy wake early and sneak into his father's room.

It was a comfortable, blissfully simple life, and she was with two people she'd grown to love. What could be better?

She tried hard to quiet the voice of doubt that said Jack was merely using her body because she was convenient. He'd still given her no pledge of love, no promises of the future. She wanted to just enjoy this time on the ranch for what it was. A glorious, happy time. A respite before she had to return to her real life and her empty apartment in Denver. But with every day that passed, she fell deeper in love with Jack Colton and his son. Leaving them, when the time came, would be the hardest thing she'd ever done.

For all the joy she felt with each new day, the specter of danger lurked at the edges of every thought, every horseback ride, every family meal. She couldn't forget that a killer still hunted her, and she spent her days looking over her shoulder, jumping at shadows.

Abra's attack remained at the fore as well. Every day, after the work of the ranch was done, the three of them would drive in to the hospital to check on Abra and Big J. Jack's father refused to leave his wife, choosing instead to eat, sleep and shower at the hospital, despite his family's urging to get some rest at home. Day after day, Abra remained in the drug-induced coma, her condition stable but serious.

On the afternoon of her eighth day of living at Jack's house, Tracy stepped out of the shower, having needed a second one that day thanks to a messy incident involving a rambunctious little boy and a muddy holding pen. The house was eerily quiet, and she was anxious to dry off, re-dress and find Jack and Seth.

She spotted Jack near the stable from the guest room window as she toweled dry her hair, and once she'd put on a fresh pair of shorts and sandals, she headed out to meet him.

Jack greeted her with a brilliant smile and kiss. "Have I ever told you how great you smell?"

She chuckled. "No. But it's not hard to smell better than most of the things on this ranch."

"True," he said, taking another deep whiff of her newly shampooed hair and hugging her tight.

"Where's Seth? Doesn't he need a bath, too? Last I saw him, he was pretty muddy."

"I hosed him off behind the barn."

She gave an indelicate snort. "Hosed him off? Like he was livestock?"

"He's only going to get dirty again before dinner." Jack turned back to the saddle he was oiling. "He rode out to the north pasture to help Brett and the hands with sorting, vaccinating and branding calves."

She drew a sharp breath. "Branding? Isn't that rather a…harsh thing for him to witness?"

Jack lifted a shoulder. "It's part of ranching. Something he needs to learn. He'll be fine."

She opened her mouth to disagree but snapped it closed again. Jack loved his son and raised him by different methods than she would, but that didn't make his ways wrong.

Jack moved closer to her and rubbed a thumb over the crease she hadn't realized she'd made between her eyebrows. Lifting the corner of his mouth in a grin that was becoming a familiar part of his repertoire, he repeated, "He'll be fine."

She returned a grin and nodded. "All right. I trust you."

His grin grew more amused, and he shifted his hand to cup the back of her head. "So I have your approval to raise my son as I see fit?"

An awkward flush prickled in her cheeks. "I only meant—"

He silenced her explanation with a slow and sultry kiss that she felt all the way to her toes. When he stepped back, he tweaked her chin. "What if we headed out to the branding pen ourselves and gave them a hand?"

"Me?" She blinked rapidly. "How would I help?"

"Plenty of ways." He gave her a raised-eyebrow look that sent a silent challenge. "Assuming you don't mind getting your hands dirty again."

"You couldn't have told me this before I showered?"

He flipped up a palm. "You didn't ask."

"Branding, huh?" Tracy squared her shoulders and jerked a firm nod. "Bring it on." Then glancing down at her shorts and peasant top and sandals, she added, "Let me go change into work clothes, and I'll be right back."

She stood on her toes to give him another quick kiss, gave Sleekie a scratch on the cheek as she passed the straw bale where the cat napped and marched across the ranch yard toward Jack's house.

Tracy inhaled the sweet scent of hay that was carried on the June breeze and smiled up at the wide blue Oklahoma sky. She noticed she had a bounce in her step that matched the delight that filled her chest. It surprised her to realize that she, a city girl, was truly happy here at the ranch. Sure, she was still getting used to the early hours, the hard work and the dirty jobs that went along with ranching, but when she tumbled into bed at night, achy and exhausted, she had never felt as satisfied and accomplished.

After years of teetering on a precipice because of Cliff, she finally was beginning to feel as if her feet were on solid ground.

Her cell phone buzzed in her pocket, and she pulled it out to check the message. She read the message from her landlord in Denver, asking when she planned to return and reminding her that her rent was due in three days.

Her heart gave a painful throb at the thought of leaving the ranch once the police caught The Wolf and she was safe to return to her home in Denver. While she'd formed the bond she'd hoped to with Seth, she hadn't counted on falling in love with the little boy's father.

What if—

A heavy object struck a sharp blow to her head. Pain exploded through her skull. Her knees crumpled, and as she slid toward the ground, a muscled arm caught her around the waist. A smelly rag was slapped over her nose, the bite of some pungent chemical burning her nostrils.

Jack, help! her brain screamed, but she couldn't make her mouth form the words. Her vision grew fuzzy, dimming. Her last images were of the world tilting as the brute hefted her up. Tossed her over a meaty shoulder. Then everything went black.

Chapter 18

Jack finished saddling Mabel for Tracy, tidied up a corner of the stable where Sleekie or some other critter had knocked over the bottles and cans on a storage shelf, then checked his watch for the third time. What was taking Tracy so long to change clothes? He knew women took a while to dress when they were getting gussied up to go out, but how hard was it to put on jeans and a work shirt? He'd tried calling her cell phone, but it went to voice mail.

"Dang it," he grumbled, stashing his mobile phone back on the clip at his waist. A niggling fear twisted through him. Could something have happened to her? Should he have accompanied her back to the house? The distance to his house was short enough, with hands typically milling about the ranch yard, so he hadn't deemed the precaution necessary. But...most of the ranch hands were helping with the vaccinations and branding of the calves.

Disquiet needled him. Damn it, he should have gone with her! As unlikely as it was that the gunman could have gotten this far onto the property without being noticed, The Wolf had gotten onto the ranch before, even if just an isolated pasture.

And *something* had delayed Tracy. With a huff of agitation and self-censure, he headed toward the house. He swept his gaze around the yard, looking for signs of trouble, a strange vehicle or tire tracks on the dusty ground. The afternoon sun glinted off something dark near the base of the front-porch steps. Heart pounding, Jack jogged over to the reflective item.

Tracy's phone.

Acid gushed in his stomach, and panic spiked in his blood.

He scooped up her cell phone and rushed into the house. "Tracy!" There was no answer. "Tracy!"

His own phone beeped, and he whipped it out, checking the caller ID. Tom Vasquez. He pressed ignore. He'd have to get back to the ranch hand later.

Replacing his mobile phone, he hurriedly searched every room in the house, calling for Tracy. His voice grew more desperate with every passing minute. She simply wasn't there.

Hands shaking, Jack pulled his phone back out and dialed Ryan's number. Knowing time was of the essence, he flew down the steps and raced out to the front porch, while his brother's line rang in his ear. And rang. "Come on, Ryan!"

Finally his brother answered with, "Colton."

"It's Jack. Tracy's gone." Speaking the words made it real, and viselike pressure clamped his heart. His voice was hoarse and strained when he added, "I think that Wolf bastard has her."

Jack heard shuffling sounds through the phone that told him Ryan was on his feet and leaving his office, even as they spoke. "Talk to me. Where are you? How long has she been gone?"

"I'm at my house. She's only been gone a few minutes. Maybe ten? Fifteen?" *Too long.* Anything could have happened in that amount of time. It only took a few seconds to slit someone's throat and have them bleed out. His gut roiled at the possibility Tracy could have been hurt. But the more he considered it, the more likely it seemed. If she hadn't been injured or incapacitated, she would have screamed or called out for help.

Ryan fired more questions at Jack, and he answered as best he could.

No, he saw no signs of a struggle.

No blood to indicate violence.

He'd heard nothing, seen nothing.

He didn't have any damn clues where she might be. They couldn't even track her phone, since she'd dropped it.

"I'm on my way, and I'm bringing backup. We'll find her."

But reaching the ranch, even driving at top speeds with lights and sirens, would take Ryan twenty minutes or more. "What do I do in the meantime? I can't just sit here!"

"Nothing rash. Keep looking for anything to tell us which direction they went. There has to be *something.*"

Jack gritted his teeth in frustration as he disconnected. He knew basic tracking. All of the Colton kids had learned how to read telltale clues to track lost cows. He circled the house slowly, his gaze trained on minute details. The incoming text signal sounded on his phone. Vasquez again. He swiped his thumb across his screen intending to close the message menu when the first word of the text caught his eye. *Tracy.*

Tracy woke to a splitting ache in her head. When she blinked her vision into focus, her view of the world was upside down, and her body was being roughly jostled. *What the...?*

In an instant, fear charged through her. She was draped over the back of a horse. Her hands were bound in front of her with rope, and a foul-tasting rag had been shoved in her mouth.

An angry-sounding voice barked at the mare. "Come on, you stupid animal! Move it!"

Pounding fear flashed through her in a hot wave. Tracy twisted and flailed, trying to right herself. For her efforts, she earned a stinging slap on her buttocks.

"Stop squirming! You ain't going nowhere," the man, whose lap she was across, growled.

A whimper of fear swelled in her throat, but she determinedly muzzled the sound. Inhaling slowly, she fought to calm her jangling nerves and keep a level head. Her only chance of escape depended on thinking rationally, planning. Not panicking.

The horse slowed again, taking a few side steps, then tossed his mane and snorted, clearly agitated.

"Damn nag! Go!" The kidnapper kicked the horse in the ribs, but his brutality only upset the horse further. Grumbling under his breath, the man shoved her away from his legs so that he could dismount. Once on the ground, he grabbed a fistful of her hair and yanked her head up. "Don't try anything stupid, or you'll be dead before you take two steps."

Pinpricks of pain shot through her scalp, and she recoiled when she met the chilling gray glare of the man's feral eyes. *The Wolf.* His moniker suited him. Frighteningly so. His breath stank of cigarettes, and her stomach soured at the acrid stench.

She tried to swallow, but the dirty rag in her mouth left her tongue dry, her throat arid. Despite her fear, she narrowed her eyes in a defiant stare. She was through with cowering for bullies. She'd let Cliff push her around, intimidate her and ruin her life far too long. But in the few days she'd spent with Jack, she'd seen how a real man treated a woman. He'd showed her respect, patience, tenderness. He'd encouraged her to find her inner strength and fight for what she wanted from life.

And what she wanted was Jack. She wanted a chance to make a family with Jack and Seth. She wanted the happiness she'd found here at the Lucky C.

Because she loved Seth...and Jack. The realization flowed through her like warm honey and filled her with the will to fight.

"Come on, damn you!" The Wolf screamed at the horse.

Despite angling her head, Tracy couldn't see what had upset the horse and made it stall, but she knew enough from her few riding lessons that The Wolf's abuse and harsh tone were upsetting the horse further. Good. Any delay had to work in her favor, didn't it?

How long would it take before Jack worried about her and came looking? And once he did realize she was missing how would he find her? She had to do something to help him find her. But what?

Tracy kidnapped. Horse stolen. In pursuit on foot. East.

Jack read the text message twice, his heart in his throat. Though his worse fear was confirmed, at least he had a lead where Tracy had been taken. And someone was already following her. God bless Tom Vasquez. The ranch hand would definitely be getting a bonus in his next paycheck.

Regrouping, Jack ran toward the garage where the utility vehicles were stored, praying the hands didn't have all of the ranch's transportation at the branding pen.

East. Jack mentally pictured the terrain east of the ranch buildings. Mostly idle pastures and old, unused buildings from his grandfather's time. An equipment shed in bad repair. A dilapidated barn where hay bales were stored. Fields where they grew the hay.

He skidded to a stop at the garage and threw open the side door. The bay was empty except for an older SUV with two flat tires.

Damn it!

Wasting no time, he raced toward the stable, remembering he had Buck and Mabel saddled and waiting. Not as good as a motorized vehicle, but faster than racing after the kidnapper on foot.

As he ran across the ranch yard, he redialed Ryan's number. He quickly relayed what Tom had reported. "I'm headed that way…on Buck."

"Jack, don't do anyth—" Ryan started, but Jack disconnected and dialed Tom's number.

"Where are you now?" he asked without preamble when a breathless voice answered. "Any sign of her?"

"I can see them…ahead of me…but they're moving too fast…for me to…keep up."

"Where? Give me a landmark." Jack grabbed the saddle horn with his free hand and swung up on Buck's back.

"Miller's creek. They're near…the old hay barn."

"Can you tell…" Jack's lungs tightened, and dread speared his gut. "Is she hurt? Can you tell if she's…" *Dead.* His throat closed, not allowing him to say the word.

"I can see…her moving, struggling…to get free," Vasquez wheezed.

Relief flooded Jack so hard and fast that his head spun.

"I can't follow…anymore. I'm sorry. I—" Jack heard Vasquez retch.

"On my way." Pausing only long enough to tap out a quick text to Brett, alerting him to the kidnapping, he headed out. With a slap of his reins, he and Buck bolted toward the eastern fields. Silently he prayed he wouldn't be too late. If The Wolf was headed toward the old barn, did Jack have time to get there before the assassin carried out his mission to kill Tracy? He didn't like the odds.

Fear twisting through him, he gave Buck a kick, urging his mount to run faster.

The Wolf reined the stolen horse to a stop and shoved Tracy off his lap so that she tumbled with a jarring thud to the ground. Hands bound as they were, she hadn't been able to break her fall and ended up biting her tongue. The metallic taste of blood filled her mouth, adding to the nausea and anxiety that roiled inside her. After finally coaxing the horse to cooperate, The Wolf had set off at a gallop, unmindful of how the pace bounced Tracy in her awkward position. The only good thing she could say about the jolting ride was that she'd been able to work the rag out of her mouth and spit it out as they raced along. Her head reeled, and her ribs throbbed from the assault, but she shoved thoughts of her pain aside, focusing only on how she could escape.

She glared up at the man who towered over her, his imposing brow and menacing eyes sending icy trepidation down her aching spine. "They know who you are, you know. You won't get away with this. The Baxters confessed everything. The cops are looking for you even now."

Her news earned a brief hesitation, and the quirk of one dark eyebrow. "Oh, they did, did they? Well…" He scoffed. "I'll take care of them when I finish here."

He stalked toward her, and she scuttled back on her bottom as best she could with her encumbered hands. "No! Get away from me!" She kicked her legs, aiming for his knees, his crotch, any vulnerable area she thought she could hit.

Her captor managed to dodge all but a few cursory blows. "Stop it, bitch!"

"Help!" she screamed as loud as she could from her bruised chest. "Help me! Someone!"

A slinging slap found her cheek, and her head snapped back. Her ears buzzed from the force of the blow.

"Shut the hell up!" he snarled in her face, his cigarette breath making her gag.

For a moment, she flashed to the few times Cliff had let his temper turn violent, and her instinct was to curl inward, to protect herself and end the threat faster by becoming submissive. But a new stronger voice in her soul shouted down that first instinct.

This man intended to kill her, and she refused to go meekly to her death. Not when she now had so much to live for. Jack, Seth, a fresh start in life.

"Get up," he barked and caught her under her armpits. As he dragged her to her feet, she scrambled mentally for some way, *any way* to call for help, to signal her location or free herself from his grasp. He was too strong to overpower him. Her hands were tied, limiting her ability to fight. But she hadn't seen a weapon yet. If he was unarmed, then how…?

Her brain shied away from finishing that question, but

the sentiment remained. Where was his weapon? Was there any chance she could snag the weapon from him and use it to defend herself?

She scanned his body with a frantic gaze, looking for a telltale lump that might be a hidden gun or knife. The only obvious bulge she saw was at his chest pocket, where he'd clearly stashed his cigarettes. Her spirits wilted. Small paper-wrapped sticks of tobacco would hardly be helpful in freeing herself.

"Let's go." With a biting grip on her arms, he shoved her towards a dilapidated barn. He'd been so purposeful in bringing her here, she realized he must have planned it out. She knew he'd been on the ranch property before when he'd shot at her and Seth. The idea that he could have been lurking nearby all these weeks, learning the territory and plotting her murder sent a chill through her.

There was a sick logic to bringing her to this old barn. By killing her here, away from the main ranch property, he could make his escape before anyone found her body. Did that mean he also had his weapons stashed here? Would he kill her outright or torture her first? The man seemed sadistic enough to want to watch her suffer.

The hinges of the barn door screeched as he pushed her inside. Her heart thumped wildly, and she continued her frenzied search for a plan. She stumbled through the barn door and blinked as her eyes adjusted from bright sun to the dim light. Was there something close by she could use as a weapon?

The ground was primarily hard-packed dirt except for an animal stall with a thick layer of rotting straw where rusting farm equipment had been abandoned in a back corner. Dust motes swirled in the thin beams of sunlight that seeped through cracks in the roof. Disturbed by their presence, a bat swooped low then fluttered near the rafters before resettling in the shadows. A bent saw, some baling wire and a pair of pliers were hung on a Peg-Board on one wall, but they were too far away for her to reach.

He aimed a finger at the floor. "Sit down."

She didn't budge. If she was going to have a chance, she needed to stay on her feet, stay mobile. "Didn't you hear what I told you before? The Baxters gave you up. You won't get paid for killing me, so why not let me go?"

"Because I have my own reasons to want you dead."

His reply stunned her. "What reasons? I've never met you before. What could you possibly have against me?"

"You cost me thousands of dollars."

She shook her head, baffled. "How?"

He curled his lip in a sneer. "I had a business arrangement with your husband. Now that he's dead, that source of income is gone. Word on the street is he was chasing his runaway wife down when he was the arrested."

"What kind of b-business arrangement?" she rasped.

"We were selling Girl Scout Cookies," The Wolf said, his curled lip matching his sarcastic tone. His expression soured further, and he glared darkly at her. "What difference does it make, seein' as how he's dead, and it ain't going to pay off no more."

"Look, i-if it's money you want, I'll pay you."

"Only one form of payment I'd want from you." He looked her up and down with a leer that made her skin crawl. "Don't think I haven't considered having a taste of what you've got before I off you." He licked his lips like a hungry dog, and an oily revulsion rolled in her stomach.

"No," she rasped, her body trembling despite her efforts to be brave.

"If only I had more time..." He dismissed the idea with a lifted shoulder, then stuck his nose in her face and bared his teeth. "Now, *sit down*."

With that, he grabbed her shoulder in a painful grip and shoved her toward the floor. Weak with fear, her knees buckled, and she crumpled. Without use of her hands, she again landed hard and toppled onto her side, her face pressed to the dusty floor. The low rumble of a male laugh penetrated the swoosh of blood past her ears. She gritted her teeth as fury, humiliation and determination spiked in her, a triumvirate of rebellion and refusal to be subjugated again.

You have a core of inner strength, Jack had told her, and feeling her choler rise, she believed him. *Fight back*, the long-buried warrior inside her whispered.

Drawing a deep breath for courage, Tracy rolled to her back and sat up, working her legs under her.

Eyeing her with dark purpose, The Wolf bent at the waist and tugged up the leg of his pants. She saw the grip of the handgun poking from the top of his boot, and cold terror slithered through her. She was out of time, out of options. She had to act *now*, do *something*! Or die like the submissive wimp Cliff had convinced her she was.

She tensed, ready. And the instant The Wolf's gaze shifted from her to the gun, the second he reached for his weapon, she lunged. With a primal roar that shocked even her own ears, she pounced on him. Her tied hands clawed at his face, her feet swinging for his shins. Like a rabid wildcat, she attacked, flailing, leaping on his back, biting…whatever outlet she found she used in a whirlwind of desperation and anger. She'd caught him off guard, which gave her the upper-hand for a few precious seconds, and she battled for all she was worth.

But his superior strength and size soon turned the tide. His arms snaked around her thrashing body, and he pinned her arms down, her body facing his. He grabbed a fistful of her hair and jerked her head back. When she quit struggling, in deference to the painful grip he had on her hair, he jammed the handgun into her face, growling, "That's going to cost you, sugar. Do you know how many nonlethal holes I can put in you before I finally end your suffering?"

She moaned involuntarily, the lightning pain in her scalp making her eyes water.

"Here's a hint. This here PX4 Storm SubCompact holds ten rounds." He jerked her closer, snarling, "That's ten holes, sweetcakes."

Tracy seized what might be her last chance. She sank her teeth into the fleshy part of his gun hand, just below his thumb and bit down. Hard.

The Wolf howled in pain, pushing her away and flinging his hand to shake her off. And losing his grip on his weapon.

Seeing the gun spin across the dirt floor, she dove for it, her bound hands grappling in the straw until she held the gun between her shaking palms.

Hand in his mouth, sucking on the bloody wound she'd inflicted, he glared at her. "You won't shoot me. You don't have the guts."

Her breath shuddered as she took aim. "You sure about that?"

"You won't be able to live with the guilt." He inched toward her, and she scuttled back. "Have you ever seen a man die? It's not pretty."

Her heart clenched. She'd seen Laura die. She'd watched the life ebb from her cousin after their car crashed. Laura hadn't given her life, winning Tracy's freedom, just to have her cousin die months later at the hand of a hired assassin.

But Tracy's mind recoiled from the notion of killing a man in cold blood. She swallowed the bitter taste of bile that rose in her throat and scrambled for her next move. The Wolf continued to close in on her. He crept steadily toward her as if knowing a sudden move might make her panic and pull the trigger. She met the feral, chaotic gleam in his eyes and shivered. His hair was disheveled from her attack. His shirt pocket was ripped and dangling by a few threads. His cheeks bore long red scratches, and blood from his hand had smeared on his lips and chin. He looked like his namesake animal after a vicious hunt. Wild, ferocious, predatory.

Her back bumped the rusted old hay baler, preventing any further retreat. In a few more steps, he'd be on her, would overpower her and reclaim the gun. A cold sweat beaded on her lip. Either she shot him now, or…

The flicker of light, as the bat stirred again in the hayloft, drew her attention upward. Tracy followed a gut instinct, a rash idea. Just keep the gun away from him.

Swinging her tied arms between her legs for more heft, she flung the gun up and forward.

"Hey!" he roared as the gun sailed toward the upper loft.

The weapon discharged when it landed in the hayloft, startling the bat from its perch.

The Wolf blinked once, clearly startled by her move, then his face contorted in an ugly snarl. "You bitch!" He rushed her, grabbing a fistful of her shirt and shaking her like a rag doll. "All you've done is delay me. And piss me off!"

She gasped as he seized her wrists and dragged her to the end of the hay baler.

Unknotting the rope binding her arms, he looped the ends through a large-toothed iron gear wheel and quickly retied the knots. He jerked the ends hard so that the rope cut into her flesh. "I'll be back, bitch. And it won't go well for you."

Her stomach filled with acid, the bitter taste rising to the back of her throat, but she held his glare, fighting the urge to cower. She was through being anyone's punching bag or foot mat.

He stalked away, climbed to the loft using a half-rotten wooden ladder and began searching the piles of hay for his weapon.

Tracy knew she had precious little time to think, to plan, to come up with her next move. Frantically, she twisted her wrists, trying to angle her fingers so that she could loosen the knotted rope. But the binds were so tight, she was already losing feeling in her hands.

Next she scanned the hay baler, looking for a sharp edge she could use to fray the rope, but saw nothing within her limited reach. Shifting her gaze to check The Wolf's progress, a glint of metal on the dirt floor caught her eye. Next to the scattered pack of cigarettes that had fallen from his shirt pocket when she tore it, a sunbeam glimmered off a silver butane lighter. A throb of anticipation and hope skittered through her. If she couldn't cut her wrists free of the rope, could she burn through them?

Her mouth dried knowing she'd burn her wrists, but weren't burns better than surrendering to him and inevitable death? And he'd all but sworn to torture her first.

Sliding as far down to the floor as her tied wrists allowed, she stretched her leg toward the lighter. The toe of her sandal nudged the lighter closer, then a few more inches. Her awkward position strained her wrists, the binding knots gouging and pinching her skin, but she refused to give up. Every bit of pain was worth it if she could save herself. For the first time in many years, she had a future she looked forward to. A relationship with Seth, the opportunity to build a career of her own…and Jack. She'd only just realized that moments earlier, just before The Wolf grabbed her, and she hadn't had the chance to tell him her feelings. How would he react to her feelings? Would he ever give marriage a second chance?

She gave her head a brisk shake. That was a debate for another time. She had to focus on freeing herself, surviving her current ordeal.

The lighter was only a few inches from her now, but with her hands tied to the baler, she couldn't bend to get it. With a glance to check on her captor's progress, she kicked off her sandals. The Wolf was grumbling bitterly in the loft, clearly not having any luck finding his gun in the mounds of molded hay. Using her toes to grip the lighter, she wiggled and lifted her foot as high as she could. She dropped it once and had to start over, but finally got the lighter close enough to her fingers to clasp it between her hands. Working slowly, her hands trembling, she tried to flick the igniter. After a couple attempts, a flame danced up, and she exhaled the breath she'd been holding. Careful not to let the flame go out, she wrenched her arms to an awkward angle hoping to touch the ropes to the small flicker.

A few of the fibers glowed red as the rope struggled to catch fire. Tears of frustration and pain filled Tracy's eyes as she continued to hold the flame against the rope with only marginal success. Singed fibers dropped from the smoldering rope onto her skin, and she fought the instinct to flinch, to jerk her hands back from the heat. Her progress was slow, but the rope was burning, bit by bit. *Please, please, please!* This had to work. She had no other ideas, no other options, and no more time.

The Wolf's footsteps thudded as he crossed the wooden floor of the hayloft, still searching for his gun.

"I have other ways to kill you, ways that are less merciful than a bullet." When he came to the edge of the loft and shouted down at her, she curled her fingers around the lighter to hide it from him. "You think you've won a victory, but this only means you'll suffer more."

He drew his dark eyebrows into a frown and lifted his nose to sniff the air like a predator scenting his prey. "What's that smell? Something's burning. What—" His gaze narrowed on the ropes around her wrists.

Tracy glanced down. The spot she'd been burning smoldered, trailing a thin wisp of smoke.

"Like fire, do ya?" The Wolf cast his gaze around the old barn. "You're right. This place would go up like a tinderbox, all this weathered wood and straw." His grin was pure evil. "And you with time to think about burning up like a campfire marshmallow…"

An anxious whimper escaped her throat, the sound loud to her own ears. Loud enough that she almost missed the shout from outside. The voice of her salvation. Jack!

"Tracy!" He was clearly still a good distance away, but…he was coming after her!

She stretched her body trying to see out the nearest window. Fresh tears of hope rushed to her eyes. "Jack! Help me!"

The Wolf, too, moved to a spot in the hayloft where he could look out through one of the many gaps in the dilapidated walls. Growling a bitter curse, The Wolf headed back toward the ladder. Then, as if having second thoughts, he changed direction and disappeared into the shadows of the loft.

Tracy's anxiety ratcheted up a notch. Not knowing where The Wolf was and what he could be doing was somehow more frightening than his looming presence.

"Tracy!" Jack's voice was closer now, accompanied

by the pounding of hooves. Though she still couldn't see Jack, the jangle of reins drifted in from just beyond the barn door.

"Jack!" Her heart almost burst with a surge of relief when the barn door crashed open.

Rather than race into the barn, he hovered by the door, sweeping the interior with a keen gaze and leading with a gun clenched between his hands. Clearly he'd realized who'd kidnapped her, but he was walking into an unknown situation.

"Jack, look out!" she called in warning as he zeroed in on her and hurried inside the barn. "He had a gun… in the lo—"

Before she could finish, a large dark figure pounced from above. The Wolf landed on Jack's back, knocking him to the ground and causing him to lose his grip on his gun.

A startled scream slipped from Tracy's throat, and her anxiety spiked as the Wolf lobbed a punch into Jack's chin. Her cowboy's head snapped back, and his attacker snaked an arm around Jack's neck.

Tracy held her breath, her heart in her throat, as she watched the two grapple. Jack grunted with effort, his face reddening from lack of air as The Wolf held his forearm tight across Jack's windpipe.

A sob welled inside her, seeing the abuse The Wolf unleashed on Jack. If anything happened to Jack, how could she forgive herself? He'd come to rescue her, and now his life hung in the balance.

Chapter 19

Despite the viselike grip of the arm that choked him, Jack managed to find his footing and renewed leverage. Bracing his feet, he threw his head back into The Wolf's face. The assassin howled in pain as blood spurted from his broken nose, hitting Jack's neck in a warm spray. Jack followed with repeated blows from his elbow to the man's ribs.

Under counterattack, The Wolf cringed in defense, and his hold on Jack's throat loosened. With a twist of his body, Jack wrenched free of his opponent's grip. He stumbled to his feet and gulped air into his burning chest.

His gun. Where had his gun landed when he fell?

While The Wolf clutched his broken nose and sucked shallow gasps into his bruised lungs, Jack cast a quick glance around the floor his feet. He spotted the pistol about two yards away at the same time his opponent lunged for it.

Jack hefted his boot into the man's jaw just as The Wolf's hands closed around the barrel of the handgun. Determined to keep the weapon out of his assailant's hands, Jack stomped with all his weight on The Wolf's wrist.

The assassin shouted in rage and grabbed Jack's ankle with his free hand. Yanking hard, The Wolf managed to pull Jack off balance. Oxygen whooshed from him as he crashed to the hard-packed dirt, but he continued to kick, battering The Wolf with blows, striking him in the head and face with the heel of his boot. Though blinded by Jack's barrage of kicks, the assassin fumbled the pistol into his fingers. The Wolf aimed in the general direction of his opponent and fired. The heat of the bullet streaked past Jack's cheek. A sting on his ear told him he'd been knicked.

"Jack!" Tracy screamed.

When The Wolf rolled to his back and shifted the weapon toward her, Jack landed one last resounding kick to the assassin's gun hand. The jolt knocked the pistol from his hand, and the gun skittered toward Tracy. Out of his reach, but also out of The Wolf's reach. Good enough. That evened the odds.

Gathering his focus and strength, Jack sprang to his feet, ready for The Wolf's next attack.

He didn't have to wait long. The dark glare of the hired killer narrowed as he surged toward Jack. But the man's hands weren't empty. He'd found a piece of steel rebar and swung it at Jack's head.

Jack ducked, just in time, and flicked a fast look askance as he dodged the next arc of the swinging bar. Finding the stack of rebar, he grabbed one himself and met The Wolf's attack with a practiced parry and riposte.

A *Prise de Fer* and *remise*. Jack met The Wolf's startled look with a smug grin. "Come on, bastard. Bring it."

Tracy gasped as Jack's gun landed a few feet from her. She might be tied to the baler, but she had to do something to try to keep the gun out of The Wolf's hands. As she had in retrieving the lighter, Tracy scrunched low and extended her foot as far as she could. She toed the gun closer, closer...

The clank of metal brought her head up, her attention back to Jack's battle with The Wolf. Her gut roiled seeing the heavy bar the assassin swung toward Jack. A blow from the steel rod could do serious damage, could even be fatal if it struck him in the head. She bit her bottom lip, willing herself not to cry out and distract Jack. After a moment, she realized Jack had the upper hand in this battle. His moves and countermoves were skilled and effective in both tiring The Wolf and landing strikes that diminished his opponent's ability to fight back.

A strike to the arm, a jab in the gut, a blocked thrust.

She flashed back to her recent visit to Jack's home office and the small swords he kept in the display case. *Of course.* Fascinated, she followed his moves, his footwork.

An optimistic buoyance lightened the pressure in her chest. Jack was in his element.

Monitoring the fight with half her attention, she went back to her pursuit of the gun. Another couple inches. And again...

Finally she was able to twist and pick up the weapon, but in doing so the lighter slipped from her hands. Didn't matter. Jack was here. He'd free her once he handled The Wolf.

A loud curse and groan yanked her focus to the men. The Wolf clutched his chest and crumpled on the dirt floor. Jack stepped back, panting, and eyed his quarry critically. The Wolf coughed, spitting out blood, and his eyes rolled back as he hugged his ribs.

Jack pulled the rebar away from the downed man, then cut a glance to Tracy. "Are you hurt?"

"Not much." She showed him the gun she'd retrieved. "Here."

"Good girl," he said, lifting a corner of his mouth as he strode toward her, the rebar swords still in his fist. When he reached her, he tossed the bars into a corner of the barn and pulled her head close for a kiss. "Thank God you're all right. If anything had happened to you…" Rather than finish the sentence, he kissed her again.

She closed her eyes, relief rushing through her and weakening her knees. "I was so scared."

He took the gun, slid it in the waist of his jeans at the small of his back, then took a small folding knife from his pocket. "Let's get you out of here."

Tears filled her eyes as she watched him saw on the ropes binding her hands. "How did you know—"

A sudden movement, a scuffling drew her gaze and Jack's across the barn. Too late.

The Wolf had seized another steel bar from the original stack and lunged, staggering toward them. He swung the steel rod in a downward arc at Jack.

His hands occupied with cutting her ropes, Jack's reaction was a fraction of a second too slow. The rebar cracked a glancing blow to his head, but he fell backward and didn't move.

"Jack!" Tracy sobbed, her heart plummeting to her toes.

Still swaying on his feet and holding his side, The Wolf cast his gaze around, clearly looking for the gun. When he spotted the lighter, he stooped and scrabbled it off the floor. "This was a gift…" he paused and wheezed a gurgling breath "…from my father."

Grabbing a handful of straw from the stall, he lit the stalks and let the flaming tinder land on the pile.

Horror streaked through Tracy as the flames caught and the hay ignited in a bright, fast fire.

This place would go up like a tinderbox, all this weathered wood and straw. And you with time to think about burning up like a campfire marshmallow… The Wolf's taunt replayed in her mind, and her heart galloped. The smoke was already making her cough and gag.

The Wolf backed toward the barn door, his steps weaving and his grin pure evil. "Time to go."

Tears prickled her eyes. From fear. From smoke. From guilt. Bad enough that her in-laws' assassin would kill her today, but Jack…

Her chest squeezed. Seth would be an orphan. Both of his parents' deaths would be blood on her hands.

"Jack?" she called, nudging him with her foot. *Please, please wake up!* She had to revive him before the smoke overwhelmed them both. Before the flames crept any closer or blocked their only exit.

When Ryan got the call about Tracy's kidnapping and Jack's pursuit of the assassin, he'd had already been planning a trip to the ranch, bringing his latest intel on The Wolf. The killer had been identified as Wayne Parnell and a partial fingerprint of Parnell's had been found at a service-station restroom where he'd been ID'd from security-camera footage. Now, minutes later, after driving at top speeds with lights and sirens, he'd commandeered a ranch four wheeler and was bouncing across the fields to the old hay barn. He had a rifle with a sniper scope strapped to his back in addition to his department-issued side arm.

He'd just picked up Tom Vasquez, who'd abandoned the pursuit after Jack galloped passed him. An asthma attack had left Vasquez winded, but he was able to direct Ryan where they needed to go. Their destination became all too clear when a billow of smoke rose over the horizon, just past a large hill. Ryan's gut pitched. If that was the old barn burning, as he feared, the aged building would be ashes in minutes. God help anyone trapped inside. And *anyone* could be Tracy. Or Jack.

Fresh urgency whipped through him, and he squeezed the throttle.

"Hang on!" Ryan told the ranch hand who rode behind him. He gunned the engine, and it whined with effort as they shot up the incline.

Thick smoke filled the barn quickly. Within minutes, Tracy's skin stung from the heat of the flames, and her throat and lungs were raw and scorched. Her eyes watered as she tried again to revive Jack, rasping, "Please! Please, Jack, wake up!"

Her head felt muzzy from lack of oxygen, but she fought the pull of unconscious oblivion, knowing she had to get Jack out. Even if she was going to die here. "Jack…please!"

She poked him weakly with her toe again, the effort almost more energy than she had left to give. Finally he stirred, coughing and raising a hand to his head wound. *Thank God!*

"Jack, you…" *cough* "…have to get out!"

He blinked up at her, in confusion for a fraction of a second before clarity lit his gaze and alarm filled his eyes. "Not without you!"

Groaning and choking on the thick smoke, he rolled to his hands and knees, scanned the floor until he found the pocketknife he'd dropped when he'd been attacked, and began sawing again at the ropes.

"Leave…me…" she said, then gave over to a fit of racking coughs.

"Like hell," he said, his voice a low scrape. "I lost…one woman I loved…and didn't fight for. I won't lose…you."

Ryan spotted Jack's horse and a brown gelding prancing restlessly outside the barn as he crested the hill. He scanned the area carefully looking for his brother, for Tracy…and for The Wolf. Wayne Parnell. A man with a lengthy rap sheet and a brutal history of merciless killing.

"Jack!" he shouted over the roar of the ATV.

A movement in his peripheral vision caught his attention at the same time that Tom Vasquez aimed a finger toward the same tree-shaded ravine a hundred yards down the other side of the hill. A tall, dark-headed figure lumbered and lurched into the shade of the trees. Ryan brought the ATV to a skidding halt. "Check the barn," he barked to Vasquez, as he swung off the four-wheeler and pulled the rifle from his back. "Jack and Tracy have to be around here somewhere."

The ranch hand hurried toward the burning barn, covering his mouth and nose with his shirt.

After checking the rifle and chambering the first cartridge, Ryan crouched low and took up a position from which he could monitor Parnell's movement.

"Do you see them?" he called to Vasquez.

"I think so. But the fire's too hot to go in the front." Vasquez raised his arm to shield his face from the heat and stumbled away from the flames licking the barn door.

Ryan set his jaw. No way in hell was he letting his

brother perish in that fire without even trying. "Then we have to create a way for them to escape out the back."

"Ideas?" the ranch hand asked.

Ryan's gaze darted to the four wheeler and the tow chain mounted on the rear. "Let's rip a hole in the wall."

I won't lose you.

Tracy heard the words, and her heart gave a light flutter of recognition, but her eyelids drooped. Staying awake took too much strength. He legs were rubbery. The only thing keeping her upright was the rope that bound her to the baler, and it cut into her flesh as her weight sagged against the constraint.

The smoke was so dense. Jack was awake. She could just...

"Tracy!" he growled when her head lolled. "Stay—" *cough, cough* "—with me!"

"Can't..." The ropes tugged at her wrists as he cut. "I love...y—"

The ropes dropped loose, and she toppled toward the floor. Muscled arms caught her. Lifted her.

She curled weakly against Jack's chest, her breathing no more than a feathery wheeze. Beneath her cheek, his chest heaved and rumbled when he coughed.

I love you, Jack. She longed to say the words, but her head was too fuzzy, her body too weak.

Jack had started for the front door of the barn, before realizing the fire blocked the exit. Tracy lay draped in his arms, limp and unresponsive. A bitter ache lashed his heart at the thought of losing her.

Hang on, darling. I'll get you out of here. I promise. Just hang on a little longer!

Adrenaline fueled his legs as he changed direction,

searching for another way out. Without protection from the smoke for his mouth and nose, he was rapidly succumbing to the acrid cloud filling the barn. He had just turned, searching the dark recesses for an alternate escape route, when he heard a familiar voice shouting his name. Relief and gratitude pricked the bubble of tension swelling in his chest, but he didn't call back. He saved his oxygen for rescuing Tracy.

Ryan was there, but could his brother do anything to help them get out? And what about The Wolf? Was the killer lying in wait to pick them all off as they fled the burning barn?

He heard a distant roar, a loud screech and a crash. A large piece of the back wall tore away, and bright beams of sunlight streamed in through the dense smoke. Weaving through the maze of flames, Jack rushed towards the gaping hole. Fingers of fire reached for him and floating embers scorched his skin, but he didn't slow his step. His only thought was of getting Tracy out that barn and reviving her.

"Jack!" Tom Vasquez shouted. "Bring her over here!"

Sucking in fresh air as he emerged from the conflagration, Jack staggered to the shade of a nearby tree where Tom met him.

"Tracy!" His voice was choked by emotion and phlegm as he set her carefully on the ground. He slapped her cheeks lightly to rouse her, and she blinked against the blinding sunlight that peeked through the branches above her.

She groaned hoarsely, her head rocking side to side in distress. "Jack…" she whispered, her voice crackling roughly.

He pressed a kiss to her forehead and shushed her. "Easy, darling. You're safe now."

Her body convulsed as she coughed and wheezed, and Tom helped her sit up.

Jack, too, cleared his lungs as best he could, spitting out the dark taste of ash that lined his throat, before turning back to Vasquez. "Where's...The Wolf?" he asked between gasps for breath.

"Down in that ravine," Tom said, aiming a finger past the idling four wheeler. "Your brother is watching him."

Jack rubbed his gritty eyes, which stung from the smoke, and narrowed his gaze on the dark figure huddled under the trees in the ravine. He drew his gun from the small of his back and rose from his knees. "Stay with her, will you? I have unfinished business."

He stalked past the blazing barn and dropped weakly on the ground beside Ryan.

His brother gave him a side glance. "You okay?"

Jack nodded and coughed.

"Tracy?"

"Alive, but..." He drew a rattling breath. "She needs medical attention."

"You both do. Go. I've got this." Ryan peered through the sniper scope. "He's not going anywhere."

At that moment, The Wolf dashed from the cover of the trees, charging them. Jack didn't wait for permission. He aimed his pistol. Fired.

A second shot blasted at the same time. Ryan's rifle.

The Wolf dropped, writhing on the ground, holding his leg.

Ryan glared at Jack. "I said I had it."

Jack slumped with fatigue and relief, raising a hand to his aching head.

His brother grunted and hitched a thumb over his shoulder. "I'll take it from here. I have backup on the way. You get out of here. Get Tracy and yourself to a hospital."

At the foot of the hill, The Wolf had stopped moving, his eyes in a fixed stare. Assured that the killer was no longer a threat, he jerked a nod to Ryan and stumbled back to Tracy's side.

Wide blue eyes met his as he dropped to his knees next to her. "W-Wolf," she rasped, grabbing his hand.

Jack stroked her cheek. "We got him, Trace. He's dead."

Chapter 20

His living room resembled Grand Central Station.

Having heard about the incident at the old hay barn, Jack's heroic rescue of Tracy and the death of the assassin who'd been stalking their guest, every Colton and hired hand had assembled in Jack's living room.

"I'm fine," Jack assured Big J for the tenth time when his father cast him a worried glance. "Eric said the CT scan showed no concussion. I have a hard head apparently."

Tracy, too, had been treated for minor wounds at the ER and released. Now, she sat on his sofa with Seth on her lap and Greta hovering beside her. Jack wanted to be the one keeping vigil over Tracy, but his turn would have to wait until his sister, Brett, and half of the ranch's staff including Edith, who was a force of her own, finished buzzing worriedly about her.

"I know you probably could use something stronger,"

Tom Vasquez said, handing Jack a glass of iced tea, "but your brother says alcohol doesn't mix with whatever painkiller he gave you at the ER."

Jack smiled his thanks, keeping half of his attention focused on Tracy even as he answered questions for the curious hands who surrounded him.

"You're all being so kind," Tracy said, squeezing Greta's hand and tugging Seth close for another one-armed hug. "Really, all I need is a good night's sleep. I'm just glad the ordeal is over, and none of you were hurt." Her eyes lifted to Jack's then, and he read in her gaze the same fear that had shaken him to the core when he'd learned she'd been kidnapped. The bone-deep terror of losing her.

"So now that the threat to your life has been eliminated, will you move back to the main house?" Greta asked.

Tracy hesitated, drawing a slow deep breath. Her expression darkened, Jack's only warning before she said, "Actually, I think the time has come for me to leave. I've already imposed on your hospitality and protection far too long."

Jack's gut swooped, and his muscles tensed. She was *leaving*?

"What?" Greta said, frowning.

"No, Miss Tracy! Stay here!" Seth whined, tugging her sleeve.

"I'm sorry," she said, "I never intended to stay this long. If not for the threat I was under and Jack's insistence that I stay here, I'd have gone last week."

"You're not an imposition. We've all loved getting to know you," Greta said.

"Thank you. Really, but I must. There are things back in Denver I have to—"

"Nooo," Seth groaned again, tears welling in his eyes. The hurt and disappointment on his son's face left a hard, cold pit inside him. Everything he'd tried to protect Seth from when Laura left, everything he'd felt when his wife had abandoned him and their son, everything he'd tried to repress for five years so that he could make a happy home for his boy came crashing down on him in that instant.

Tracy said something quietly to Seth he couldn't hear over the roar of blood in his ears. His fingers tightened around his tea glass, and he gritted his back teeth so hard his molars ached. A tremor started low in his belly and worked its way outward until his limbs trembled. He turned without speaking to anyone and stalked outside. He needed air. He needed distance. He needed to punch something.

He'd opened his home, his life, his heart to Tracy. And she was walking away.

Tracy's gaze followed Jack as he stormed out of the living room, and her heart sank. She'd hoped for a chance to talk to him privately and explain her decision before telling the rest of the family, but when Greta asked, she'd been honest with her new friend about her plans. What she hadn't told Greta, what she couldn't put into words even in her private thoughts was the devastation she'd felt when she'd seen Jack crumple on the barn floor. In those moments when she thought they'd both burn to death, when she considered the danger and anguish she'd unwittingly brought to the Colton ranch, her guilt and despair had been a vicious animal gnawing her soul. She was jinxed. She had been responsible for her cousin's death and nearly cost Jack his life. Tragedy followed her, and she wouldn't allow the train wreck of her life to hurt anyone else she loved.

She would keep in touch with Seth, as she'd promised, but lingering at the ranch any longer, allowing the little boy to grow more attached to her—and vice versa—would be selfish and cruel, knowing she couldn't stay permanently.

And Jack…

Jack would be the hardest to leave. She'd fallen in love with him. Losing him from her life would be like ripping out her heart. Like living underwater with no air to breathe. Already the pain was suffocating.

Maybe things could be different if she thought he loved her. If he'd ever said anything about a future together. If he'd asked her to stay—not because she had to to save her life, but because he wanted her there.

But his silence was deafening. Shattering. Conclusive.

Even the small hope she clung to that he was waiting for the crowd of relatives and friends to clear out of his house to speak his mind proved futile. He was decidedly closed off, sullen and terse with her as they prepared Seth for bed.

He remained withdrawn the next morning as she packed her bags. When she tried to broach the topic of her departure, he'd brushed her aside and stalked outside to the stable. He remained hidden in the shadowed stalls with the horses, even when she sent Seth with a message for him that she was ready to go.

"He said to tell you he was busy, but to have a safe trip," Seth reported when he returned.

Brett and Greta had both turned out to wish her well and say their goodbyes, and Jack's siblings exchanged a look of disbelief.

"Tracy, I'm sure he just—" Greta started.

"No, it's okay. I understand," she said as bravely as she could and flashed them all a smile she didn't feel.

She cast one last look toward the stable, and the crack in her heart widened. With a sigh of resignation and heartache, she pulled Jack's son into her arms for a final hug. "I'm going to miss you, sweetie. But I'll call, and we can Skype, and you can visit me anytime you want."

Seth's chin quivered. "Bye, Miss Tracy. I...l-love you."

"Oh, Seth, I love you, too." She gave his rumpled hair a kiss, fighting not to lose her composure in front of the child, then hurriedly climbed into the rental car and closed the door.

Jack moved with stiff, jerky motions as he worked in the stable, killing time until he heard the engine of Tracy's rental car rev and the tires crunch over gravel as she drove away. He slammed things down with more force than needed and smashed his finger in a stall gate.

Spitting a curse out under his breath, he stuck his injured finger in his mouth and sucked on the throbbing wound. If only he could find a similar balm for his seared heart.

He heard the thud of booted steps and glanced up to see Brett striding toward him with his mouth set in a grim line. "You're an idiot and a bastard, Jack Colton!"

Jack fisted a hand and returned his brother's glare. He didn't want to punch his brother, but he was itching to hit something, and if Brett provoked him... "Leave me alone."

"You couldn't even come out and tell her goodbye? That's more than rude, man. That's just..." Brett flattened his mouth again and shook his head in disgust.

Self-preservation, Jack finished mentally.

"Cold," Brett said. "And pathetic."

Jack heaved an exasperated sigh. He felt bad enough about Tracy leaving without his brother heaping on guilt.

He grabbed a rake and started shuffling straw around the stall floor. "If you have a point to make, do it. I'm kinda busy here."

Brett seized the rake handle and yanked it from Jack's hands. "Did a bull kick you in the head, bro? Why did you let her leave?"

"Let her?" He scoffed. "I can't keep her here against her will. That's called imprisonment, and it's illegal. Ask Ryan."

"She wanted to stay!" Brett waved a hand toward the stable door. "Anyone with eyes could see that."

"Really? Fine way of showing it. I thought packing her suitcases and hopping in her rental car at her first opportunity said she was eager to leave." He stepped closer to his brother and put his hand on the rake, trying to grab it back. Brett held tight.

"Well, from what I can tell, you didn't put up even a token resistance. Does she know how you feel about her? Did you tell her?"

Jack stilled, and his insides grew cold. "I don't know what you're talking about."

Brett laughed without humor, shaking his head. "Man, you *must* have been kicked by a bull." He stared at Jack for a few seconds with an incredulous look furrowing his brow. "Is it because of Laura? Are you going to let Tracy walk out of your life without a fight because you think this is somehow a repeat of what happened with Laura?"

Jack heard the quaver in his inhaled breath, felt the sting of moisture in his eyes. "Leave me alone, Brett," he gritted through his teeth.

His brother released the rake and curled his fingers in the front of Jack's shirt, tugging him close enough to stick his nose in Jack's face. "It's not the same. Don't screw this up because you're scared of what you're feeling for her."

Jack couldn't breathe, couldn't make his lungs loosen enough to take in oxygen. He held Brett's stare and fought the surge of emotion that stampeded through him.

"She was happy here. You'd have to be blind not to see that. You made her happy." Brett cocked his head. "She loves you, Jack. Hell, even I could see that!"

"He's right."

Jack jerked his gaze to Greta, who'd sneaked up on them undetected.

"Listen to him, Jack. Our bonehead brother is making sense. I saw it. Tracy blossomed in the last couple weeks, even with the threat of that killer hanging over her. Because of you. And Seth. She's leaving because she's scared, too."

"Maybe I'm letting her go to protect Seth," he said defiantly.

"Bull," Brett said with a snort. "She loves Seth, and he loves her. You let her go to save your own sorry hide. From what, I don't know, because it's pretty obvious she's perfect for you."

Greta stalked closer. "Jack Colton, if you love her, go after her. Don't let her leave here thinking you don't care."

Jack's pulse ramped into high gear. Laura had left because she didn't belong on the ranch. The life of a rancher didn't suit her, and she never loved him enough to overcome her unhappiness. But Tracy *had* taken to ranching, messy chores and all, like she was born to it. She'd smiled when she woke in his arms, excited for a new day. Despite the stress she was under from The Wolf.

And *he'd* been happy, damn it! As happy as he'd been in a long time.

His stomach bunched as he cast a glance toward the ranch yard where Tracy had just driven away. "It's probably too late to stop her. She must be to the highway by now."

Greta squeezed his arm. "Maybe not. She was going to stop at the main house to tell Maria and Edith goodbye."

Blowing out a nervous puff of breath, Jack pushed past his sister and tugged Buck, saddleless, out of his stall. If he wanted to catch up to Tracy, he'd have to hurry.

Tracy sat at the entry gate to the ranch, wiping away tears as fast as they filled her eyes. She couldn't read the rental car's GPS device for the moisture blurring her vision.

Where do you want to go? the screen read.

The ache in her chest swelled. "I want to turn around and go back," she said with a sniff. "But I can't."

Fumbling for the rental car papers, she looked for the address of the rental agency where she would return the vehicle. She started tapping the address onto the electronic keyboard when a low thundering noise rumbled through her open window. She raised her head and checked for storm clouds, but the Oklahoma sky was a bright, clear blue. The sound got louder, and as she scanned the highway for hot rods or large trucks, a movement in the rearview mirror snagged her attention.

A horse was galloping up behind her at a full run. The rider's head was down, and he hunched forward over the horse's neck, clutching his mount's mane. Startled, and somewhat alarmed by the sight, she blinked hard to clear her eyes. Everything about the horse's speed and the cowboy's tense position screamed trouble.

Then she recognized the gelding, the black cowboy hat, the dark, unruly hair of the rider.

"Jack…" she whispered with a shuddering breath. What was wrong? Why—?

"Tracy!" he shouted as he rode past her and reined Buck in front of the car, blocking the driveway.

Limbs trembling, she clutched the steering wheel and gaped at him in dismay. What in the world? He'd ridden bareback, not even bothering to saddle Buck, and now he swung off the gelding in a smooth motion and rushed to the driver's-side door.

"Tracy!" he gasped, out of breath from his jarring pursuit. "Don't...don't go." He snatched open the car door and pulled her arm to coax her out.

Unsnapping her seat belt, she slid out of the front seat and narrowed a concerned gaze on him. "Jack, what's wrong? What's happened?"

"Not wrong..." he panted. "Right. I fell..." He paused as he swallowed hard and dragged in a lungful of air. "I fell in love with you."

"I— What?" She felt fresh tears fill her eyes, and she held her breath, almost afraid to move for fear she'd shatter the moment and it would be lost.

"Stay." His fingers gripped her shoulders, and the desperation and sincerity that lit his eyes stirred a flutter under her ribs.

"Wha—"

"You belong here. You belong with me."

Her eyes widened in surprise, and her mouth opened in a silent question.

Jack grunted in frustration and scrubbed a hand over his face. "Let me start over." He drew and released a cleansing breath. "I don't want you to leave, Tracy. I love you. Seth loves you. You belong with us, not in Denver."

"But..."

"You were happy here. Weren't you?" For the first time a flicker of uncertainty flashed in his gaze, and she quickly nodded, assuaging his doubt. Even as she admitted the truth, though, her own uncertainty lashed at her.

"B-but…I'm jinxed, Jack. I've brought trouble and tragedy to everyone I love. You were almost killed because of me. I can't bear the idea of anything happening to you or Seth because of me."

He scowled at her and shook his head. "Don't be crazy. There's no such thing as a jinx. What you brought me and my son was a second chance to be a complete family. You brought love and happiness and laughter. We need you, Tracy. Don't go."

"I don't want to leave, but—"

"But nothing, Trace." He framed her face with his hands and pressed his forehead to hers, their bodies touching head to boots. She felt the tremor that rolled through him as he feathered kisses across her cheeks. "Say you'll stay. Say you'll be part of our family and grow old with this stubborn, surly cowboy."

The shock and joy of the moment overwhelmed her. Her emotions tangled and knotted in her throat, choking her voice, while happy tears spilled from her eyes.

When she didn't answer, he leaned back from her, a dent of worry in his brow. "Tracy?"

Again her mouth opened and closed without a sound.

His hands slid from her shoulders to grasp her hands, and whipping off his cowboy hat, he dropped to one knee. "Tracy McCain, I love you and want you in my life. Please say you'll stay. Say you'll marry me."

Joyful laughter bubbled up from her soul, and despite the grip her happy tears had on her throat, she squeaked out, "yes!"

* * * * *

MILLS & BOON®

The Thirty List

At thirty, Rachel has slid down every ladder she has
ever climbed. Jobless, broke and ditched by her
husband, she has to move in with grumpy
Patrick and his four-year-old son.

Patrick is also getting divorced, so to cheer themselves up the two decide to draw up bucket lists.
Soon they are learning to tango, abseiling, trying
stand-up comedy and more. But, as she gets
closer to Patrick, Rachel wonders if their
relationship is too good to be true...

Order yours today at
www.millsandboon.co.uk/Thethirtylist

MILLS & BOON®

The Chatsfield Collection!

Style, spectacle, scandal...!

With the eight Chatsfield siblings happily married and settling down, it's time for a new generation of Chatsfields to shine, in this brand-new 8-book collection! The prospect of a merger with the Harrington family's boutique hotels will shape the future forever. But who will come out on top?

**Find out at
www.millsandboon.co.uk/TheChatsfield2**

MILLS & BOON®
INTRIGUE
Romantic Suspense

A SEDUCTIVE COMBINATION OF DANGER AND DESIRE

A sneak peek at next month's titles...

In stores from 19th June 2015:

- **Surrendering to the Sheriff** – Delores Fossen *and*
  The Detective – Adrienne Giordano

- **Under Fire** – Carol Ericson *and*
  Leverage – Janie Crouch

- **Sheltered** – HelenKay Dimon *and*
  Lawman Protection – Cindi Myers

Romantic Suspense

- **How to Seduce a Cavanaugh** – Marie Ferrarella
- **Colton's Cowboy Code** – Melissa Cutler

Available at WHSmith, Tesco, Asda, Eason, Amazon and Apple

Just can't wait?
Buy our books online a month before they hit the shops!
visit www.millsandboon.co.uk

These books are also available in eBook format!